# Darby's Cafe

**CORI COOPER**

Immortal Works LLC
Grantsville, Utah 84029
Tel: (385) 202-0116

© 2025 Cori Cooper
www.coristories.com
Cover Art by Megan King

All rights reserved, including the right to reproduce this book or portions thereof in any form whatsoever. For more information visit https://www.immortalworks.press/ This book is a work of fiction. Names, characters, businesses, organizations, places, events and incidents either are the product of the author's imagination or are used fictitiously. Any resemblance to actual persons, living or dead, events, or locales is entirely coincidental.

ISBN 979-8-330532-17-9 (Paperback)

ASIN B0DS6Y399N (Kindle)

*To: Grandpa and Grannie Farr*
*For living in Southern Utah so I could have the BEST childhood memories!*

# Chapter One

*Timid Young Blond (TYB) Seeks the Guts to Talk to the Hottie at Work. Maybe He Could Make the First Move? Otherwise, This Might Take Awhile.*

She wasn't a stalker.

Darby dared any red-blooded woman in the world *not* to stare at Myles Cook with her mouth hanging half open and her tongue wagging out.

It was impossible.

He was just so dang beautiful.

His blue eyes, behind those black hipster glasses, were bright and swoony. The way he focused all his attention on the newspaper in his hands made Darby feel just a teensy bit jealous of the newspaper.

What woman doesn't want a man to stare at her for almost an hour like she's the most interesting thing in the room?

As yummy as his eyes were, his lips were even better. Sometimes, when he read, he'd mouth the words. Darby spent an enormous amount of time when she was supposed to be wrapping utensils in napkins, trying to decipher what he was reading based on the shapes his lips made.

Every once in a while he ran his hand through his blond, wavy hair, wrecking the perfect Ken doll gel job. The best part happened next, when one stubborn lock dropped back into his eyes. Darby dreamed of one day reaching over and smoothing that lock into place for him. Or, even better, transforming herself into that lock of hair just so he had to brush her with his fingers.

Okay, that was a little weird.

Borderline pathetic.

Actually, the whole crush was pathetic.

She was pathetic.

Myles had come into the Corner Café every morning, at precisely seven thirty, for the last six weeks, and the only reason Darby knew his name was because she rummaged through the register to find his credit card receipt after he left that first day.

Pathetic.

And, okay, yes, fine, she was a little bit of a stalker.

She sighed and dropped the last utensil roll into the bin under the counter.

And missed.

Of course.

Because nothing ever went smoothly for her.

Because, oh yeah, the universe hated her.

Darby squatted to pick it up, hoping that her boss, Gretta, hadn't noticed. The napkin would have to be thrown away and the utensils washed again just in case any part of them touched the dirty floor. Gretta wouldn't like that at all.

As Darby rose, she misjudged where the mugs were and knocked them with her elbow. This set off the coffee mug symphony orchestra which meant Darby's chances of going unnoticed just tanked hard.

Darby let out a long breath as she steadied the mugs with one hand. They were quiet now. She was just stalling to put off the moment she had to turn around and face Gretta.

Gretta and her Gremlin Face.

Darby fixed a smile into place and spun around on her heel, careful to keep her elbows glued to her side. Gretta was watching, of course, because there was no way Darby's crappy luck would let Gretta be busy when something embarrassing happened.

Crappy luck was pretty consistent that way.

Gretta's lips pressed into a thin line. "I need you to pay better attention to what you're doing."

"I know." Darby nodded, gluing her eyes to Gretta's face. Gretta's voice only had one volume, loud, and Darby didn't want to see who else was witnessing her moment of shame. For the first time ever, she was glad Myles hardly ever looked up from his newspaper.

"The person at the counter is the first thing people see when they come into the Corner Café. They're gonna judge the whole place by what you do. Any more of this," Gretta swept a hand toward the mug display, "and you're moving to the kitchen."

Not the kitchen.

Anything but the kitchen.

Darby's face flushed. Gretta probably thought the threat of scrubbing ovens and congealed pots was enough to scare Darby straight, but that wasn't it at all. She could wash dishes with her eyes closed. It was everything else about the kitchen that freaked her out.

"I get it." Darby scuffed her toe against the wilted vinyl. "I'll be more careful."

"I hope so." Gretta didn't look all that hopeful. Her Gremlin Face made it clear her expectations were dangerously low. "The corner booth is free. You know what to do."

Darby nodded again, not daring to point out that since she worked the counter, someone else, like Meredith, should clear the booth. Gretta didn't love back talk. Meaning, any talk that contradicted what she said *or* thought. More than once since Darby started working at the café she wished she could read Gretta's mind. It was exhausting trying to guess what she was thinking all the time.

Darby kept her eyes trained on the floor so they wouldn't sneak over to Myles as she walked by.

Not even a peek.

This was her penance for being such a spazz.

The small family of four that previously occupied the corner booth was still making their way out of the café. Darby stopped to let them pass and then hurried to the table. That booth was a favorite spot, so Gretta was a stickler for making sure it was always available as quickly as possible.

"Hey, Myles! Man, how are you? It's been forever!"

Darby ducked behind the high back of the booth and froze with her hands hovering over the stack of sticky, syrupy plates. When she got the guts to peek over the top, it was just in time to see two guys pull away from a very manly back-slap hug.

"Are these your kids?" Myles' eyes lit up as he leaned over to see the little girl at eye level. "I'm Myles, I knew your daddy in high school. What's your name?"

Darby's heart pounded in her ears.

Gorgeous and good with kids?

Did he drop from heaven, or what?

The little girl hid her face in her mom's pant leg.

"It's okay," the dad said. "Myles is super nice. Remember I told you about that time I hurt my leg real bad in football? Myles was the one who got me off the field."

"Oh, man!" Myles laughed. "I can't believe you still remember that!"

"Course I remember that! There was that five-hundred-pound gorilla bearing down on me. He would have killed me if you hadn't pulled me out of the way. So," he poked his daughter in the arm, "you should tell Myles thank you for saving your daddy's life."

Gorgeous, good with kids, humble, and part superhero?

Yes, please!

"T'ank you." The little girl chanced one small glance at Myles, then scooted behind her mom.

"Her name is Sophie." The mom laughed. "And usually we can't get her to stop talking. Maybe you should come over while we're trying to watch a movie, or, you know, have a conversation during dinner."

"Anytime." Myles swung his hair out of his eyes. The movement was so perfect, Darby was pretty sure her heart stopped beating for that one second.

"Man, it's good to see you!" The dad said again. "Do you still live in Hurricane? What are you doing?"

"Yeah, I'm here, for now." Myles' eyes shifted to his newspaper, a crease forming between his eyebrows.

It was delicious.

"I was in the Bay Area for a couple of years, going to school. But, now I'm back."

"Yeah, I think I remember that. Didn't you get a business degree? Wait, you started a business, didn't you? I think I heard that you started a business or something."

"I did." Myles chuckled at Sophie as she shrank down into a little ball behind her mom.

It was pretty hilarious that little kids thought they could disappear by getting smaller, or they couldn't be seen if they had their eyes closed. Right now, Darby just wanted to shake that little girl's hand because hearing Myles chuckle that way pretty much made her day.

Actually, her week.

Okay, fine, her life.

"I actually have three businesses. I'm looking into starting a fourth somewhere closer to my parents."

Gorgeous, good with kids, humble, part superhero, successful, and family-oriented?

Oh, mama! Darby was a goner.

"Wow, man, look at you." The dad pulled out his wallet and rifled through it until he emerged with a business card. "I feel kind of lame now. But, here, take my card and give me a call sometime. Yeah? We can hang out."

"And do dinner." The mom added. "I was serious about that." She patted Sophie's back. "Say goodbye to Myles, Soph." Then waved the arm of the baby on her hip.

Sophie mumbled into her mom's pant leg again, and everyone laughed.

Darby stifled a gasp. Myles' eyes literally sparkled when he laughed.

He was too good to be real.

Like fat-free ice cream.

Or unicorns.

"What in the world are you doing?"

Darby jumped and fumbled with the skirt hem of her white linen uniform. "Wha-what?"

Gretta stood in front of the booth with hands on hips and a frown firmly in place. "I said, what in the world are you doing right now, Darby Reynolds?"

"Uh, clearing up the booth." She didn't dare peek back at Myles with Gretta watching her so closely, even though she wanted to very badly. "Of course, that's what I'm doing. We need to keep it clear, right?"

"Hm," Gretta's lips pressed into a thin line. "It don't look to me like you were doing much more than staring holes in the back of that young man's head."

Could Gretta lower her voice for like one sentence? Just that one sentence? If Myles heard what she just said, Darby might actually die.

"Oh, no, uh, I wasn't, um, staring. . . ." Darby looked around for inspiration because telling her boss she was crazy-butt-in-love with a dude she hadn't even talked to was not an option. "I was, uh. . . ."

"Forget it." Gretta rolled her eyes. "Just get that booth ready for the next group who walks in here."

"Of course." Darby dropped her head.

Gretta poked a finger close to Darby's nose. "No more daydreaming, staring, or scheming, got it?"

"I wasn't . . ."

Gretta walked away without looking back.

" . . . scheming." Darby sighed heavily. She'd just missed the end of the exchange with Myles and his high school buddy, as well as the part where Myles paid for his breakfast and left the café.

Such a shame, really, watching him walk away was her favorite part.

In fact, walking away would become a positive thing if more people got to watch Myles do it.

Dang.

The boy could strut.

Now all that was left of his presence in the café was the empty plate with crisscrossed utensils and a half-empty mug off to the side.

Rotten, rotten luck.

Her luck had always been rotten, the fact that it kept getting worse wasn't a shocker. It was disappointing though. After all her pep-talking and courage gathering before she came to work this morning, there was nothing to show for any of it.

What a waste.

Stupid, stupid luck. If she hadn't dropped the utensils and knocked the cups, she wouldn't have caught Gretta's attention. Then she would have been at the counter when Myles looked up from his newspaper to talk to his old high school buddy. She could have grabbed his attention with something amazingly witty and right now they'd be planning a vacation together in Aruba.

So, thank you rotten luck.

Thank you soooooo much.

Darby sighed again and started stacking plates on her forearm. She could get all these dishes into the kitchen in one go, then come back with a rag and have the table wiped down before Gretta had a chance to huff for the third time.

On second thought, she'd better make two trips. With her luck she'd slip on something that appeared out of nowhere and break everything in her arms. Darby set half the things back on the table and carefully picked her way to the kitchen, then returned for the rest of the dishes.

As she headed back to the counter, after dropping the second load off with the dishwashers, the bell over the door rang the next person into the Corner Café.

Not just any person.

Kenya.

Today she wore a long, flowered skirt, a peasant blouse, a fringed suede vest over the top, and a bright yellow crocheted cap. Her long, dark brown hair was straightened with a middle part that made her chocolate brown eyes look ginormous. A garish headband to keep all that hair from swinging in her face when she sat down at the counter.

Darby glanced at Gretta, who wrinkled her nose. "You're working, don't you forget that. And if she ain't buying anything, she's got five minutes."

"I know. I remember. Thanks."

Darby couldn't stop the smile from taking over her face as she met Kenya at the counter. "Hey! Are you finally done with work?"

Kenya nodded, plopping onto the stool. "I am so wiped out! All that YMCA-ing and booty shaking, it's exhausting! Seventies dancing is not slow if you know what I mean."

Darby had no idea what Kenya meant since she was born a full twenty years after the seventies were over. So was Kenya, for that matter. That's where the work part of Kenya's party planning business reared its head, she'd spent most of the last two weeks researching the seventies, then telling Darby all about it when she came in for breakfast. Darby was pretty sure the two of them knew more about the era than the people who lived through it.

The rest of what Kenya did was technically play.

"I really think you have the funnest job in the world," Darby said, keeping one eye on Gretta. When the woman started shifting, it meant she was losing patience. Throat clearing was a death sentence. Darby usually had a solid five minutes before the shifting started, but Gretta seemed to be in an especially ornery mood today.

Kenya's back curved into a C-shape. "It's fun, don't get me wrong, but after nights like this one, I'm thinking Costco would be a great career. Predictable hours, steady pay, same thing every day."

Darby anchored her hand on her hip. "Yeah right, you wouldn't last a week at Costco, or anywhere else. You'd be bored out of your mind."

"You think so?"

"I know so."

In fact, Darby would have bet money on it. Kenya was the opposite of predictable, steady, and consistent. That's partly why Darby loved her so much, Kenya was so different from herself. Talking to Kenya was kind of like living a vicarious life, one where she wasn't so dang scared to put herself out there again.

"You're right, as always." Kenya glanced over at the sad remains of Myles. "Hey, where's Lover Boy?"

"Don't say that so loud!" Darby hissed.

Kenya didn't even lower her voice. "Why not?"

"Someone might hear you." Darby's eyes shifted down the counter. It was empty, but still.

Kenya's eyes followed the same shift with the same result. "Mmm hmm. I see what you mean. All these people, listening in."

"I don't want Meredith to walk by and overhear. She's like an evil villain and gossip is her superpower. Whatever you say she will hear, then totally misconstrue."

Kenya still looked skeptical, but leaned forward to whisper, "Where's Lover Boy?"

"Gone," Darby whispered back.

"Already?" Kenya frowned, then scooted over to the stool where Myles had been sitting. "He's usually still here when I come in." She picked up his abandoned newspaper. "You know he's probably the only dude our age in the world who reads an actual newspaper, right? Super old school."

Darby knew. That was what caught her attention on her first day of work. The more she thought about him, and that happened pretty much constantly, the more she decided she loved that about him.

Kenya fluffed the newspaper. "Let's see what he was reading today, shall we?"

Darby moved down the counter along with Kenya to start clearing the dishes Myles used. The stoneware clanged together as Darby stacked things into, and onto, each other. "What did you discover?"

"Well . . ." Kenya snapped the newspaper upright and peered closer, ". . . he's interested in this car for sale, see, it's all smudged right there. And, oh, ho, ho! This is interesting! Lover Boy McHottyson likes him some personal ads."

"Nuh-uh." Darby leaned over the counter to look. "They do not still run those things."

"They sure do, listen to this." Kenya's voice lowered and took on a pompous accent. "Elegant Dame Wanted, that's EDW for you laymen out there. Middle-aged country boy, who recently inherited a fortune, in need of a sophisticated woman to teach him how to navigate posh society."

"You are making that up!"

"No, for real, look!" Kenya pointed to the text. "All true."

Darby leaned back, a low whistle escaping through her teeth. "I don't know if that is adorable, or completely pathetic."

"Yeah, me neither. I just wish I knew which one of these ads your Lover Boy was drawn to. It would clue me in on who he really is."

"Based on which ads he was reading?" Darby gave Kenya an incredulous look.

People were more than what they read, watched, and listened to. At least, Darby liked to think so. She would hate it if people judged her solely by her fetish for Hallmark movies.

"Nope, it's completely reliable." Kenya flicked the paper so it made a satisfying crinkly noise. "When I met Mitch he was totally sucked into Steve Young's biography."

Okay, yeah, Kenya's boyfriend, Mitch, was a total sports nut, but Darby was still skeptical. Mitch reading books about sports wasn't really who he was, it was what he was interested in. And a sports biography was way different from a newspaper. There was a cornucopia of information on just one page of the news. It would be impossible to figure out who a person was from the article on the school board's decision to move to year-round school, to the article about the expected heatwave next week, to the editorial on recycling.

"Oh, come on." Kenya swatted Darby's arm to get her attention. "You're overthinking it. People are not that complicated. Do you think you could peek over Lover Boy's shoulder tomorrow morning when he comes in to see which ads he reads? Do some surveillance?"

Darby could barely get her tongue off the roof of her mouth when he was in the café, so, yeah, she sincerely doubted it. His cologne might send her into a swoon from which she would never recover.

She shook her head as she reached for his mug and balanced it on top of the plates.

Kenya pursed her lips together. "I could have casually spied on him this morning if he hadn't left so dang early. What's up with that, anyway? What happened?"

Darby clutched Myles's dishes and wished with all her heart that she had something she could tell Kenya besides the truth. The truth stank. She was a buffoon and Myles left without so much as glancing at her. Okay, maybe he glanced at her, but it didn't count because she didn't see it. "Nothing."

Such a desolate word. Nothing, nothing, nothing.

"You didn't talk to him?"

Gretta cleared her throat loudly.

Steeeeee-rike one.

Both girls glanced her way, then leaned forward so they could talk lower and still hear each other.

"No."

"Why not? We had a great plan! You were going to take his order and then segway into what he was doing today. It was almost foolproof."

Almost was the key word, there.

It was like the theme of Darby's life.

Almost . . . could have . . . if only. . . .

Kenya was right though, the plan was foolproof, or it would have been foolproof if it wasn't for, oh yeah, Darby's luck. She wasn't about to bring that up to Kenya again. Kenya thought that luck was hooey. Of course, she'd only known Darby for like eleven months. That wasn't enough time to fully appreciate the scope of Darby's misfortunes.

Aside from the luck thing, Darby wasn't all that great at talking to hot guys. Whenever she tried, words turned into toffee and stuck to the back of her teeth. In the silence, she just stared and blinked occasionally while her brain tried to figure out how to start working again.

Kenya's voice softened. "You chickened out?"

No!

Okay, kind of.

But really, it was the luck's fault.

Stupid, rotten luck.

Darby reached for the dishes on the counter. "I better get these back to the dishwashers before the egg dries into concrete. The guys hate that. Be right back."

"Mmm hmmm."

Darby could feel Kenya's eyes follow her through the swinging doors to the kitchen. Since Kenya had the attention span of a squirrel, there was a good chance she'd forget what they'd been talking about by the time Darby got back.

A girl could hope.

Darby took an extra long time stacking the dishes next to the sink before she went back to the counter. When she returned, Kenya was sitting in her original spot, tapping a tune with her fingernails on the napkin dispenser. Darby raised an eyebrow as she walked by Kenya and went to greet the couple that had come in while she was lolly-gagging in the kitchen. She slapped the orders on the window for Samson, then returned to her friend.

"You chickened out," Kenya said immediately. Her voice was more matter-of-fact than it was judgy. "Of course, you chickened out. That's understandable. Myles is gorgeous. Everyone who went through middle school knows it's hard to talk to gorgeous guys. We need a better plan, that's all." Kenya bit the insides of her cheeks so that her face was all cheekbones. "Maybe if you memorized some phrases, or maybe it would help if we rehearsed. I could totally be Myles."

Darby snorted loudly and then covered her mouth, glancing over at Gretta.

Who cleared her throat.

Strike two, meaning Gretta was almost out of patience.

Darby shot Kenya a look. This was the one that said, 'If you don't order something right now you're going to get tossed out of the café.' Kenya got the hint and pulled a menu upright in front of her face. "Yes, I'll have the garden omelet with country potatoes and orange juice."

"No biscuits and gravy?" Darby raised an eyebrow above the order pad. The only thing consistent about Kenya was her addiction to biscuits and gravy. Darby didn't think Kenya had ordered anything else in all the time she'd been coming to the Corner Café.

"Not today, my good ma'am. I gotta go home and sleep after this. Biscuits and gravy would interfere. I'd end up gloriously stuffed, binge-watching something stupid, then be super cranky at the Sock Hop tonight."

Darby finished jotting down Kenya's order, then stuck it on the window into the kitchen. "Sock Hop? That sounds fun!"

It really did sound fun, of course, but more than that, it sounded awesome to change the subject away from her dismal failure with Myles. Darby tucked her notepad away, then reached under the counter for a clean glass to fill with orange juice.

"It is fun, super fun! Sock hops are my favorite thing. Though,"

Kenya eyed the glass as it slowly filled. "I gotta stop scheduling things back to back like this. I am so wiped out, did I mention that? Hey, you should come tonight!"

Darby was already shaking her head.

"Oh, don't give me that look! It's a singles thing, for the community, anyone can come. Please? It would be *so* much more fun if you were there!"

Darby crossed her arms and leaned forward. "I can't party all night and work all day, *then* go to school all evening. Just picture that...." She held her arms out in front of her, eyes half closed, and groaned her best zombie impersonation. "Can I fill your eggs? How do you want your glass?"

Kenya got a case of the high-pitched giggles that made Gretta start snapping her fingers in their direction like she was getting after a disobedient dog. It was lucky the café was bustling, keeping Gretta busy schmoozing customers, or they would both be in for a tongue-lashing.

And no one tongue-lashed like Gretta.

"Okay, seriously though," Kenya wiped away her smile with surprising ease. "This is my serious face, are you taking me seriously?"

"I'm sure trying." Darby pursed her lips.

"Okay, because I got a call last night, or was it this morning? Hm, it's all a blur. Anyway, it's for a wedding reception in three weeks."

"Three weeks?" Darby's eyebrows leaped. "That's soon. Really soon. Don't people usually schedule stuff like that months in advance?"

"Probably should have. They also should have hired a professional caterer instead of a family friend who thinks they are an amateur chef."

"Ah," Darby nodded. That was a mistake. Even Darby, who had never been married, or even close to it, knew people should never hire friends for wedding caterers. Or photographers. For some reason, those two things had a long history of tragedy. Kenya liked to joke about her sister-in-law, who'd been married to her brother for twelve years and still brought up their crappy wedding photos at every family dinner.

" . . . and that friend had something come up at the last minute and can't do it."

"Well, that stinks."

"Right? So, they looked up every party-related business in Southern

Utah and made frantic phone calls until they found me." Kenya jabbed a thumb at her chest. "Except, there is one problem with this whole thing."

"Only one?"

"Well, no, but only one at the moment." Kenya gave Darby a mock glare. "And that problem is that it's a wedding party of five hundred. That's way too much work for one little me. So, I started thinking about people I could hire to help me out. If only there were someone who was an amazing chef who would be willing to cater the reception with me. . ."

Darby froze, her stomach clenching into a wall of concrete. A fiery chasm opened up in her mind. It was going to swallow everything. "Kenya—"

Kenya dropped all nonchalance and grabbed Darby's hand in a death grip. "Please, Darbs? Please, please, please? It would be so fun to work together and I'd rather hire someone I can trust than call the temp agency again. Last time they sent me some guy who thought getting baked and baking are the same thing. They are not, by the way. You'd be doing me the biggest favor. Me, your bestest friend in all of Hurricane. Don't say no, please, please, pretty please say yes!"

Darby tugged hard to extricate her hand. "I can't, Kenya. Remember that conversation we had a few minutes ago about working all day and doing school all evening? I don't have time."

That was a real reason. She wasn't just making excuses. Darby *was* super busy with work and school. But it wasn't the only reason. In reality, if she did some juggling, she could probably find time to help Kenya.

Except that she *couldn't*.

She really, just, couldn't even with cooking. Just the thought of standing in a kitchen for longer than it took to drop off dirty dishes made shivers run up and down her back.

"Order up." Samson banged his ladle on a pot to get Darby's attention. Darby could have kissed him for interrupting. Except that he was somewhere between fifty and eighty with seven grown-up kids and an adorable wife who always gave Darby a hug and a lemon drop when she came to visit Samson at work.

"Hold on," Darby whispered to Kenya, then grabbed the plate

from the window and whisked it to the older man at the end of the counter. He wasn't a regular, so she didn't say his name when she set the plate in front of him, but she did refill his apple juice and slid the ketchup next to his plate before he had a chance to ask, so that was a win.

It rattled her just a little that she could feel Kenya's eyes watching her from one corner of the room and Gretta's glare singeing her neck from the other corner.

"Man, she's grumpy," Kenya whispered, her eyes flickering to Gretta, when Darby was across the counter again. "She glared at you the entire time you were doing your thing. What's her deal, huh? We should do something about that."

There weren't many times Darby felt grateful for Gretta's bad attitude, but she did right now. If it distracted Kenya from the catering thing, Darby was all about the bad attitude.

She leaned closer to Kenya so the chances of being overheard were much lower. "Like what?"

"Saran wrap her toilet seat? Silly string her purse?" Kenya's face erupted into a wicked grin.

Darby gave her a look. "Cause we're in middle school now?"

"Oh no," Kenya shuddered. "Stop, no, forget I said anything, 'cause yikes. Bad memories. I think that guy needs a refill." Kenya jerked her head towards a man sitting a couple of stools away.

"Just one sec." Darby went to check on him, then made the rounds, refilling everyone else's everything. She returned to Kenya just in time for her order to come up.

"Do you want hot sauce?" Darby slid the plate across the counter to Kenya.

"If it's, like, Cholula or Sriracha, and not that picante crap."

Darby grabbed a bottle of sriracha from the cluster of mini bottles behind her and shook it in the air until Kenya nodded. Kenya proceeded to douse her entire plate with it.

"You're such an Arizona girl." Darby watched in awe. "No one else I know puts hot sauce on their eggs and potatoes."

"I will take that as a compliment." Kenya picked up her fork. "Now, seriously, what are we going to do to get that boss of yours to stop breathing down your neck all the time? It's stressing me out and I don't even work here."

"We could always throw her a party," Darby said as she reached under the counter for extra napkins. The dispenser on the counter was getting low.

Kenya stopped with her fork halfway to her mouth. "Are you serious right now?"

Darby shrugged. She actually wasn't sure.

"Don't you tease me with a good time," Kenya said. "You say the word party and I instantly go into planning mode."

"It just popped out, I don't know if I meant it or not."

Honestly, now that Darby was considering the idea, she couldn't think of a single reason why she, or anyone else for that matter, *would* throw a party for Gretta. The woman was such a crank.

On the other hand, maybe that's exactly why they *should* throw her a party.

"You know," Darby leaned one hand on the counter. "Grammie always used to say that you make cookies with a cup of sugar, not a cup of salt."

Kenya swallowed her bite of omelet and tipped her head to the side. "What the heck does that mean?"

"Oh, come on," Darby rolled her eyes. "Obviously, it means being sweet is better than being salty."

"Obviously," Kenya repeated with a sassy toss of her head. "So, are you being serious about the party thing? I honestly can't tell right now. I thought Gretta drives you crazy."

"She does, sort of. I mean, she's hard to work for. That's all."

The words came out a jumbled mess because Darby's insides were a jumbled mess. There was part of her that totally understood Gretta. It wasn't easy owning a restaurant. There was a lot of pressure on the lady that no one else ever saw.

"I don't know, maybe it would help her be nicer." Darby shrugged. "Anyway, it would be interesting to see what happens. You know?"

Kenya grabbed her knife to cut the rest of her omelet into bite-sized pieces. "Okay, let's just go there. What kind of party would you throw for her?"

Darby had no idea. She'd been at the Corner Café for almost a year but didn't know when Gretta's birthday was. They weren't big on birthdays around here. Darby brought in a cake for Samson's birthday a week ago and everyone acted like that was the weirdest thing ever.

The café also didn't do holidays. Easter was a week ago and it came and went like it was nothing.

"How about a Gretta Appreciation Day Party?"

"That's not a thing."

Darby flicked a napkin at Kenya. "Well, then let's make it a thing. You aren't a Utah-famous party planner for nothing."

Kenya straightened, a smile spreading like the sunrise. "Utah-famous, huh? Give me some more of that sugar! Come on, butter me up. Tell me how awesome I am and how you desperately need my help because you can't plan a party without me."

Well, that was easy, because it was all true.

Darby grabbed a spoon and held it to her mouth like a microphone, but was very careful to keep her volume low. "Kenya Sparks, party planner extraordinaire, was recently commissioned to plan the Gretta Appreciation Day Party for Gretta Robinson, the owner, and manager of the Corner Café. It's no secret Gretta has been aching for some appreciation, her scowls have gotten scowlier, her throat is raw from clearing it more than ever before, and her eyebrows have become one in the center from drawing together so often. The only person with the mettle—"

"Mettle?" Kenya chewed on the word along with a bite of omelet. She clearly wasn't enjoying the flavor.

Of the word, obviously. Darby knew the omelet was perfect. No one could omelet like Samson. He was the best short-order cook in Southern Utah.

"Okay, okay. The only person with the innovative creative genius . . . yeah?"

Kenya nodded.

"Innovative creative genius needed to execute, no, no, produce, um, to fabricate, assemble, churn out. . . . I'll come back to that. Kenya was the only person qualified to make the perfect Gretta Appreciation Party. Wasn't she the girl who put together the most amazing fiftieth high school reunion just last night? Complete with disco ball, the belliest of bell bottoms, and moves that would make Travolta bolta? Yes, yes she was. Lucky ducky Hurricane High class of 1972! Goooooooooooooooooooooooooooo Redskins!"

"Okay, okay, okay." Kenya's face was bright red. She took a huge gulp of orange juice and a very deep breath. "Girl, you have to stop or I'm going to choke. But, you're right. If you really want to do this, you obviously need me. We wouldn't want this to end up like Samson's birthday cake with icing that turned everybody's lips purple."

"Purple is a great color."

"Not for lips. It makes everyone look like they're in need of some serious CPR."

Darby wiggled her eyebrows. "Bud seemed like he would be pretty excited to practice mouth to mouth on you. Mitch better watch out, huh?"

Kenya set her fork down. "Stop right now or you're going to see that omelet come back up again all over your uniform."

Darby hid a smile and kept her comments to herself, like the comment about how most of the dudes working at the Corner Café would give their beat-up truck for Kenya's phone number, or the comment about how interesting it was that Kenya was jotting party ideas on a napkin and humming to herself when just a few moments ago she was contemplating a career change to Costco.

She obviously loved her job.

An unexpected clench gripped Darby's stomach again.

No.

No no no no no nononono.

"Hey, do you need more juice?" She asked to distract herself.

Kenya nodded and pushed her glass closer to Darby. "When would you theoretically want to do this Gretta Appreciation Day thing? I need to get it on my calendar."

Darby looked at the ceiling. "Um, I don't know, we should probably wait until after your wedding reception."

Oh!

Shoot!

Darby wished she could catch all those words and stuff them in her pockets.

Kenya's eyes flickered. "Yeah, speaking of that, are you going to help me out, or what?"

The only thing that could save Darby now was the brunch rush. The bell over the door started jingling before Darby stopped hemming and hawing, and didn't really let up until after Kenya finished her food. Darby didn't get another chance to talk to her, even though she hung around for a few extra minutes. When it was clear her spot at the counter was needed, Kenya waved and left.

Darby knew she'd have to face Kenya eventually. She just hoped by then she'd have a super good excuse. Something ironclad and unavoidable. Maybe one of her business professors would assign a boatload of homework that night, or a major project that would take forever. Well, not forever, yuck, just until the wedding reception was over.

An excuse would make that conversation easier, for sure, but with a good excuse or without one, there was no way Darby was catering a wedding reception. What a wreck. Darby, in charge of the most important day of a couple's life?

No way.

Not with her luck.

She'd just screw the whole thing up.

Like she did with everything.

# Chapter Two

*Aspiring MatchMaker (AMM) Seeks the Perfect Match for her Best Friend. Breaking Hearts is Not Allowed. Don't Respond if You Have a Track Record.*

Darby got out of her Intro to Entrepreneurship class right on time with zero major looming projects.

Well, that stank.

Her professor wasn't a fly-by-the-seat-of-his-pants kind of guy. If he hadn't assigned something ridiculously time consuming by now, it wasn't going to happen. Her Business Applications professor, on the other hand, was fond of overloading the students with spreadsheets that made their eyes cross, but Darby didn't have that class until the next day. That meant she'd have to face Kenya in the morning, totally excuse-less.

Fabulous.

The first thing she did when she stepped out of the building was check her phone. It had been dancing the rumba in her backpack pocket for the last hour.

She didn't recognize the number, and everybody knows there's only one thing to do when you don't recognize a phone number.

Darby called it back.

"Hello?" said the unidentified male.

"Hi, this is Darby Reynolds, I have a couple of missed calls from you. . . ."

"Darby Reynolds? Darby . . . oh, yeah. Apartment 1A, right?"

It gave Darby the creeps that some strange dude knew her house number. She turned on her heel and went back into the lighted building. The dark and spooky parking lot combined with the shivers up her spine was too much all at once.

"Uh, yes. Who is this?"

Don't say Jack the Ripper.

"Oh, heh, heh, sorry, it's Al, the superintendent of the building?"

Darby probably should have recognized that name, but she didn't. She might, if she did more than sleep at her apartment. Once a month the flier from Red Rock Duplex Community came without fail, filled to the margins with news and events that Darby probably would have thought were way fun if she actually stopped to read what they were. The newsletter ended up in her garbage can, head first, everytime. There was no point in getting to know a bunch of random people when she didn't plan on staying there long. As soon as she finished her degree she was going back to the city.

But maybe she should have at least learned the superintendent's name. That would have been useful in a moment like this.

Darby pushed open the door and headed back out to the parking lot.

"Yes, hi Al, how are you?"

"Well, I'm good. Wish I could say the same for your duplex."

Wait, what?

What was wrong with her duplex?

Darby's brain went nuts with worst-case scenarios that were so consuming that she didn't pay attention to where she stepped next. As her luck would have it, someone left a glass sprite bottle on the sidewalk even though there was a garbage can an arms length away.

Darby's foot hit the bottle at the perfect angle to pitch her into the nearby bike rack. She grabbed onto the nearest bike with both hands, to keep from rearranging her teeth on the asphalt, and dropped her phone into a pile of junk hanging out in the gutter.

Come on!

Seriously?

The bike Darby gripped teetered back and forth for a minute, then fell, dragging Darby with it. She landed hard on her palms and watched the other bikes clang to the ground in sequential order.

Bang.

Bang.

Bang.

Bang.

BANG.

That last one was an overachiever, obviously.

Darby blew hair out of her eyes and glared at the mess of tires and chains. Why didn't people actually chain their dang bikes to the rack instead of just setting them there? If the bike she'd grabbed had been chained, it wouldn't have fallen over, and then half the people in the parking lot wouldn't be staring at her through their car windows right now.

Apparently everyone in college needed to get a Netflix subscription. Darby was not that interesting.

Her neck burned as she crawled to the pile of leaves. She took a few deep breaths and closed her eyes, then she plunged both hands into the depths. If she touched something hairy or breathing, she was totally going to freak out. Thankfully, her fingers brushed the hard case of her phone right away. She fished it out of the mess and held it to her ear.

Close, but not touching.

Cause, ew.

Al was still talking on the other end, like nothing happened.

She only half listened as she struggled to her feet and went to fix the bike situation. It wasn't all that easy with just one hand. It took a lot of clanging, and the unfortunate squashing of three of her fingers, but Darby finally got the bikes back where they were before she knocked everything over.

Just as Al stopped talking.

Silence.

Not just silence though, expectant silence.

She was obviously supposed to say something.

Except that she had no idea what they were talking about.

She swallowed what was left of her pride, not that there was much to swallow, and laughed awkwardly. "Al, I'm sorry, I didn't catch what you said."

"Oh, heh, heh, technology, huh? Gotta love it."

Yeah, Darby was just going to let him think that it was technology's fault. That's right. It had nothing at all to do with her terrible, terrible luck.

"I was just calling to let you know there's an infestation of cockroaches in your apartment and the one next door. Your neighbor discovered a nest in their mattress and gave me a call. I hope you don't mind, I couldn't get a hold of you so I went ahead and let myself in. Sure enough, there's a nest in your place too."

Cockroaches? For real? Darby almost dropped the phone. Her tongue slid out of her mouth as her stomach heaved. She hadn't eaten dinner yet, so there was nothing to come up, but her stomach sure was trying to empty itself anyway.

A couple of deep breaths and she kept the contents of her stomach where they belonged. Good thing too, Darby couldn't imagine explaining to the owners of the bikes why she'd knocked them over and then thrown up all over them.

But really, come on!

Cockroaches?

That was just messed up on so many levels.

"I'm sorry," Darby said in a small voice. The less she opened her mouth right now, the better. "I didn't hear what you said after the bug nest thing."

"No worries, now, heh heh, I was just telling you how the exterminator roped off your building. Apparently, those things breed like nothing else. They're gonna do a full fumigation, don't you worry, good as new when they're done. Except you don't want to go back to your place for at least three weeks. Maybe four."

"Four weeks?" Darby looked down at her café uniform, now covered in gutter guck. She'd gone to class straight from work. "I can't grab clothes or anything?"

"Trust me, you don't want nothing from there right now. Those roaches lay their eggs in everything, and I mean everything. If you take something with eggs in it, say, your toothbrush, then they could infest your car, your work, the grocery store. . . . No, we want to let the professionals get in there and take care of it."

Darby dry heaved again.

Her toothbrush?

Why did Al have to say that? She couldn't make that mental image go away now.

Ew, ew, ew.

Darby interrupted right in the middle of his monologue. She'd heard enough. More than enough. Yikes, she might seriously never recover from this conversation. "Okay, okay, yeah, I get it, I'll figure it out. Thanks for letting me know."

"Wish it was better news."

Darby let out a laugh, one that was dry and brittle, completely lacking in humor. Better news? She had no idea what that even meant. Better news and Darby were not acquainted. And she didn't even want to talk about *good* news. Ha, what was that?

"I'll give you a jingle when it's all taken care of. Good luck to you."

"Thanks," Darby said with an extensive roll of her eyes. Good luck? Yeah, that was the same as good news. Unknown and unattainable.

Darby hit the end button on the call and stared at her filthy phone.

What the heck was she going to do?

She'd come to Hurricane Utah on purpose because she didn't know anyone here. Grammie grew up in Hurricane and loved it, so it seemed like a great place to escape from Salt Lake. Now Darby realized she was a nincompoop. Not having a friend or family member you could call when you had a cockroach crisis was a very big problem.

She didn't have enough money to stay in a hotel or a Vrbo for three or four weeks. Maybe she could sleep in her car? She'd just watched something on the news about more and more people doing that, especially in expensive places like California where housing costs were atrocious. If those people could do it permanently, Darby could do it temporarily.

Maybe.

She reached her two-door sedan and looked at it with a critical eye.

A friend had given her a great deal on it. It was a reliable little car. But, a house?

Yeah, not so much.

The phone vibrated in Darby's hand, tickling her palm. She looked down at it but didn't answer right away. What if it was more bad news?

She didn't think she could take more at the moment.

Carefully, she turned the phone over so she could see the screen and the person who was calling.

Oh, it was Kenya.

Darby answered, trying not to let the phone touch her face as she leaned into the driver's side door.

"Hey, Kenya."

"Hey, girl! Where are you?" Kenya shouted over Elvis, who was getting all shook up in the background. "I've been trying to call you for over an hour!"

"Oh, sorry about that. I was in class."

"Duh, me, I knew that. You're out now, right?"

"Yes," Darby fumbled through her purse for the keys to her car. Exhaustion poured over her suddenly, making her knees feel like pancakes.

"What's wrong?"

"Huh?"

"What's wrong? Something's wrong. You don't sound right."

Darby looped the keys around her fingers so she didn't drop them. She was pretty sure she remembered a horror movie that started that way and she didn't have any luck to press.

"It's just been a long day."

"Hmmm." Then a looooooong pause. "Nope, that's not it. What's going on with you?"

"I'm fine. It's fine. Everything is fine."

"Yeah, that's what people say when they are really not fine. Come on, spill your guts. I'm not hanging up until you do."

Darby sighed deeply. There was no point in delaying the inevitable. "I got a call from my super, apparently my apartment is infested with cockroaches and I can't go home."

"Oh, my nasty!" Kenya's voice squeaked. "Are you kidding me?"

"I wish, see, I told you, I have the worst—"

"Don't say luck!" Kenya interrupted. "There is no such thing as luck. Remember? Grammie always said you make your own luck."

"Grammie did not ever say that." Darby laughed despite herself. Introducing Kenya to Grammie's sayings was opening a whole bucket full of worms.

"Of course she did, you just don't remember. That is totally something Grammie would say." Kenya said firmly. "Luck is not real. We're not here on this planet to get kicked around by some mystical Karma and domineering Luck. It's hooey. You are the boss of your own life!"

Well, look at that. Kenya should have ditched the party planning track and gone into motivational speaking. She could pull sayings out of nowhere like a magician.

"What are you going to do?"

"I don't know." Darby thought Kenya was the best, but they were just café chums. They weren't really close enough for Darby to share her money woes. They'd met at the café shortly after Darby started working there, so less than a year. Kenya came in dressed like a clown. Darby had to ask what that was about, cause how could she not, and that was the eginning of their friendship.

So, they were friends, yeah, but it was like a see-you-at-the-café-every-morning kind of friendship, not a bear-your-whole-soul kind of friendship.

Well, except for that one day when Darby let it slip in a weak moment that she used to be a chef. That was a mistake. She'd been way more careful what she said to Kenya after that.

"Darby?"

"What?"

"I thought so, you weren't listening. No worries, I got you. You're staying with me."

Darby was already shaking her head. "I can't do that!"

"Of course, you can! My house is huge, like four bedrooms. My costumes need one, and my party junk needs another, so that means there's one for you."

Darby bit her lip.

Hanging out with someone at the café was one thing, living in the same house with her was another. Seriously, stuff like this destroyed relationships. Darby didn't want to lose the only person in one hundred miles that she could talk to.

"Where else would you stay?" Kenya said. "Do you have another option?"

Darby clamped her mouth closed.

Yeah, that was a no.

"Then it's settled," Kenya said. "You're coming home with me. Look at that, you didn't even have to buy me dinner."

Darby tried to smile. It was watered down and pathetic, but the best she could do after the day she'd had. "Thanks, Kenya, that's really nice of you. I appreciate it."

"Nice, nothing." Kenya grinned. "I'm bribing you, so you'll help me with the wedding reception. Plus, it will be so fun! Like having a sister. I always wanted one of those. Now, drive your booty to the community center. Seriously. You gotta be here, like, right now."

Yeah, but did she, though?

"Kenya, I worked a bazillion hours today and then put together a proposal for a make-believe lemonade stand business."

Not to mention the bikes, the dirt, and cockroaches.

"I am seriously exhausted."

"Trust me if you don't come right now, you're going to regret it for the rest of your life."

Darby opened her car door and plopped into the worn seat. Just the thought of loud music, tons of people, and white bobby socks made her want to hide in the middle console. "Are we talking regret like there's a hot guy that is so beautiful he will make my eyes melt and I have to see him or regret like the Elvis impersonator got his wig stuck in the ceiling fan and it's super funny?"

"Not saying. You have to see this for yourself. But it's not the second one so hurry up!"

And then she hung up the phone.

A hot guy so beautiful her eyes would melt?

As fun as that sounded, Darby didn't have a great track record with hot guys. Kenya probably figured that out by now, she'd been trying to help Darby get up the guts to talk to Myles for like eight months.

Since Darby had no idea where Kenya's house was, she couldn't just go straight there, so it looked like her next step was made for her. She tossed her purse over to the passenger's side and slid the key into the ignition. She pulled out of the parking lot and took a right toward the community center.

Her thoughts were noisy as heck the whole drive there, but she told them to can it. She was just going to go to the stupid Sock Hop, see what Kenya wanted that couldn't wait, then crash at her house for four weeks while her duplex got fumigated.

It was fine.

She was fine.

It was all fine.

The Patsy Cline song playing at the community center was cranked so loud, Darby could hear the warble before she even saw the building. She found a parking spot about a million yards from the front door, of course, because there were never empty spots near the front for her, then turned the engine off and got out of the car. Before she followed the music towards the front door of the community center, she tried to brush dirt off her uniform.

It didn't really work, because her hands were equally filthy.

Oh well, she wasn't there to fling or hop so it didn't really matter what she looked like. The lights were usually dim at these singles things anyway. It was better for people all around if they couldn't get a good look at who they were dancing with.

Darby stopped in the entrance to look around for Kenya. She'd only scanned a corner of the room when someone grabbed her arm and tugged hard. Darby found herself stumbling behind the refreshment table to the back of the photo prop booth.

"Okay, take a deep breath, and then look to the right of the DJ. Hurry." Kenya hopped up and down, jerking Darby's arm with her. To get away from Kenya, who was possibly shaking her brains loose, Darby did what she said.

She peeked over the side of the photo booth, her eyes flickering around the DJ table. Nothing stood out there, so she started focusing on the people milling around that corner. A girl in a pink poodle skirt with bright red lipstick. A guy really working the James Dean thing. Another guy....

Darby gasped.

Was that . . . ?

Kenya pulled Darby out of sight, her own bright red lips tugged into a smirk. "Mmmm hmmm, I told you! You're welcome."

Darby peered around the side again, her eyes finding Myles easily this time. "What's he doing here?"

"It's a community singles event, what do you think? He's probably here to find himself a woman."

"Wow, Kenya."

Just . . . wow.

"What? You know what I mean. A partner, a significant other, a boo, call it what you want. That's what they're all doing out there." Kenya peeked around Darby. "He hasn't been trying too hard, though. Obviously, he's just been waiting for you to show up. Get out there and show him what he's missing."

"Get out there?" Darby looked down at her rumbled uniform. There were all kinds of stains on the knees of the skirt and a bright white rectangle where her name tag was usually pinned on her right shoulder. At least she'd thought to take that off before she came inside. "I can't do that! I'm a mess. And I'm not dressed up like everyone else is. I can't talk to him like this."

"Okay, you are a mess, what happened?" Kenya pursed her lips, then waved one hand. "Never mind. It's dark out there, Fifties and diners were a thing. You fit right in. Waaaaaaaaay better than that hot mama."

Darby looked where Kenya gestured. A supermodel thin girl with a high ponytail danced her booty off with a guy in a checkered jacket. She wore a simple white shirt, so tight Darby could count her ribs, and toddler-sized capri jeans. How in the world did she move in those things? They looked like they were painted on before she went out for the night.

She was in desperate need of Samson's biscuits and gravy.

"Come on, girl, you've been talking about talking to Lover boy for weeks. He's right there, all alone, waiting for you. You're never gonna get a better chance than this."

Darby let herself imagine for a minute that she was the type of girl that could walk right up to Myles and talk to him like it was nothing. She imagined herself strutting across the room and saying something super confident like, 'Hey baby, dance with me'.

Ha!

Who was she fooling, if she had confidence like that, she wouldn't be in Hurricane at all. She'd be in some big city, making things happen.

"I can't, Kenya, I really can't."

Kenya opened her mouth, then stopped and planted both hands on Darby's shoulders. She peered so closely into Darby's face, Darby could see the yellow ring around her dark brown eyes.

It made her squirm.

"What are you doing? It's creeping me out."

Kenya didn't pull back, but she did purse her lips and wrinkle her forehead. "I know you're holding back on me, and you got your reasons, but I also know you're gonna regret it if you leave here tonight without talking to him."

Darby hated to admit Kenya was right. It's just that she would much rather talk to Myles for the first time when she was well rested, wearing clean clothes, and not homeless. Was that too much to ask?

"Look, look! He's moving." Kenya whirled Darby around and nudged her forward.

Darby poked her head around the photo board and watched Myles cross the room toward them. He had such a cool walk, sleek and confident. Darby could watch him all day.

He stopped in front of an arrangement of sugar cookies decorated with royal icing. They were so fantastic, she got distracted and stared at them instead of Myles. Jukeboxes, poodle skirts, Ford Thunderbirds, and leather jackets. Decorated sugar cookies used to be so fun to make. Darby's fingertips tingled as she took in all the little details.

"Darby?" Kenya waved a hand in front of her face.

"Those cookies are awesome, did you make them?"

"Heck no," Kenya said. "I ordered them from a bakery in St. George. I'm good, but not that good. Now, focus, this is your moment, Darby. He's three feet away. Go talk to him."

"What do I say?"

Kenya looked at the ceiling. "Darby, I swear! You say hi, then you ask him to marry you. Duh!"

Darby opened her mouth, then couldn't get it closed again.

"You look like a dying fish. I was joking. Say hi, and then ask him if he likes Elvis, or if he comes to this place often, or what he thinks about them Dodgers, whatever, just get out there! Oh, and take this with you." Kenya pulled the knot of the pink scarf around her neck and dangled it in front of Darby's eyes.

Darby looked at it like it had venomous fangs.

"It will complete your costume. Now go. Take this and go make your own dang luck."

With shaking fingers, Darby took the scarf, then secured it around her neck with a nice square knot.

Maybe she could do this.

It wasn't that big of a deal.

She was just going to talk to him.

She talked to people all the time.

It was fine.

She was fine.

"Okay. Okay, okay, okay, how do I look?"

"Lemme do something about that hair." Kenya stuck her hand in the pocket of her cardigan and came out with a couple of ponytail holders. "I always carry spares in case they break. What am I saying? *When* they break. Come here."

Darby bent her head so Kenya could reach it and tried not to wince at the pulling and tugging. When Kenya patted her head a few minutes later, she felt like her scalp had gone through an egg beater.

"Perfect, you should do a high pony more often. You got some cheekbones! Go get him!"

Go get him.

Darby took a deep breath and lifted her foot to step forward, then she stalled. "What do I say to him, again?"

She seriously couldn't remember a single word in the English language.

Kenya let out a huffy breath and shook her head. "You've been talking since you were a toddler, start with hi and let the rest happen.

Trust yourself. Come on, he's gonna end up with someone eventually, why not you?"

Why not you . . . ?

Why not . . . ?

Why not me?

The thought of Myles ending up with someone else made Darby's stomach flip-flop uncomfortably.

She had to do this.

She had to, or she would regret it for the rest of her life.

Okay.

Okay, okay, okay, okay, yes, she was ready.

Kenya pulled her own ponytail tighter and then gave Darby a little nudge. "Stop stalling! Go get him."

Darby nodded.

Go get him.

Go get him.

Go get him.

She shook out her hands and stepped out from behind the photo prop. Myles was still at the refreshment table, just a few steps away.

And he was still alone.

The women in this place were idiots.

Darby let out a long breath and commanded her feet to move forward. The first step was laggy, but then her feet got the hang of it and carried her quite smoothly toward Myles. He was really absorbed in the refreshments, he didn't look up as she got closer.

Just another foot or so to go.

She opened her mouth to say hi.

Okay, that didn't work.

She took a deep breath and then opened her mouth to try again.

"Hi!"

Myles' eyes slid by Darby. She turned to see who the infiltrator was. There stood the girl Kenya had pointed out earlier. The hot mama. She was staring at Myles with smokey blue eyes and red pouty lips. Obviously, she'd ditched the checkered jacket guy and crossed the room with one purpose in mind.

"Aren't you going to say hi back?"

"Hi," Myles said, then turned back to the refreshment table.

Darby wanted to give him a high five.

At the very least.

The girl looked stunned for a moment but recovered quickly. She sidled over to Myles and draped her arm on his shoulder.

"Hey baby, dance with me."

Darby almost laughed out loud.

Those were the exact same words she imagined herself saying to Myles!

But she was totally joking, there was no way she'd say them in real life. Even if she did have the confidence. Now she was super glad she didn't, because when the girl said those words, they sounded completely ridiculous. Kinda desperate and demanding.

Myles shrugged her arm off and stepped to the side.

One step closer to Darby.

The girl huffed. "Are you seriously not interested in dancing?"

He picked up a cookie and placed it on the plate in his hands without answering. His non verbal cues spoke for him just fine.

"Then, what are you doing here?"

Myles finally looked at her. Darby wished she stood at a different angle so she could see his face. His voice sounded incredibly frustrated. "I'm here with my friend." He swung out his arm towards the James Dean look alike. "He needed a wingman."

"You're so funny!" The girl gave a gushing laugh as she shoved his shoulder.

Myles looked at his arm but said nothing. Darby didn't blame him exactly. There wasn't anything particularly hilarious about the word wingman.

"Oh, I love this song. Come on, dance with me."

It was a Buddy Holly slow song, perfect for wrapping yourself up with another person and swaying.

"No, thanks," he said.

Darby couldn't believe the girl was still trying after so many brush-offs. She was either incredibly determined.

Or incredibly stupid.

"No, come on." She grabbed a hold of Myles' hand and tugged, but he stood his ground.

"You go. I'm sure you can find someone else to dance with."

Well done, Myles!

The girl gave Myles full range to her perfect red pout. "You seriously can't tell me you came to a dance, and you're not going to dance at all?"

Myles didn't answer.

"Seriously?" She narrowed her eyes. "You want me to go out there and find another guy to dance with?"

"You want to dance." Myles shrugged. "I don't. It kind of makes sense."

Both of her hands found their way to her tiny waist. "What if I don't come back?"

Myles stared at her.

Darby did too, in total fascination. How in the world was a person supposed to answer that?

Your loss?

That's too bad?

Byeeeeeeee?

Darby was still thinking of responses when the girl flounced into the crowd. She latched on to an extra from Grease and started dancing like the two of them were velcroed together. Every once in a while she'd shoot a look back at Myles, like showing him what he was missing.

Myles breathed out a huge sigh. It made his shoulders lift almost to his ears, and then lower. Darby was close enough to see the whole progression. She was also close enough to tap one of those shoulders without even stretching her arm that far.

What would happen if she did?

Myles started to move like he was going to turn around, so Darby did the most logical thing she could think of.

She dove into the ficus tree next to the refreshment table.

It wasn't her smoothest moment, that was for sure. The tree jostled the refreshment table, knocking over some of the napkins. Which, of course, caught Myles' attention. He picked up the napkins and dropped them into the nearby trash can, then he examined the tree with a confused look on his face. Darby held as still as she could, didn't even breathe. After a moment, he looked away and went back to his in-depth inspection of the refreshments.

Darby might possibly be stuck in the ficus plant until the end of time.

She couldn't get out while he was standing there, it would draw his attention again, and he definitely didn't look like he was moving anytime soon.

And the worst part was that her nose itched super bad.

One of the leaves would reach forward with her inhales and tickle the tip of her nose. Inhale, tickle, exhale, relief. Inhale, tickle. . . . Now that she was hyper aware of it, she wasn't sure she could hold the sneeze in much longer.

Myles glanced over his shoulder, away from Darby, and she seized her chance to rub the itchy tip of her nose.

This gave her a moment of reprieve.

Just a moment.

Before the most explosive sneeze of all time erupted from her nose and mouth. Darby's cover was blown, literally. She kept her eyes squeezed shut for a moment to gather herself. There was no way to explain to Myles why she was hiding in the tree. She was just going to have to step out and admit she was ridiculous.

She opened her eyes, then bent to avoid whacking her head on the branch as she stepped forward.

Or tried to.

Something held her back, but she couldn't see through the dang branches. Darby yanked her foot.

And the room went dark.

People gasped, someone screamed, and Darby bent over to confirm her suspicions.

Yep, that thing holding her back? That would be an extension cord.

And since she was already Sherlocking it up in here, it was important to note that the extension cord was the main power source of the strings of twinkle lights on the ceiling.

And also the music.

Elementary, dear Watson.

What happened next was a series of unfortunate events that would have made Lemony Snicket proud.

Someone nearby pulled out a lighter and flicked it to make a small circle of light. Small, but powerful enough to allow others to find the flashlight on their phones. Darby held out her hands to feel her way out of the tree, to the photo prop where she hoped Kenya waited with her phone light. Darby's was still in her car. No idea why she left it there, seemed like a good idea at the time.

Darby's fingertips found the photo prop for just one moment before the clouds parted and the universe shouted, I hate you Darby. The photo prop crashed to the floor. More shrieking. The person with the lighter jumped out of the way, lost his balance and landed on the edge of the refreshment table.

It's fine, the napkins broke his fall.

And then they went up in a bright flame of orange and yellow.

Apparently party napkins are incredibly flammable.

Good to know.

More screaming as the flames licked the fake ficus, which was also incredibly flammable. Darby was glad she'd moved. The whole top of the tree was lit.

And not in a good way.

Then, the flames reached high enough to attract the attention of the sprinkler system.

Meaning, the sprinklers went off.

All over those expensive phone flashlights.

A whole new chorus of screams joined the party then, a couple of octaves lower than the screams before. Lights disappeared as people tried to protect their phones from the torrential downpour.

And, without light, no one could see where they were going.

There were thumps as bodies slipped and hit the floor, crashes as people bumped into expensive things that should have stayed upright, and a series of synchronized clangs as a bunch of metal chairs fell against one another.

Darby covered her face with her hands, waiting for the next bad thing. She knew her luck was awful, obviously, but she had no idea it could go atomic on her. The best thing to do would be to teleport herself, with her mind powers, of course, to the parking lot and hide in her car.

But Darby hadn't really figured out that teleporting thing, plus she was afraid to move. With her luck . . . seriously? She'd run across a hidden bomb or something and all that would be left of this Sock Hop was a smoldering crater.

Someone had the presence of mind to flip the switch for the overhead lights, since those weren't affected by the extension cord. Darby gave herself to the count of ten for her eyes to adjust, and then she bolted. It wasn't quite teleporting, but it was a mad dash, so that was almost the same thing.

When Kenya came out, about an hour later, Darby was still sitting in the driver's seat with her forehead resting on the steering wheel.

She looked up as Kenya approached her car. "Are you sure you want me to stay at your house? It might implode when I walk through the door."

There was no way Kenya would deny the power of rotten luck now.

"What are you talking about?"

"Seriously?" Darby blinked. "Did you not notice that big fat mess I made of your Sock Hop?"

"That?" Kenya waved her hand toward the building. "That could have happened to anyone."

Darby scoffed. "Are you kidding me?"

"Come on, Darby. It stinks, yeah, it's disappointing, sure, but stinky and disappointing things happen sometimes. This doesn't have to mean anything about you or your supposed luck. It can just be a freakish accident, you know?"

"You should be so mad at me right now."

"Why? Before everything went pear-shaped, people were having a great time. So, mission accomplished. We got it all cleaned up and the community center discovered that the sprinkler system works. See, it's all good."

Darby groaned and thumped her forehead back into the steering wheel. "I can't leave this car. I can't face people ever again. I don't know why you aren't yelling at me. I seriously ruined everything."

Kenya laughed. "Did you see hot mama running out of there in those heels with a platter over her head" She covered her mouth and snorted unabashedly.

"Missed it," Darby said.

It wasn't funny yet.

"Make-up running down her face, hair all stringy, screaming like a goat. Seriously worth all the hard work. See, bright side. There's always at least one."

Darby raised her head to give Kenya a look. "You're weird."

"I know," Kenya slapped the hood of the car, making Darby jump. "Follow me, okay? I need a shower and you need sleep. You look like death." She hummed 'you ain't nothing but a hound dog' as she danced to her car.

Darby turned the key to start the engine and tried not to listen to the boxer in her head. The one that was really good at throwing words like punches that usually hit the mark just right. She wasn't an idiot. If Kenya thought it was no big deal, then maybe Darby could just let it go too.

Eventually.

Like in a week, when she was done torturing herself over and over by reliving every horrible moment.

She did see a bright side though. Kenya would be proud. Myles had been too enthralled with the cookies to notice Darby there. See that was good new cause if he had seen her, Darby wouldn't be able to go to work ever again.

And she really needed her job.

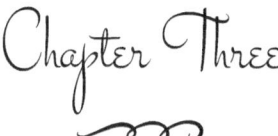

# Chapter Three

*Determined Twenty Something (DTS) is Ready to Try Again. Maybe*

That dream again.

The one where she stood in the middle of her bright, shiny restaurant, holding a tray with an assortment of appetizers. She smiled so hard her cheeks were going to hurt for a week afterward. Slowly, she rotated in a circle so the cameras could catch each individual antipasto and puff. Reporters called out praise that would end up in five star reviews she could hang on the wall of her office.

It was the most glorious moment of Darby's life. She'd worked so hard for this. She wanted this moment to last forever.

But, it didn't.

It never did.

Darby's beautiful restaurant dissolved into a blur of blacks and reds. Suddenly, she was outside, standing on the brink of a bottomless fiery chasm. Darby watched her restaurant slip off the edge of the chasm and disappear into the darkness.

Brick by brick by brick.

Darby pulled herself out of the tangle of super soft leopard print blankets on Kenya's spare bed and grabbed the clock from the bedside table.

Fabulous.

It was three in the morning.

Of course, it was. She should have known she wouldn't sleep well after that mess at the community center. She shouldn't have been a bit surprised. This always happened when her terrible luck reared its ugly head. All those awesome feelings from last year came bounding forward like a billion bouncy balls.

And by awesome, she meant awful.

Memories of her supreme and utter failure.

This was exactly the reason she stayed busy, never stopping long enough to think about the past. Not only did it change nothing, but letting her mind go back there brought on the dream.

Every time.

And it sucked.

This was all Jackson Wilcox's fault.

Even thinking his name made her stomach clench. Did Jackson Wilcox have any clue of the long-reaching consequences of his article? What would he think if he could see her now? What would he say about Darby leaning over the edge of her bed, rubbing her bloodshot eyes? How would he feel if he knew he continued to ruin Darby's life long after that fateful day last March?

Darby snorted.

She knew the answer to all of those questions.

He would think, say, and feel nothing.

Because he had no soul.

And possibly no heart.

Okay, so, maybe he needed to have a heart actually, to be alive, but Darby had her theories about that.

Cyborg, for one.

Zombie, for another.

Darby rose from the bed and walked over to the cork-board above the desk. There were tons of inspirational quotes tacked there on all different colors of paper. The words jumped at Darcy, mocking her thoroughly.

*You believe in you.*
*You are capable of the impossible.*
*You are unstoppable.*
*You have everything you need to do everything you want.*
*You are the architect of your life.*
*The only failure is not to try.*
*No one can make you feel inferior without your permission.*
*You can do anything you put your mind to.*

Darby leaned back to survey the board all at once, in all its colorful glory. There were many more quotes that she didn't bother reading. No offense to Kenya, Eleanor Roosevelt, and George Clooney, but Darby thought most of those phrases were a load of crap. She did not *ever* give Jackson Wilcox permission to make her feel inferior, but he still did it.

And she did try.

But she still failed.

Maybe those quotes only worked for everyone else. They must, right? Or they wouldn't still be circulating the internet, producing more and more memes. Maybe it was just Darby who couldn't do what she wanted, no matter how badly she wanted it. Maybe she was the only person in the world who worked her butt off for years and still crashed spectacularly

Now, there was a chipper thought.

Stupid luck.

Darby gripped her hands into fists, her fingernails digging into her palms. She hated, with a fiery passion, that Jackson Wilcox could get away with demolishing a person and be paid a boatload to do it. He didn't just get away with it; he was exalted for it.

Darby's eyes stung.

Stupid Jackson Wilcox, and stupid three in the morning. It was impossible to think clearly at this hour. Everything felt huge and horrible. The nicest thing she could do for herself was jump back into that adorable, comfortable spare-room bed and go back to sleep.

So that's exactly what Darby did.

Well, the jump back into the bed thing. The sleeping thing was more elusive. Every time she closed her eyes she saw Jackson Wilcox's headshot poised next to the byline of his article. Perfect hair and perfect teeth.

Then she had to try and convince herself not to imagine punching him in the face, which took a lot of energy that should have been focused on falling asleep. Eventually, she did though.

It just didn't feel like it.

She woke up groggy, with the sun peeking through the curtains, a few hours later. The café opened at seven. She didn't have time to lollygag, as Samson loved to say. It was time to stop wallowing and start moving.

Darby flung herself out of bed, leaving all her thoughts sticking to the down feather pillow. She showered, then dressed in her uniform and the same underclothes from yesterday. That was not going to work for much longer. She'd have to hit Walmart after her shift, then maybe go to a thrift store for pajamas, jeans, and shirts. Work was covered, there were a bunch of uniforms in the closet at the café in all different sizes. She should be able to find one that fit.

Well, maybe.

She definitely shouldn't hold her breath. There was probably nothing in her size.

Darby was rubbing her phone down with another Clorox wipe to get rid of any residual gutter grime from the night before as she walked to the kitchen for breakfast. She was so intent on her work, that she almost bumped into the back of Kenya's chair. Kenya sat at the kitchen table, all hunched over, nursing a huge mug of hot cocoa that smelled like peanut butter.

Darby jumped back just in time, banging her elbow on the wall instead of Kenya's head. "Whoa, sorry, I didn't think you'd be up this early."

Kenya looked up with puffy eyes. "I'm usually not, but I wanted to see you before you went to work. You know, make sure you don't leave with your bra on the outside of your clothes or something."

"What? I have never done that."

"Yeah," Kenya grinned. "But you might."

Darby couldn't even be offended. She certainly wouldn't do that on purpose, but if she was distracted enough, who knew?

"Are you hungry? There's cereal in the pantry and milk in the fridge."

Darby walked toward the door Kenya indicated. At home she just ate meals at the cafe, so she wouldn't have to shop or prepare food. It was the mention of the word pantry that got her. Darby had an unnatural obsession with pantries. There was something about rows of colorful varieties of food that spoke to her soul. The invitation to scope out Kenya's pantry too much to resist. She went to the door and pulled it open before she could talk herself out of it and gazed at the shelves of food.

Glorious.

Amazing.

Beautiful.

And it was making Darby's stomach clench again.

She hurriedly pulled out a box of cereal, who knew what kind, and carried it onto the table, then went to the fridge for the milk. "Bowls and spoons?"

"There and there." Kenya pointed.

Darby gathered the rest of the supplies for a classic bowl of cereal and plopped into the seat across from Kenya. "What are you reading?"

"Personal ads."

Darby poured cereal into the bowl and then covered it in milk. "Why?"

"Research." Kenya didn't look up.

Darby waited until it became very clear that Kenya was not going to elaborate. "Research for what?"

"For you."

Again with the long silence.

"What does that mean?"

Kenya finally raised her eyes from the paper. "That means I think you should put a personal ad in the newspaper for Myles."

Darby dropped her spoon into the bowl, making milk splash out onto the table. "What?"

"It's perfect. Hear me out." Kenya's voice gained momentum with each word. "Myles reads the paper every morning, right? He's kind of obsessed with it. And we know he's checking the personal ads. All you gotta do is write one that catches his attention and then see if he calls."

Darby gaped, it was all she could do.

Kenya didn't let that stop her. She held up one finger. "It will be wildly romantic, for one," the next finger, "a great story to tell your kids, for two," and then a third finger, "and super fun, for three. Yeah?"

"No," Darby tried to keep her voice from rising to levels of hysterics. "No! That's so. . . . It's so. . . . It's weird."

"No, it's not! Have you seen this?" Kenya lifted the paper and shook it. "A billion people write into these things, even with all the online dating and apps. That's gotta mean something."

The word 'desperate' came to mind, but Darby didn't say it.

"Come on, Darbs! We write an ad with hints in it, so he can easily guess it's you, and then, when he calls, it's proof it's meant to be! How can you not?"

"What if he doesn't call?" Darby poked at a puddle of milk on the table with her spoon.

Kenya waved her hand. "He will."

"No, Kenya, what if he doesn't?" Darby looked up, repeating the words, emphasizing every consonant. With her luck, this was crazy talk. "What if I get phone calls from creepers that live in their mother's basements? What if I get stalked? What if I disappear and they never find the body?"

Kenya rolled her eyes with a dramatic sigh. "Gimme a break! I've been thinking this through for hours—"

"Wait," Darby pressed her palm into the tabletop. "Did you ever go to sleep last night?"

"Nope."

Fabulous.

Someone needed to tell Kenya the universal rule of women and decision making. Never, never, never make any, at all, *ever* when sleep deprived, hopped up on chocolate, or PMSing.

"Girl, I got you. I figured it all out. We get you a temporary phone, so no one knows your real number, and we make sure we write the article really clearly so it's obvious what you're looking for. Since it's so specific to Myles, no one else will even answer. It's gonna work."

Darby seriously doubted it. She put the spoon back in the bowl, intending to eat. Mostly to distract herself. Only to discover that her cereal had turned soggy and gross.

"The reason you're doing this is to get Myles' attention. Just his. You don't gotta talk to anyone else. See, no creepers. Yeah?"

"Kenya. . . ." Darby lifted a hand, but it dropped back to the table, palm up. Was there was way to tell Kenya nicely that she was completely insane?

"I have to go to work, let's talk about this later?" Darby stood up to take her bowl to the sink.

"Sure, I guess," Kenya twisted around in her chair to face Darby. "I thought you'd be a little more excited. This is your big chance, right?"

Darby leaned against the counter. "You caught me off guard, is all. It's kind of unconventional. I mean, do you know anyone who ever placed a personal ad? Or answered one?"

"No," Kenya pursed her lips. "But I don't think that matters. For Myles, this is the perfect plan."

"An ad is so tacky, though. Who does that?"

"I don't know, who reads them?" Kenya's left eyebrow shot upward.

That was fair.

"It's unconventional," Darby said again. The words sounded lame to her own ears, which meant they probably sounded double gimpy to Kenya. "I don't know, Kenya, you saw what happened last night. I'm a disaster. Maybe it's better if I just like Myles from afar, so he doesn't get maimed or something."

Kenya stood up and extended one hand. "Let me ask you a question and you gotta answer without overthinking it."

Like that was even possible.

"Do you want to date Myles?"

How was she supposed to answer? She did want to date Myles, of course, but. . . .

There was a but.

A big, huge one.

"Girl, you are overthinking again," Kenya's voice went from stern to wheedling in a surprising one-eighty. "What if you just did it? Huh? What if you just took a chance? It could work spectacularly."

Or it could fail spectacularly.

As if Kenya could read Darby's mind, she went on. "Even if it doesn't work out, it's a story for your grandkids, right? They could tell all their awesome little friends about their Grammie who had the guts to do amazing things—like answering a personal ad."

That wasn't really the lasting legacy Darby had envisioned for herself. "I don't know. . . ."

"That, right there!" Kenya jabbed a finger toward Darby. "That's the attitude that gets you nowhere. You gotta know! You gotta pick a side, take a stand, do stuff! You have to work for what you want. Get out there. Stop letting things happen and start making them happen."

That was like an explosion of Kenya's inspirational corkboard right in Darby's face. It all sounded quite lovely, unfortunately, Darby knew from sad experience that was not how things worked in real life. A person could positively affirm their butt off, but sometimes things just didn't work out.

No matter how hard she worked.

No matter how hard she tried.

No matter how hard she wanted it.

Kenya studied Darby's face for a moment, then sat back in her chair. "I see. No, I get it. You think this isn't going to work out because of your luck. You know that's not how life works, right?"

Darby didn't know that, at least, not deep down where it mattered. She gave a half-hearted shrug.

"Can I ask you a question?" Kenya went on without pausing to let Darby answer. "Where did this whole bad luck thing come from? Like, how did it start?"

Darby's stomach tightened, the start of a world-class clench. She didn't want to talk about it. It was cowardly, she knew. Grammie would be so disappointed. The woman who always said you have to get out there and grab the corn by its husk. Just thinking about Grammie eased the clench.

Enough that she could . . . maybe . . . talk about it?

A little.

Darby took a deep breath. "Before I moved to Hurricane—"

"Wait!" Kenya leaned forward, all signs of sleepiness long gone. "Is this your origin story? I've been waiting to hear this for months. Go on, go on."

Darby chewed on her lip. "It's just, I don't like to talk about it, but I'm going to tell you a bit, so you understand me better . . . I guess. . . ."

"Go on, go on!"

"Yeah, so, I lived in Salt Lake City—"

"Awesome, and?"

"Downtown."

"Fabulous."

"And just a block away from my apartment was an adorable little restaurant squished between a German market and a deli."

"Cute, and?"

"And," Darby looked at the ceiling, "it was my restaurant."

"Your restaurant?"

Darby nodded.

"What the what! Are you serious? You *owned* a restaurant! Why didn't you tell me this before? What kind of restaurant was it?"

"Oh." Darby flipped a hand in the air. She'd been so overwhelmed by the prospect of getting all those words out, she hadn't prepared herself for questions. Who knew it was so emotionally taxing to relive the past? "It was just a, like, an everything restaurant."

Kenya's forehead wrinkled. "What does that mean, exactly?"

Darby folded her arms, then clasped them in her lap. "I just served, like, everything. The menu was huge."

Kenya grinned. "So, I could go to your restaurant and order pizza or chow mein or schnitzel or osso bucco?"

"Yeah, pretty much." Darby looked away.

"So unique! How did you even come up with that?"

Darby ran her finger along the top of the table. "I went on a sabbatical after I graduated from high school. I wasn't sure what I wanted to do next, besides travel, so that's what I did. Grammie went with me. We went all over Europe and Asia for a couple of months. I guess I got so excited about the different cuisines that when I got home and decided to start a restaurant, I couldn't narrow it down."

"Aw man." Kenya fell against the back of the chair. "I wish I'd known you then. I'd love a restaurant like that. So would Mitch. What happened next? With your restaurant?"

Jackson Wilcox happened, that's what.

He was the most sought-after food critic in the United States.

Last time Darby checked, he had over five million followers on Instagram and a wait list six months long. Jackson Wilcox was the leading foodie influencer, young and hot and unstoppable. Everything he said was gospel. Her restaurant was lucky to catch his eye.

At least, that's what she'd thought until his article came out.

Stupid Jackson Wilcox.

Stupid.

Stupid.

Stupid.

"I don't really want to talk about that part." Darby let out a long breath like she'd been holding it, even though she hadn't. "It was just, a total disaster."

"No way!" Kenya waved a hand in the air. "I know you. I bet your restaurant was great!"

The restaurant *was* great. It was amazing, despite what stupid Jackson Wilcox said.

"Thanks." Darby looked down at her hands. "It's fine. I'm fine. It'll be better next time."

"Next time? You're going to open another restaurant?" Kenya sounded so surprised it put Darby on instant defense.

"I mean, yeah." She had to prove to Jackson Wilcox that he was wrong about her, and her restaurant. She wouldn't be able to let this go until she did.

Kenya's lips twitched into a smile. "But what about your luck?"

That was the very question that made Darby hot and cold at the same time, but only when she let herself ask it. Which wasn't often.

"I get you now, Darby." Kenya clasped her hands and rested her chin on top. "You think you have bad luck because you failed that one time."

Darby hated that word with a fiery, flying passion.

Failed.

It was so...

Awful.

"It's not just that. . . ." Darby started to squirm, then locked her knees to keep her legs from twitching. "I really have to go, the café opens in fifteen minutes."

"Okay," Kenya nodded. "One question, though. What's going to happen when you finish your business degree?"

"I'm going to open another restaurant."

Kenya raised an eyebrow. "Really? Because I'm pretty sure Grammie had something to say about that."

It was no fair how Kenya always used Grammie against her.

"I never should have told you about Grammie."

"Just say it. You know, say the thing Grammie would tell you right now."

"I don't know what you mean."

"Yeah, you do."

"Grammie said a lot of things."

"Darby! Say it!

Darby glowered. "She would say you don't just become someone different overnight. You are who you were unless you do something different than you did."

"Ha!" Kenya jabbed her finger at Darby. "And what are you doing right now?"

"I'm taking classes." She lifted her chin high. "I'm getting a business degree so I know how to run a business better. I'm doing it the right way this time."

Kenya nodded. "Yes, you are, and you're going to do a bang-up job. But what about cooking? Huh? You never cook anymore."

"How do you know that?" Darby interrupted.

"You told me about it when you told me you used to be a chef."

Apparently, Darby needed to keep her big fat mouth shut from now on because Kenya's memory was impeccable.

"You work at a restaurant right now. Well, a café," Kenya went on. "I would think you'd be picking Gretta's brain all the time to learn how she—"

"I observe!" Darby protested. "I'm learning a ton!"

"Mmm hmm." Kenya stared until Darby started to get squirmy again. "If you want to run a restaurant again, you gotta cook. And if you want Myles, you gotta start talking to him." Kenya tapped her finger against her elbow. "How about we make a deal? You go to work today and if you talk to Myles on your own, then we do nothing. If you don't talk to him, we place the ad."

"You need a hobby." Darby started towards the door.

"I'm too busy for hobbies. And besides, I gotta prove something to you." Kenya followed close behind. "I gotta prove that one failure doesn't mean a whole forever after of failures. You can do whatever you put your mind to. Despite your stupid luck."

"So, you admit my luck is stupid?"

Kenya shook her head as she placed a hand on Darby's arm and turned sympathetic eyes her way. "Darby, I think you're the cat's pajamas, girl. I just love you. I want you to have all the things you want, right? That's it. I'm really just trying to help."

"I know," Darby sighed.

"So," Kenya wiggled her eyebrows up and down so quickly Darby couldn't help but laugh, "do we have a deal?"

"Fine," Darby said slowly. "Before you freak out, we agree that if I talk to Myles today then no personal ad, right? The ad is the very, very last resort."

"Well, you have to have a real conversation, not just take his order, and junk. It has to last longer than three minutes. Like, a real connection."

That was practically impossible to quantify.

Even if Darby felt like there was a connection, there was no guarantee Myles would feel the same way.

Kenya saw Darby's look. "Okay, you have to talk about something other than food for more than five minutes. That's the deal."

Okay, Darby could do that..

Right?

"Okay, deal."

"Yes, yes, yes!" Kenya stood with her fists in the air. "Now go to work, and come home so you can tell me all about it. I can't wait!"

Darby shook her head with a smile. "I'm going."

\* \* \*

Darby was refilling water glasses at a booth near the back when Myles walked into the café. He paused in the doorway, unraveling the scarf around his neck, and looked all over the room. When his eyes met hers, he nodded.

The cool guy head tilt thing.

Was that for her?

She almost dropped the pitcher into Mr. Saganey's lap.

"Oh, sorry, I got it." She steadied the pitcher and finished filling his glass without watering him. It was tough; her eyes wanted to slide over to Myles' stool the entire time.

"Alright, you're all set. Let me know if you need anything else." Darby smiled big and walked away, barely hearing the thanks. She was already at the counter in her mind, staring into Myles' perfectly blue eyes.

Looking at him.

Talking to him.

A real conversation.

Connection.

That wasn't so hard.

Maybe she could do this. She tugged at the too-big uniform she'd found in the closet and hoped it didn't make her look like a marshmallow with legs.

"Welcome in," Gretta called from her desk behind the counter.

"Thanks." Myles plopped into his usual stool and pulled a menu from the stack. After looking at it for approximately three seconds, he set it down.

Just in time for Darby to reach him.

They made eye contact briefly, then Myles sighed. "I don't know what I'm in the mood for."

The tips of Darby's fingers tingled with nerves. She was having the darndest time remembering how to speak English.

"Uh, how about I get you started with something to drink?"

"Just water."

Darby ducked under the counter for a glass, careful to note where her head was in relation to the edge of the counter, then took a pitcher from the counter behind her. "Ice?"

"Naw."

She filled the glass slowly, giving herself time to regroup. "The, uh pancakes here are great. Have you tried them?"

"Yeah." Myles nodded, taking a sip from the glass when Darby pushed it toward him. "I get those every morning."

Darby knew that, actually. She also knew he preferred real maple syrup and always asked for extra butter. She just didn't want him to know that she knew that.

"Have you, uh, tried the blueberry almond pancakes?"

That was a rhetorical question, she already knew the answer.

"No." Myles opened the menu again and bent over it to scan the pages "Are those on the menu? I know I've had the blueberry, but I don't remember anything about almonds."

Darby took a deep breath and leaned forward. "They're off menu. But, uh, trust me, they are the best pancakes you will ever have."

"Off menu, huh?" Myles closed the menu and leaned his chin on the top. "I can tell you are a valuable ally. What else is off menu?" He tipped his head to squint at her shoulder where her name tag lived. "Darby?"

Darby's heart flipped at the sound of her name on his lips. A bubble of courage rose from her toes to her throat.

She shook her head. "I can give you one tip a day, that's all."

Was this flirting?

It'd been so long, Darby didn't know for sure, but she thought it might be flirting.

Myles' lips quirked up to one side. "Really? What's that about?"

Darby shrugged.

"Fine, I'll take the blueberry almond pancakes. They better be good."

"They are." Darby made a note in her order pad. "Do you want maple syrup or blueberry syrup?"

Myles opened his mouth, then closed it and looked at her. "You choose."

"Me?"

"Yeah, whatever you think is best. Bring me that."

It was way hard to concentrate when he looked at her that way.

"That's not how ordering works, Myles."

His eyelids fluttered. "You know my name?"

Crap.

"You, uh, come in here every day," Darby said in such a rush the words were probably impossible to distinguish from each other.

Myles looked at her a moment longer, then gave a low chuckle that sent shivers flying up Darby's arms. "Have you ever seen the movie Ratatouille?"

The cartoon?

"Yes, I think so. Is that the one with the rat who is a chef?"

"That's the one, my niece used to love it when she was a little kid. I've seen it five thousand times. You know that part where they ask the food critic what he wants and he says surprise me? That's what I'm in the mood for this morning. I want you to surprise me."

Food critics.

Darby's stomach was so busy clenching, it took her a minute to process what Myles said after those two, horrible words. "So, you want me to bring out the syrup I think you'd enjoy the most?"

Myles saluted with two fingers.

"But, what if I'm wrong and you hate what I bring you?"

"I trust you." Myles smiled his heart-stopping smile and picked up the newspaper, flipping it open in front of his face.

When she could no longer see his smile, the room somehow looked so much dimmer.

# Chapter Four

*Personal Ads Stink (PAS)*
 *But I've Lost Faith In Humanity, so What the Heck. Might as Well Give it a Whirl. Call Me if You're Sick of the Dating Crap but Still Want to Find Someone to Love.*

The moment Darby walked through the door, Kenya peeked her head out from the kitchen "Hey! How was work?"

Darby tossed her keys in the basket on the side table, dropped a bunch of shopping bags next to the door, and groaned as she slipped her feet out of her shoes.

"That good, huh?" Kenya laughed.

"I gotta get some better shoes." Darby moved to the kitchen table and sat in a chair to rub the arches of her feet. They ached something fierce. "These were supposed to be all cushy, but my feet are killing me."

"Want some Epsom juice?" Kenya asked.

"What the heck is Epsom juice?"

"Really? You never soaked your feet in Epsom juice?" Kenya began ticking items off on her fingers. "Epsom salt, lemon juice, tomato juice, and water. Sometimes I throw in some mint leaves, just for fun. It actually, really makes your feet feel amazing with the added bonus of smelling like marinara sauce for a week."

Just the thought made Darby crave spaghetti. "I'm good, thanks. I'm just going to sit here for a minute."

"Your loss, babe. What'd you buy?"

"Clothes—what are you working on?" She asked the question to distract Kenya away from her shopping bags. Darby was so tired after work, and, because of that three am thing, she'd probably made some terrible fashion choices.

In fact, she knew she had.

She only shopped the fifty percent off rack at the thrift store and she was in a hurry. The chances that she walked out of there with something that fit right and looked decent were not good. On the plus side, she had a whole package of clean under things in the Walmart bag, so the trip wasn't a complete bust.

Kenya turned around. There was a streak of flour across her forehead and another on her pant leg. "I'm making macarons for the Maben's fiftieth wedding anniversary this weekend."

"Are those the coconut cookies, or the colored Oreos?"

Kenya slapped her hand over her heart and closed her eyes. "For the sake of our friendship, I'm going to forget you just said that."

"What?" Darby honestly didn't know what was wrong.

Kenya pursed her lips. "Macarooooooooooooons are crunchy coconut cookies. Maca-RONS are amazing almond flour buttercream sandwich cookies with different flavors that are so not Oreos. Also, they have feet. You seriously just pierced my soul. How can you know so much about food and not know the difference between a macaroon and a macaron?"

"They sound practically the same. It's confusing." Darby bit back a laugh. It was super hard. The wounded look on Kenya's face was hilarious.

"Still," Kenya sniffed.

Darby watched her shift almond flour into a bowl. "How many of those things do you have to make?"

"Mmmm," Kenya looked around the kitchen. Stacks of trays of

resting macarons were on every inch of the counter. "This is the last batch. Total I should have fifty dozen."

"Holy pound cake, Kenya, that's a ton!"

"Nah, it's only six hundred. I'm in a groove."

Darby counted the trays with her eyes, her mind whirling. "It's Tuesday. Why are you making them so far in advance? If they go stale, you'll have to make them all over again."

That would be a ton of work wasted.

"They actually get better the longer they sit, as long as they are stored the right way. Which they will be." Kenya tossed her head. "I have an event every night for the rest of the week, I won't have another chance to bake for the Mabens until Saturday morning, so it's gotta be now."

There was a tingle in the tips of Darby's fingers. That familiar itch to pick up a whisk or turn the knob on an oven. Her mouth half opened to offer to help Kenya bake when she realized what she was about to do. She clamped her lips closed and sat on her hands until the tingle started to go away.

Kenya turned off the mixer and began to fold egg whites into the almond flour. She looked over her shoulder after a couple of turns. "I'm almost done with this part and then I want to hear all about your day." She wiggled her eyebrows before she went back to her bowl.

That was obviously code for she wanted the nitty gritty details about what happened with Myles.

Darby sighed and leaned her cheek on her hand while she watched Kenya pipe circles onto a cookie sheet, then lift the tray and drop it against the counter.

"This is so incredibly satisfying." Kenya grinned as she lifted another cookie sheet about chin height and let it drop to the counter.

Darby laughed, "You're having waaaaaay too much fun with that."

Kenya struck a dorky pose and grabbed another cookie sheet. When the noise from the bang faded, she said, "Do you know why I'm doing this?"

Of course Darby did. Banging the sheets on the counter like that got rid of the air bubbles so the macarons could grow feet. Since that was a signature part of a macaron, it was kind of a big deal.

But she didn't want to talk about baking and food anymore. She needed her brain power to come up with a way to explain to Kenya that her conversation with Myles counted toward their deal so she didn't place that weird newspaper ad. Even though she'd only talked to Myles about his order and foodstuff, she really felt like they had a connection.

It counted.

It *should* count.

Kenya set a timer on the oven, then joined Darby at the table. She let out a deep sigh as she untied her apron and plopped into an empty chair.

"Okay, I'm ready. Tell me everything."

Darby did.

It took about three minutes.

"And then he ate his breakfast, and left."

"That's it? Really?"

Darby nodded. It might not sound like much, but it felt big.

"So," Kenya said. "He didn't tell you if you guessed right with the blueberry syrup?"

"Nope, he just paid at the register, waved, and left."

Kenya's lips curled with obvious disappointment. "It started so promising. If that was a book I was reading, I would have thrown it across the room."

Yeah, Darby had the same feeling.

Kenya sat up so suddenly she made the table sway. "Well, now we really gotta try out the personal ad thing." She brushed her hands together like that was that.

"Yeah, about that. Could we . . . not?"

"Darby." Kenya's voice grew stern. "We made a deal."

"Yeah, but I did have a connection with Myles. I could feel it. It was more than just taking his order, I think it should count."

Kenya looked at Darby for so long, Darby's shoulders couldn't carry the weight of her stare, they curled forward into a slump.

"Okay, fine, let's just get this over with," Darby said.

"Ah ha! Grab that pen." She gestured to the counter behind Darby, then reached the other direction for a pad of paper. "We're writing this thing right now, then posting it in the paper first thing tomorrow morning."

Darby groaned a loud, painful groan as she plucked the pen off the counter.

"Oh please, you are totally going to thank me someday. In fact, you're going to name your firstborn daughter, Kenya, and tell her about the amazing roommate that made her existence possible."

"What if I have a firstborn boy?" Darby rolled the pen toward Kenya, then dropped her chin to her arms.

"Kenneth, called Ken." Kenya flipped the top few pages over until she found a blank one, then set the pad on the table. "Okay, we have to do something mondo clever. Something noticeable. Something between the two of you. What did you guys talk about?"

"Pancakes. . . . Ratatouille."

"Excuse me?"

"The movie, you know, Pixar?"

Kenya still stared like Darby's eyebrows were cauliflower. "Wow, okay, so, we'll just come up with something that will make him want to answer the ad. But not so obvious that he instantly knows it's you. Subtle." Kenya tapped the pen against her bottom lip a few times, then leaned over and began to scribble.

"What are you writing?" Darby asked before she could remind herself she would rather not know.

"Hold on, hold on, give me just a second." She scribbled some more, then turned the pad toward Darby with a flourish. "Check it out. I should have been a writer. This is good stuff."

Darby pulled the pad closer and let her eyes glide slowly over the words.

*Dreamer Seeks Dreamboat (DSD)*
*Food-loving, educated single lady is ready to find out if dreams can come true. If you love to eat as much as I love to cook and you like to dream big, we might just be the perfect match.*

. . .

Darby groaned and dropped her head to the table with a thump.

"Oh, come on." Paper rustled as Kenya snatched the pad out of Darby's hands. "It's awesome."

"I can't believe people really write this garbage." Darby said. "Or respond to it."

"Yeah, about that. I looked it up. Guess what, girlfriend? There was a whole Oprah special on people who got together through personal ads and are still married like a hundred years later. Come on! It works!"

Darby lifted her head. "We are not posting that. It's embarrassing."

"That's fine, it was just an example, you write one."

Darby couldn't seriously write an ad like.

But she might be able to write it *without* being serious.

Darby grabbed the pad of paper and began to scribble before she talked herself out of it.

*Cook Seeks Sous (CSS)*

*Food-loving Single Lady ready to cook up some romance with a like-minded Fella, a one-dish kind of guy who craves commitment, gobbles gallantry, and is hungry for honesty. If you've put a toothpick in it and you're done with wishing and waiting, call today.*

Kenya snatched it away as soon as Darby lifted the pen and read with the pad in front of her face. When she lowered it, her smile was enormous.

"This is *perfect*!"

The fact that Kenya loved it made Darby second-guess herself. It was less like a compliment, and more like the start of a really bad idea.

"I don't want to give out my real phone number," Darby said.

"Oh, yeah, no, of course not. I already thought about that. I have an old flip phone we can reactivate. I'll do that tonight. I am so excited!"

Well, that made one of them.

Darby dropped her head onto the table again. It was way too late to back out now, she was going to do what Grammie always said and sleep in the bag she unrolled.

\* \* \*

The next morning, as Darby worked, her heart just about jumped out of her throat every time the bell over the door rang. Gretta gave her the stink eye at least a dozen different times, but Darby couldn't help it. She was so keyed up.

This was kind of a big deal.

Kenya bounced into the café two hours after opening time. She sent a glimmering smile to Myles, hunched over his newspaper, and saluted Gretta, who grunted.

"It will be in tomorrow's paper." Kenya covered the side of her mouth with her hand like they were discussing their plot to take over the world.

Butterflies started up a conga line in Darby's stomach. They'd just been fluttering all morning, now they were getting serious. She would never, in a billion years, admit it to Kenya, but she was really excited.

Crazy, nervous, but also excited.

She'd stayed in bed for a few minutes after she woke up, daydreaming about what would happen if this actually worked.

What if Myles answered her ad if he was super interested, and then . . . ?

Darby tried on a wavering smile and aimed it right at Kenya. "Okay, so what happens next?"

Kenya grinned, "Well, first you bring me a big old mug of Mexican hot chocolate and one of those banana muffins I could smell all the way down the street, and then we wait until tomorrow to see what happens."

"What the heck is Mexican hot chocolate?"

"Oh shoot," Kenya frowned. "I keep forgetting I'm not in Arizona anymore. Could you just, like, sprinkle some cinnamon in the normal hot chocolate? That's close enough."

Darby pulled out a huge mug, the one with the speckled turquoise dots that Kenya loved, set it on the counter, then went to the back for a muffin and the cinnamon shaker. She didn't dare try to guess how much cinnamon went into hot chocolate to make it Mexican, she'd let Kenya work that out herself.

They chatted while Kenya ate, interspersed with clearing tables and greeting customers. The counter was the easiest place to work and have a conversation, that's why it was Darby's favorite place in the café. The other waiters and waitresses thought she was a loony for loving it, but that was where Myles always sat, so....

Speaking of Myles....

"Check, please," Myles called as Darby passed to refill someone's coffee. She worked up his receipt and slapped it on the counter in front of him.

"How was everything today?"

"Not as good as yesterday." Myles gave her a knee knocking smile. "Maybe I should let you order for me all the time."

Darby was too busy trying to stay upright to really think about how she should respond. "Maybe you should."

Myles checked the amount on the receipt and pulled out some bills. "Well, then maybe I will." He dropped the bills on the counter and then saluted.

Darby let herself indulge in watching him walk to the door for precisely ten seconds before Gretta cleared her throat.

Sigh.

She reached for his newspaper to fold it up and throw it away, but one of the personal ads caught her eye.

*WCI, which stands for Wedding Cake Ingredients, by the way. One whole, real woman. 5'6 or shorter. 18-30. Two parts undiluted love. Three heaping cups of honesty. Four-ever on the clock. Set a timer for one month, then it's gonna go up in flames.*

Yikes.

So cheesy.

Darby couldn't believe she'd agreed to this.

But, on the other hand....

Her eyes found Myles, standing outside the café, looking at his phone.

If it worked....

Gretta cleared her throat again, so Darby tucked away her hopes and dreams where no one could see them, then gathered the money from Myles and made it right with the cash register.

Kenya smacked her arm when she came back around. "Look at you Ms. Flirty McFlirtyson!"

"Yeah." Darby hesitated, then leaned forward to whisper. "It's way easier to talk to him now. I think because we're talking about food and it's kind of my thing?"

"Or maybe it's just time." Kenya hugged herself. "I'm coming straight here after the hoedown. I have such a good feeling about tomorrow. Darby, mark my words, your luck is about to change."

## Chapter Five

*Anxiously Seeking the One (ASO)*
*Not the Two, so Don't Even Think About Answering if You're Already Taken*

The significance of the day smacked Darby in the face the moment she woke up.
The ad.
The ad would be in the newspaper.
Her ad.
She squelched all thoughts of worst-case scenarios and what-ifs. What's done was done. She couldn't change it now. The best thing to do was go to work and see what happened. Not the most comfortable option, but much better than driving herself nuts with all the ways her bad luck could make things go ka-blooey.

When the bell over the door jingled her into the café, Darby's eyes went right to Myles' usual spot. He wasn't there yet, obviously, the café wasn't even open yet. That gave Darby space to indulge in a daydream for the first time in a long time.

She imagined him sitting on his favorite barstool, with the newspaper spread out on the counter, Myles would read her ad, crack up laughing, then call her over to see for herself. He'd declare the writer of the personal ad the girl for him and then wonder aloud where he could find her.

That's when Darby would say. . . .

"What the heck are you doing just standing there? We open in twenty minutes, hop to it!" Gretta grumbled as she walked by with a broom.

Darby hopped to it with all her might.

If Gretta was in a tolerable mood when Myles came in, Darby might get the chance to talk to him about the ad. Then maybe they could stare into each other's eyes and. . . . Yeah, she had no idea. The café wasn't exactly the ideal place for a romantic interlude. She'd have to come back to that part later.

Darby worked alongside the other waitresses and waiters, prepping, arranging, cleaning, and organizing. At seven a.m. when the café officially opened, their first customers were waiting outside in a line.

At the very end was Myles.

He looked so good in the morning. Seeing him was the equivalent of waking up to sparkling rays of sunshine and birds chirping. He was checking something on his phone with the newspaper tucked into his armpit. The way he stood, leaning slightly over his phone, made that delicious lock of hair hang near his eyes.

Today.

Today.

Today could be the day!

Darby unlocked the door, then stood out of the way while people filed inside. Myles let everyone go ahead of him, gentleman that he was, and when he passed by Darby, his smile made her heart kick up a notch.

"Morning, Darby."

"Hey, there. I'll be over in just a sec to take your order."

He shook his head. "No order today. Today we do another Ratatouille. Bring me whatever you think I want for breakfast."

Darby put a hand on her hip. "Just how am I supposed to know what you want?"

Myles laughed, creating wrinkles around his eyes that were so adorable, Darby had to move her hands behind her back to resist the urge to smooth them out.

"You knew last time. And this was your idea. You said I should let you order for me again."

Had she said that? It was hard to remember anything with his blue, blue eyes staring into hers. She'd never seen a color like that before. Myles' eyes were the blue to rule them all.

"I'll see what I can do."

He saluted and strode to the counter. There weren't any more customers coming in, but Darby waited by the door anyway, just so she could watch Myles walk away.

Gretta cleared her throat, reminding Darby that she couldn't actually stand there and ogle a customer all day. She let the door go and slipped behind the counter. There were a number of people at the counter today, but Darby went straight to Myles. He never cracked open his paper until his food was in front of him and today, she wanted that to happen sooner rather than later.

"Are you serious about wanting me to pick your breakfast?" She tapped the top of her pen on the counter to make the ink nib appear.

Myles folded his hands on the counter in front of him. "Serious? Absolutely."

Darby pursed her lips as she studied him. "I can't decide if that makes you adventurous, or a lazy bum."

"I'd go with the adventurous option if I were you." Myles grinned. "It sounds cooler."

"All right." Darby tapped the pen against her lip, then jotted a couple of things down. If she were in the kitchen, this was exactly what she would make for him. It used to be one of her favorite things to cook.

Emphasis on used to be.

Obviously she didn't do that anymore.

A twinge of regret went through her stomach, but Darby was really good at pushing it away. She was done with cooking. It didn't have to be her thing now just because it was in the past.

She peered at Myles over her note pad. "I'm writing down your order. In just a minute I'm going to slap it on that window, there, into the kitchen and they will start making it. You sure you don't want to give me some valuable feedback before I go?"

Myles shook his head.

Darby ripped the paper off the pad and slapped it harder then she meant to. The impact stung her palm. She glanced over her shoulder at Myles, who watched with an endearing grin. Darby wished with all her soul that she could stay right there and stare at him forever.

The doorbell jingled, quickly followed by the smell of hay. Kenya hurried to the stool at the opposite end from Myles and waved Darby over.

Darby finished taking the orders of everyone down the line and got them to Samson before she let herself go over to meet Kenya. Gretta was always more patient when Darby kept up on her stuff.

Once she was close enough to grab, Kenya clamped onto Darby's arm and pulled her down until their heads touched. "Well, well? What happened? Has he read the paper yet?"

"No," Darby whispered. "His order is in, though, so it won't take long."

They both looked at Myles, who was staring into space with deep contemplation.

Either that or he'd fallen asleep sitting up.

"Well, I'm glad." Kenya sat back as she blew out a gust of air. "I hurried as fast as I could, I didn't want to miss anything."

"You didn't miss anything at all," Darby said. "How was the hoedown?"

"So super fun!" Kenya's full grin revealed something Darby had never seen before. She didn't want to be rude, but she totally couldn't unsee what she's seen.

"Did you know you have black stuff all over your front tooth?"

"Oh, shoot. I totally forgot." Kenya grabbed a napkin and started scrubbing. "Is it gone?"

Darby shook her head. After a couple more scrubs, Kenya smiled wide and turned her head so Darby could see from all angles.

"You're good. What was that stuff?"

"Oh," Kenya flipped her hand through the air. "I blacked out a tooth. People always think it's hilarious. It's like, pigtails, straw hat, and flannel are good, but black out a tooth and it is next level!"

"That's kind of weird."

"You don't have to tell me." Kenya agreed. "Anyway, I grabbed a newspaper on my way here, you know, just to make sure everything went through the way it was supposed to. I was going to check online, but sometimes the formatting is wonky. I wanted us to see it the way Myles will see it."

That was incredibly thoughtful.

"And?"

"It's perfect!" Kenya grinned, black tooth free and radiant. "It looks amazing. It's right about the middle of the page in the first column. They used a handwriting font, as I asked, so it stands out way more than the others. I also had them color the box around it red. That was more expensive, but, again, worth it."

"Kenya, how much was it? I should pay for that!"

Kenya flicked her fingers like she was shaking off water. "I got you. You just concentrate on getting through school so you can open another amazing restaurant."

"But—"

"Seriously, what's the point of being a Utah-famous party planner if I can't use my riches to help out my friend? Can I have a blueberry muffin? I have to do something with my hands or this waiting is going to destroy me."

Darby hesitated, not sure if she should give in. The bald facts were, though, that she couldn't really afford to pay Kenya back. "Thank you," she sighed. "You really are the best."

"You know it! Remember that when you have all those riches from your world-famous restaurant. I love jewelry."

Darby winked and went to the kitchen for Kenya's muffin. When she got back, Myles' order was up.

This was it.

Darby slid the plate with a blueberry muffin snug in the center to Kenya, then grabbed Myles' order and took it to him.

"Crepes!" Myles' eyes lit up, making Darby feel like she'd found the cure for cancer. "That's incredible! I was just talking to my sister about how much I love crepes. She studied in France for a couple of semesters back in the day. She makes the best crepes."

"So does Samson, just you wait."

"Are you for real?"

Darby placed a hand over her heart. "True as true."

Myles grabbed a fork with one hand and flipped open his newspaper. The smile he sent her was like a gift.

Darby floated back to the pickup window to divvy out the rest of the orders as quickly as she could. She knew Kenya was watching Myles, but she really didn't want to miss that moment when he read her ad for the first time.

When everyone was fed, watered, and coffeed to the brim, Darby took her place across from Kenya and tried to stare at Myles without looking obvious about it.

"I don't think he's read it yet," Kenya said. "I actually don't think he's on the classified page at all. He got sucked into a headline and has been reading the article this whole time."

Darby wasn't sad. That meant she was busy while he was reading random stuff and now she could watch him when he turned to the classifieds.

Which might be right at that moment, actually.

The swish of the page-turning was louder than normal. That, or Darby's senses were crazy sensitive. Every inhale and exhale lengthened as she waited.

Myles' eyes stopped about halfway down the page.

Time paused while Darby stared into the side of his head, wishing she really was a mind reader.

Then, he burst out laughing.

Gretta glared at him, then at Darby like she was responsible for the noise Myles made.

Which, in a way, she was.

"I'm sorry." Myles coughed into his napkin. "That was loud. This just caught me off guard."

"It's alright." Darby refilled his cup. It had sloshed a bit when he set it down.

"You have to read this," Myles said, moving the newspaper towards her.

Darby glanced at Gretta, then leaned over Myles' newspaper. His finger pointed to a red-bordered box with handwriting text.

"Cook seeks sous . . ." Darby read under her breath.

Holy smokes, this was just like her daydream!

Myles had called her over and showed her the personal ad just like she imagined. Next was the part where he said this was the girl for him.

"I am about to say words I never thought I'd say." Myles chuckled. "If I was ever going to answer a personal ad, it would be this one."

Darby's jaw dropped. She casually reached down to pinch her leg, just to make sure she was awake.

Okay, that hurt.

This was really happening.

How could this be really happening?

Myles went on. "I think it might be fate. I mean, come on. A personal ad like this and my last name is Cook? That's too much of a coincidence to be one, right?"

Darby nodded mechanically, her eyes not focusing on anything.

Since this was going the way she imagined it, now was the part where she told him he didn't have to call the number or look any further, she was the girl and she was right there in front of him.

There was only one problem.

She couldn't do it.

Her brain was mush and her tongue hung slightly to the side of her wide-open mouth. She couldn't get the two to connect no matter how hard she tried. There was no way she was getting any words out. Especially none that made a lick of sense.

Myles pulled out his phone and took a picture of the personal ad, saying something about showing it to his sister. It was actually hard to understand his words over the buzzing in her brain.

"Miss, can I get a refill?"

Mr. Cutchen's voice effectively snapped Darby back into the moment. She glanced over at Gretta, who was watching her with pursed lips. There was nothing fateful or romantic about that. Gretta's stink face was exactly what Darby needed to get herself out of her own head.

"Absolutely, sir, what were you drinking?"

She couldn't, for the life of her, remember.

"Cranberry juice, sweetheart."

"On my way." Darby tapped the counter next to Myles as she hurried away. She refilled the cranberry juice and checked on everyone else at the counter, all the while giving herself a stern talking-to. Yes, it was amazing that her daydream sort of came true, but it wasn't that big of a deal. Dreams came true all the time, or it wouldn't be a saying people put on t-shirts. Sure, they didn't ever come true for her, but maybe that meant her bad luck had maxed out and it was time for some good.

Mrs. Greer and her son took the last two seats at the counter as Darby was finishing up her tasks. They came in so often that they were ready to order without looking at the menu. By the time Darby turned in their orders, got them water and cleared the place of another couple who just left . . .

. . . Myles was gone.

# Chapter Six

*Text Relationship Only (TRO)*
*Young Woman Seeks Correspondent Through Text Messaging.*
*Face to Face is Overrated*

Darby collapsed on the couch at home, her arm flung over her face.

Kenya made sympathetic grunts and grumbles as she settled in beside Darby.

"I don't know what happened, Darbs. You were rushing around and I looked down at my phone to read a text really quick. One minute he was there, the next he was gone."

"I was going to do it. I was ready to tell him. I could have done it, I just needed one more minute."

Stupid luck.

"I'm sorry." Kenya puffed out her lower lip.

"He didn't even take the paper with him." Darby's words were muffled by her arm. "He's not going to call. He can't call a number he doesn't have with him."

"No, no, no! He took a pic. I saw him. He might still call."

Darby peeked out from under her arm. "That's right, he did."

Maybe that was good? A tremor of hope went through Darby's chest. Did she dare indulge it? If it got squished by her luck's big butt, she might actually cry.

"Speaking of phones!" Kenya said, her voice brightening. "I have the old one for your personal ad, I activated it this morning. I'll get it."

Darby stared at the ceiling. She wanted to activate that daydream she'd had that morning before Myles showed up. It was way more fun to think about the possibilities than it was to wallow in everything that didn't go the way she wanted it to. It was just way hard to grasp that daydream right now. Myles left too soon. That made everything feel stupid.

Kenya returned, tossing the old flip phone from hand to hand. Darby held out her palm for the phone but didn't open it. She wasn't brave enough to see if there were messages right now.

"It was too bad the café got so busy right when things were getting good." Kenya said as she tapped her fingers on the table top. Darby couldn't be sure, but she thought it might be the tune to Ode to Joy.

Joy. Pshaw. Ode to Rotten Luck was more like it.

Rotten Luck Myles left so soon.

Rotten Luck that the café was so busy.

Rotten Luck.

Rotten Luck.

Rotten Luck.

As soon as Myles left, everything went downhill. The café stayed super busy for Darby's entire shift. In fact, Gretta had to come away from her desk of power and help Darby clear the counter more than once. She took care of Myles' dishes and newspaper while Darby rang up Mr. Cutchen. That was just a fan-flipping-tastic cherry on top of everything else. Gretta was a bear when she had to step in and bail the staff out.

If Darby still had a job by this time tomorrow, she would be super surprised.

Kenya's voice was exceptionally cheerful. "But it's okay because you two had a moment. You totally had a moment."

Darby nodded absently. The phone slipped from her fingers. She bent over to retrieve it and took her time coming back to an upright position.

"Which is why things are about to change. I can feel it," Kenya said. "Let's look at that phone now. See if Myles, answered the ad."

Darby tossed the phone to Kenya and leaned back against the couch with her eyes closed.

She couldn't even.

Kenya made clicking and tapping noises as she checked the text messages on the phone. That's what Darby assumed she was doing, anyway. She didn't bother opening her eyes to check for certain.

"Oh!" Kenya smacked Darby's arm a couple of times. "Oh, Oh, Oh!"

"What?" Darby jerked her arm out of range of all the slapping.

"Darby, look, look at this!" Kenya shoved the phone in front of Darby's face so close that all she saw was a black blob.

Darby took it and held it at a reasonable distance.

Unidentified number.

*Hey, I saw your personal ad in the classifieds. I never do this, but I have to admit, I'm intrigued. I'd very much like to know more about you.*

Darby blinked and read the text again.

"It's him!" Kenya bounced on the couch next to her. "It's him, it's him, it's him!"

Darby stared at the phone a moment longer, then typed a return message.

It took forever.

How did people survive with flip phones? It was ridiculous that there were three letters on each numbered button. One word took a hundred billion years.

"What are you writing?" Kenya was so impatient her voice had reached shrill.

Darby read her message out loud.

. . .

*What's your name?*

"Way to get straight to it!" Kenya bounced a few more times. "What are you going to do if he says he's Myles?"

"I don't know."

Which was why she wanted to know who was on the other end of this phone as soon as possible. It would be so much easier to talk to him knowing it was him. And it seemed fair, she was willing to tell him who she was. He just needed to go first.

The phone wiggled across Darby's palm. Kenya latched onto Darby's arm, nails digging into her skin.

*Not so fast! Let's see if this has the potential to go anywhere before we exchange names. As I said, I never do things like this. I will tell you, for peace of mind purposes, I am single, employed full-time, under the age of thirty, and male.*

"Does that sound like him?" Kenya asked. "Is it him? Do you think it's him?"

Darby read the message three times. "I don't know."

"Doesn't matter if it sounds like him." Kenya waved her hands around. "Things always sound weird over text. Remember when I sent you that big long text about Mitch 'cause I thought he loved sports more than me and you were super busy so you just texted that you were sorry and I got all mad?"

"Yes." Darby wasn't likely to forget that anytime soon. They'd had to make a verbal agreement that if they didn't have time to text enough words to appease the other person, they had to at least tack on a couple of situation-appropriate emojis before both of them were satisfied enough to let the subject drop.

"Texts are stupid that way. It has to be Myles, we saw him reading your ad. Seriously, he laughed right out loud!"

True, true, all true.

Darby tapped the keypad with her thumbs, then started the long, slow process of putting another sentence together.

*What do you want to know about me?*

He must not have a flip phone because his big long text came super quickly.

*Everything. I'm intrigued. What kind of woman writes a personal ad like this one? I've spent hours laughing at personal ads because they are so ridiculous. You made me laugh for a different reason. There was something about your ad. It was funny. Innovative. It made me want to know more. But before we go any further, I have to know. Are you really a woman? Are you super old, or super desperate? Do you have a criminal record or purple hair? And most importantly, are you really a cook?*

Kenya had scooted closer to read over Darby's shoulder. She let out a long breath that tickled Darby's arm.

"What are you going to say?"

"I don't know."

His last question rattled her a little bit. The truth was quite complicated. Way too much information to type on this dilapidated telephone. And way more information than she'd even told Kenya. Tons of different explanations, short explanations, went through Darby's mind at break-neck speed. The only one she felt truly comfortable with was the complete and honest truth.

*I used to be.*

. . .

"Nicely said." Kenya nudged Darby with her elbow. "Short and mysterious and totally true."

Yeah, it was all of that, but it also wrung Darby's stomach like a wet rag to write the words.

Or type them.

Or whatever.

"Except for the part where you said you used to be." Kenya nudged her again with a laugh. "That wasn't totally true. You are still a cook, Darbs. You just need to start doing it again."

"Maybe." Darby stared at the screen. A message appeared before the notification had a chance to chime.

*Intriguing again. I asked a lot of questions, which one are you answering exactly? Are you saying you used to be a woman? You used to be super old or super desperate? You used to be a criminal, you used to have purple hair, or you used to be a cook?*

Darby puffed out her cheeks and held her breath for a moment. This flip phone was driving her nuts. It was so clunky. She let out a puff of air and went for honesty again.

*Old flip phone. Texting sucks.*

*Wow, okay, that didn't answer any of my questions. I don't think I could get more curious right now if I tried. Let's do this, how about I ask you yes and no questions so you don't have to text long answers for now? Then we can go from there.*

*Y*

. . .

*Come on, you have to at least give me a full word.*

*Yes :)*

*Much better! Okay, are you a woman?*

*Yes*

*My mom, and my sister for that matter, will slap me for this next question but I have to know. How old are you? (that counts, it's not yes or no, but it's a short answer)*

Darby smiled, in spite of herself.

*24*

*I assume you want to know how old I am, too?*

*Yes*

*25. While I'm volunteering information about myself, I'll include that I have a college degree in Business, I'm almost done with my MBA, and I have a successful side business I started my freshman year of college. Also, I love to eat. My favorite thing to do is ask a chef what they think I want instead of ordering off a menu. Have you ever tried that? It's a rush.*

. . .

*No*

*I just figured out the problem with your short answer thing. I can't tell from that **n** and that **o** if you think I'm awesome or weird for doing that. It's not super clear. Do you think I'm weird?*

*Undecided*

Kenya poked Darby in the ribs. "Mean!"

"No, it's not." Darby squirmed away. "It's honest. I'm not sure what I think yet."

Because her brain was spinning at warp speed. Because this was Myles. It had to be. He did that thing with her. The thing where he totally asked her to order for him.

*I guess that's fair. Let's keep going and maybe I can tip the scale. Are you married?*

*No*

*Have you ever been married?*

*No*

*That's good to know. Not a deal breaker, but certainly makes things easier. For the record, I'm not married, never have been married, and don't have any kids. Do you have any kids?*

. . .

*No*

*I will tell you I was engaged once. We met in college, she knocked my socks off, we got engaged three months after we met and then realized we made a huge mistake. She's in Colorado, happily married with two kids. We're cool. How about that convict question? Clean record?*

*Yes*

*No speeding tickets I should know about?*

If Darby wasn't on a dorkified phone she might have told him about the time she drove to visit her friend in Flagstaff and got a ticket for forgetting to use her blinker when she passed a car on the Navajo Reservation. Not that it was an exceptionally thrilling story; she was just beginning to feel like their conversation was extremely one-sided.

*No*

*Me neither. Squeaky clean. Okay, so that means I know that you are in fact a woman, single, never been married, and without a criminal record. What about the purple hair? Give me some descriptors so I don't keep picturing you like Shrek.*

What? Shrek? Of all the things she could have looked like, that was what he went to? Shrek didn't even have purple hair.

She must have hesitated too long because another text came through while she was still trying to figure out how to answer that.

. . .

*Sorry! That was weird. Obviously you're not a seven foot green ogre with a Scottish accent. I used to watch that movie with my niece so often that it runs in the back of my mind on default pretty much all the time. Maybe you're typing right now and it's taking forever because that wasn't a yes or no question? If it helps, you can just tell me your celebrity look a like. That'd only be two words. Or one if it's, like, Rihanna or Zendaya.*

Celebrity look a like? Darby tipped the phone toward Kenya so she could see the question. "What do I say? Who do I look like?"

Kenya pursed her lips and studied Darby through narrowed eyes. She did this for so long, Darby started to feel like a goldfish.

"Emma Stone."

"What?" Darby shook her head. "No way. There's no way I look like Emma Stone! She's, like, gorgeous!"

"Yes, you do look like her." Kenya said in her don't-argue-with-me voice. "Emma Stone from Cruella, with light brown hair instead of red. Seriously, your eyes are the same greenish color, you have the bangs and the waves. Emma Stone. Type it." Kenya leaned over Darby like she was going to take the phone and do it herself if Darby didn't obey.

Darby bit her lip and then typed the words, cringing the entire time.

*Like Emma Stone from Cruella? Or blond Emma Stone or Emma Stone with dark hair?*

*Cruella*

Darby cringed some more with each push of the keypad. Cringe, cringe, cringe, cringe, cringe, cringe, cringe.

"Cut that out," Kenya swatted her arm. "You look like Emma Stone. It's a fact. Quit making that face."

. . .

*Is your hair black and white, then?*

Darby shook her head. *Estella.*

*Got it! Love that movie. Okay, I think I'm beginning to get a handle on who you are. At least, what you look like. I'd like to add more to the list. What do you think?*

"Is he asking if I want to keep talking to him?" Darby blinked a couple of times in rapid succession. It was excessive, but it helped her think.
"Sure sounds that way."
"*Should* I keep talking to him?"
"Are you seriously asking me that?" Kenya turned slightly to look at Darby. "It's Lover Boy! Of course, you should keep talking to him! This is your dream, Darby. Your dream come true. You can't tell me anything about your stinky luck ever again!"

It was her dream, which was why Darby's stomach was doing backflips.

It was too good to be true.

Myles was too good to be true.

She didn't share her thoughts. She knew Kenya would come back at her with copious amounts of optimism and positivity, which wasn't super helpful when she felt so conflicted.

So, she shrugged. "I don't know. What if it isn't Myles?"
"What if it is?"
"Yeah, but what if it isn't?"
"Okay," Kenya scratched her cheek. "Let's just go there, what if it isn't Myles?"

Darby let her head drop to the back of the couch and stared at the ceiling some more. Okay, she'd go there.

What if it wasn't Myles?

Well, then she would spend some time chatting with another guy and then stop when she realized he wasn't Myles. Was that really that big of a deal?

No, it wasn't.

The real problem was she was pretty dang positive it was Myles and if that was true, then her luck was a serious concern.

She didn't want it to mess this up.

"Darby?" Kenya poked her arm. "What if it isn't Myles?"

"But, what if it is?" Darby said in a small voice.

"Is that what's bugging you?"

Darby nodded slowly.

"You're scared it is him and it won't work out, yeah?" Kenya nodded along with Darby. "You know what I think? I think you gotta make peace with the worst-case scenario or you are going to be miserable from beginning to end."

Worst-case scenario.

Darby hated worst-case scenarios.

After a person lived through one, they realized the worst-case could be so much worse than they imagined.

But, on the other hand, she *had* lived through it. That was something. It hadn't completely destroyed her.

"The way I see it, Darbs, the absolute worst thing that can happen here is that it does end up being Myles on the other end of that phone and he has zero interest in you once he discovers who you are. Right? Then what?"

Well, then she would have to face a mountain of disappointment, something she had a ton of experience with, and then she would be exactly in the same place she was before she started talking to him. Going to school, working, and turning down invitations to go to all the community single parties Kenya threw.

Darby let out a long breath. Okay, that wasn't actually that bad of a scenario. Really, she had nothing to lose.

And she was curious.

*Why?*

. . .

*Oh good, you're still there. I thought I lost you. Why what?*

Darby whined and groaned inside her head the whole time she typed the answer to his question. It was really hard to think of a response, make it as short as possible, and text at the same time. It was making her brain hurt.

*Why do you want to keep talking to me?*

There was a longer pause before he responded this time.

*That is a very interesting question coming from someone who looks like Emma Stone. Who wouldn't want to talk to you, right? Just kidding. Really, you surprise me. I meet a lot of different types of people because of my work and all of them are the same, more or less. Prestigious, pompous, overeager. It's been a long time since I came across someone who was genuine and didn't take themselves too seriously. Like your ad. It was the opposite of what I'm used to and I want to be surprised like that some more.*

Darby's fingers flubbed over the keys as she tried to write a response. It was a good thing Kenya was editing over her shoulder, or she would have sent a text with a plethora of typos, some of which were kind of inappropriate.

"Ugh, this is totally not going to work!" Darby flung the phone onto the couch next to her. "Flip phones are the worst."

"Give it to me, pumpkin." Kenya reached over to retrieve the phone. She flipped it open and was done typing something before Darby was done sulking. When she realized what Kenya was doing, she made a grab for the phone.

"Wait, what are you doing?"

"Nothing weird, just a second."

"No, really, what are you saying to him?" Darby's idea of weird and Kenya's idea of weird were very different things.

Kenya snapped the phone closed and reached for Darby's smart, beautiful phone. "What's your screen unlocking pin thingamajig?"

Darby took the phone to enter the code, then handed it back to Kenya. Why? Because it was pointless to resist. By now, Kenya had already done whatever it was she was going to do. It was too late to prevent it. Better to let Kenya finish making a mess before Darby tried to clean it up.

"There." Kenya lifted Darby's hand, palm up, and slapped the phone into her hand. "You're welcome."

"What did you do?" Darby stared at the phone as if it had suddenly turned into a fat hairy spider.

"I installed the Voxer app so you can stop glaring at me while you try to type. Now you can either leave Lover Boy voice messages or you can text him through the app. See, he has no access to your real number or personal information. I set up your account with the name Hot Cook."

Darby stared at her. "You didn't, really?"

"I didn't." Kenya laughed. "But I should have. The look on your face is crazy awesome, just imagine how much more awesome you would look right now if I'd really done it?"

Darby glared death and daggers.

"Your name is Cookgirl. That's it. Put that glare away, you're giving me the creeps."

Darby opened her phone and clicked on the new app. There was only one contact. FoodieC.

"Is this him?"

"Yeah, I told him you had a temp phone for the newspaper and it was driving you bonkers, and asked if he was on Voxer. He was, so I set up a profile for you and away you go! Again, you're welcome."

Okay, that was actually pretty awesome.

"Thank you."

"Yep." Kenya smacked Darby's knee and stood up. "I have to get some sleep or I'm going to be wrecked at this thing tonight. Tell me everything tomorrow?"

"Absolutely," Darby agreed.

* * *

Darby slept in the next morning.

It wasn't intentional.

It was bad luck.

Somehow her clock got unplugged during the night so the alarm didn't go off.

No, actually, the numbers were blinking. So that meant it was probably a power outage. So, no alarm, on top of way too little sleep because she stayed up really late thinking about FoodieC, equaled bags, and bloodshot eyes.

It wasn't like they said anything exceptionally amazing last night. They actually only messaged a few more times before he had to go.

There was nothing out of the ordinary about any of it.

So, then, why did she feel so extraordinary?

Her phone rang, shattering the warm and fuzzy feelings she'd gathered around herself like a blanket. She reached over and checked the number.

Shoot.

It was Gretta.

"Hey, I know, I'm sorry. We had a power outage last night and my alarm didn't go off."

Gretta's sigh was a mini hurricane. "Fine, just get here as soon as you can."

"I will, I'm sorry."

Gretta hung up without saying good-bye.

Darby scrambled to dress and gather her things. She didn't have time to eat breakfast; she'd have to grab something at the café.

Kenya walked through the door just as Darby reached for the knob to open it.

"What are you still doing at home?" Kenya looked at her watch. "Shouldn't you be at work by now?"

"Slept in." Darby pulled on her sweater, tugging the stubborn arms into place.

"Well, that stinks. Unless . . ." A wicked grin spread across her lips. ". . . unless you were up all night talking to Lover Boy!"

Darby rolled her eyes.

"You were, you totally were! I'll walk you to your car, you have to tell me everything!" She linked her arm through Darby's elbow and stepped back into the morning sunshine.

"There really isn't anything to tell, Kenya."

"Oh, come on, there has to be if you were up all night talking to him."

"I never said that I was up all night talking to him. You did." Darby skipped over a crack in the sidewalk.

"Oh, well, were you?"

"No."

Kenya poked Darby in the ribs.

"No, really, after you went to bed, there were only a couple more messages. Nothing even that earth-shaking."

This wasn't exactly the whole truth, but Darby wasn't about to bear her soul about something she didn't entirely understand herself.

"Well? Tell!"

Darby's flustered mind tried to piece together a response. It took a lot of work. She hated being late. Specifically, she hated the range of martyr sighs Gretta did when people were late to the café.

"We messaged through the app, so that was nice. I told him I was good to keep chatting if he was. He said he would like to get to know me better. I said the same and then his sister needed something so he had to go."

"Sister?"

"Yeah, so, that's another thing, I guess. He lives with his sister."

Kenya stopped walking, making Darby lurch to a halt. "So it *is* Myles, yeah? He's mentioned his sister loads of times."

Darby had already made this connection, so she didn't say anything as she pulled away from Kenya to unlock her car.

"Did you get a voice message from him? Does it sound like Myles?"

Darby shook her head. "I don't want to voice message yet." She was glad she didn't have time to explain why. Kenya would surely want to know and Darby didn't have a good answer. Not one that would satisfy, anyway. Besides, now that she didn't have to wrestle with the flip phone, she was good to go on messaging forever.

Well, maybe not forever.

"So, what do you think? Best idea ever?" Kenya threw in some jazz hands that made Darby smile. "Are we glad we did the personal ad?"

If Darby admitted the truth, it would only encourage Kenya to come up with more crazy ideas. She would forever after use this instance as evidence that everything else she came up with when she was hopped up on chocolate and sleep deprived was a great idea.

Darby knew this.

But she also didn't care.

"Yes," she said and got into her car.

She didn't even try to hide the smile.

# Chapter Seven

*Missing In Action (MIA)*
*Saw a Hottie at Walmart but didn't get a Name.*
*We talked about Cat Food. Call me.*

Myles was late.

It was making Darby's ankles itch.

She spent the whole drive to work figuring out how she would act when she saw Myles. She rehearsed what she could say, including multiple ways she could subtly hint at their conversation the night before without being totally obvious. He had to get here quick, before her courage completely oozed out of her eyeballs and pooled onto the tile.

A couple of teenagers took Myles' usual seat at the counter and had already, in the course of about fifteen minutes, broken a sugar shaker, spilled both of their drinks, changed their order three times, and earned a world-record amount of glares from Gretta.

Darby did her best to treat them kindly, while also encouraging them to stop acting like heathens. This was probably like being a parent, wanting to protect the kids and throw them out the window at the same time.

When they finally left, she looked at the clock and sighed.

Where was Myles?

She couldn't remember a day since she started working at the Corner Café that Myles hadn't stopped in as soon as they opened. Was he sick? Hurt? Frequenting Starbucks?

Every one of those was cause for concern.

With each tick of the clock, Darby felt more tired—droopy—and her feet ached something fierce. When Mrs. Skinner slipped Darby a roller bottle of peppermint essential oils to 'perk her up', Darby realized she'd reached a whole new level of ennui. She took the Skinners' order, slapped it on the window, then excused herself to the bathroom where she splashed freezing water on her face and gave herself a very stern talking-to.

Her life didn't revolve around Myles and his schedule. She was going to go out there with a smile on her face and treat each person who came into the café like they were the most important person in the world.

It was time to forget herself and get to work.

But before she left the bathroom, she pulled out her phone and opened Voxer. Without giving herself a chance to talk herself out of it, Darby sent a message to Myles, asking if everything was okay.

That made her feel better.

Doing something always felt better than doing nothing.

As she pushed the door open to go back to work, she almost smacked Merdith in the face.

"Oh shoot, I'm sorry."

"Don't worry." Meredith waved her hands. "I don't need my nose anyway."

"You're sure?" Darby checked over Meredith's face to make sure there was nothing broken or oozing.

"Really, yes, my hands got the brunt of it, but, come'ere real quick." Meredith peeked over her shoulder, then grabbed Darby's arm and pulled her back into the bathroom. She checked all the stalls to make sure they were empty before she faced Darby. "Did you know the café's birthday is in two weeks?"

Darby didn't even know cafés celebrated their birthdays. "No."

"Well, it is. This is the tenth year since Gretta opened this place up.

Samson wants to throw a party or something, but I think it's a waste. Gretta don't care about anyone or anything. It'd be a bunch of work for nothing. Right? Samson thinks I'm cynical, so I'm asking around. What do you think? Party or no party?"

Fate always surprised Darby a little bit. Funny that she'd just talked to Kenya about a party to cheer Gretta up and now, this. It was too much of a coincidence to actually be a coincidence.

Meredith blew a big bubble of fruity-scented gum and popped it inches from Darby's ear.

Darby took a tiny step back. "Um, can I give it some thought, let you know tomorrow?"

Meredith shrugged. "Sure, whatever. Everyone else agrees with me. So far, Samson is the only person who thinks we should do it."

Now Darby was really glad she had time to think about it. Everyone who worked at the cafe loved Meredith, even though she'd dated and dumped over half of them. If Meredith was against a party, it might be better to go along with her.

On the other hand, Samson had worked at the café since it opened and if he thought they should do a party, it was probably worth considering. She wanted to talk it out with Kenya before she made a decision.

"Good to know." Darby nodded, trying to smile. "I better get back to work." She pointed to the door, then hurried out of the bathroom. Her mind was playing tug of war with this party idea.

Gretta didn't deserve it, probably didn't even want it.

But maybe she needed it.

She wouldn't care.

Unless she really did.

It would be a ton of work.

Darby just happened to know a Utah-famous party planner who was already considering the idea.

But Gretta was a gremlin.

Ugh!

Darby shook her head, fixed a bright smile on her face, and went to work, determined to put it out of her mind until later. For now, her mission was to make the morning at the café the best part of each person's day.

Except that the tug of war refused to stop. All day long Darby noticed things that pulled her to one side or the other.

When she took some tourist's orders, she saw Gretta run over to greet poor Mr. Sullivan who could barely walk into the café anymore without the help of his wife. That moment Darby was sure they should do the party.

Then, a couple of hours later, when Gretta went ballistic all over one of the new waiters because he dropped something that didn't even break, Darby was positive the party was a terrible idea.

By the end of the day, she had a rip-roaring headache.

To make matters worse, she was on the schedule to close that day.

With Gretta.

Darby watched the last customer pay their bill and walk out of the café. Then her eyes followed all the servers, cooks, and cleaners as they filed outside and her heart dropped just a little. She really wished she was one of them.

Okay, Darby, time for another pep talk.

She only had to close up twice a month and it didn't even take that long. Gretta was fast at what she did and probably wanted to get out of there worse than anyone else. Darby remembered that feeling. Sometimes the weight of her restaurant used to be crushing, even though she loved it with her whole soul.

Darby let out a long breath and swung her arms by her sides.

Okay, okay, okay, it was fine.

She could do this.

"I'll start with the tables and booths." She said to Gretta once everyone else was gone and the door was locked behind them.

"Sure, sounds good." Gretta already had the register open and started counting bills with impressive speed.

Darby grabbed the cleaning supplies from the closet in the back and started sanitizing all the tables, chairs, booths, and condiment bottles that stayed on the tables in cute wire baskets. It wasn't hard work, just time-consuming. Usually, Darby took this opportunity to daydream about Myles, but today her mind was empty. She ran Clorox wipes over the glass salt and pepper shakers without a thought or a worry. It was strangely therapeutic.

"What are you doing?" Gretta called from across the room.

Darby looked up. "Wiping everything down?"

"No, no, I meant, what are you humming over there?"

Darby didn't actually realize she'd been humming. "Um, show tunes."

She had the theme from Phantom of the Opera in her head, so that was probably what came out.

"I love Phantom," Gretta said, then went back to the register.

Darby stared at her for a minute longer. That shouldn't have surprised her. Most people loved Phantom. It wasn't one of the most well-known and best-selling Broadway shows for nothing. But she was surprised. Kind of shocked, actually.

She didn't realize Gretta loved anything.

A strange urge to understand Gretta better welled up inside Darby's chest. She finished the remaining tables quickly, then moved to the counter, where Gretta was still balancing the register.

"When did you see Phantom?" Darby asked.

Gretta didn't even look up. "Oh, I've seen it a number of times."

"At Tuacahn?"

"Yes, there, and on Broadway. We lived in New York for ten or so years. I always got season tickets for my birthday from my. . . ." Gretta swallowed the word hard, then hunched lower over the register.

Darby watched her, trying to think what to say. It was a slippery moment, akin to tiptoeing across a sidewalk covered in ice, but she wanted to know more. So she pressed on.

"The high school did a performance of Phantom of the Opera la couple of months ago."

Gretta's hands dropped to the cash tray. Her head fell back and a deep, rumbling laugh soared out of her mouth. "I saw it! Man, I haven't laughed so hard in ages!"

"Right?" Darby giggled. "Remember when the poor girl who played Christine forgot half the lines of her songs?"

Gretta wiped her eyes with the back of her hand. "It would have been fine if she hadn't kept trying to adlib."

"I know!" Darby slapped her hands on the counter. "I don't know what she was thinking, saying 'watermelon' over and over!"

Gretta lowered her voice and sang, "'Then say you'll share with me one love, one lifetime . . .'" her voice rose to a mouse-like pitch, "'. . . watermelon, watermelon, watermelon.'"

Darby dropped her head to her forearms and laughed heartily.

Gretta's voice returned to normal. "Poor girl, it would have worked if she was in the chorus and no one could actually hear what she was saying."

When Darby looked up, her eyes met Gretta's and they both stopped laughing. There was a very long, and awkward silence as they stared at each other.

Darby cleared her throat. "I'll get this counter wiped down and then start on the bathrooms."

Gretta nodded. "Thank you."

It was the first time Darby had ever heard her say those words.

A smile spread so quickly it made her cheeks stretch.

The two of them finished working without any other conversation. When they parted ways after locking the café up tight, Darby had made her decision.

They were throwing that party for Gretta. Even if she and Samson had to do it all by themselves.

* * *

Darby was so lost in happy feelings, she forgot all about Myles until she pulled into the parking lot of her apartment complex. As soon as the car was safely in park, she fumbled through her purse for her phone.

There was a notification from Voxer.

With fingers that felt like overinflated balloons, Darby finally got the app open and clicked on FoodieC.

*How did you know? You're freaking me out a little bit. No, everything is not all right. Something happened yesterday, with my sister. It's not good, but I can't talk about it. It's not my story to tell. So instead, how about you tell me a story? How in the world did you know something was wrong?*

. . .

Darby's heart pounded. Was this the moment? Should she tell him she knew because he didn't show up at the café? Should she tell him who she was? Her fingers hovered over the keyboard.

No.

Not yet.

The night before had been so awesome. She didn't want to mar that up with reality so soon.

*It was just a feeling. I'm sorry it was right. I'd much rather that you were happy as that clam everyone is always talking about. I understand if you can't talk about it, but is there anything I can do to help?*

*Really? You just sensed that something wasn't right. Do you have the force?*

*I wish.*

*That's, just, wow. I'm still geeking out here. To answer your question, no, there's nothing you can do. There's nothing anyone can do. It's just sucky that people can do totally normal and legal things that still destroy someone else's life thoroughly. It doesn't seem right.*

Darby knew exactly what that felt like. It was so messed up that it was Jackson Wilcox's actual job to destroy the reputation of people's restaurants, and by extension, their lives.

*I totally agree.*

. . .

*Anyway, how was your day? What did you do?*

*Just work.*

*And how was it?*

*Actually pretty good, how about you? Everything going to be okay?*

*I think so. I hope so. I don't know, do you ever get restless? Like, you love your life and your job but you wonder if there's something else out there for you?*

Wow, that got deep fast. Something was so different in Myles' tone. Darby felt like she was on the edge of a cliff, clinging with her toes. If she let go now, she wouldn't be able to get back out. Before she had a chance to answer the question, Myles typed a new one.

*You told me yesterday that you used to be a cook. What does that mean?*

Again, she wasn't sure how to answer, so she bit her lip and thought hard. There was no clench in her belly, which was weird. Not that she wanted the clench to be there, she was just so used to it, the absence was unsettling. Maybe it was because Myles couldn't see her face and didn't really know who she was yet. It was strange, but it made her feel like she could talk about what happened.
    Like she wanted to.
    A little.

. . .

*I used to work in a restaurant as head chef, but I don't anymore.*

*Why not?*

*The restaurant closed down and I lost my job.*

*And you aren't a chef anymore? There are a lot of restaurants in this world, you didn't go get a job at another one?*

*No, I didn't. I really loved that restaurant. It was hard to see it go under. Really hard. I guess I didn't have the heart to start over at another one.*

*I can see that.*

Of course he could, because Myles was perfect.

*So, what do you do now for work?*

Careful Darby.

*I work at a restaurant.*

Not a café. Maybe that was enough of a distinction to keep him from guessing.

. . .

*Wait a second! You said you didn't have the heart to do that again.*

*I don't cook. I don't even go into the kitchen if I can help it.*

That was good, vague.

There was a very long pause before his message appeared.

*You know, the more I learn about you, the more I realize how much I don't know. I thought I had a pretty good vision of who you are after last night. But you keep on saying things that surprise me. This is probably the biggest mystery of them all. You had a hard experience as a cook in a restaurant, but you work in a restaurant now. You love it enough to stay in the business, but you don't cook anymore.*

It was true, Darby didn't make any sense. She knew that already, but seeing it written like that made it all the more obvious that she was kind of a mess.

*I know, I'm weird.*

*Not weird, fascinating. I told you before that I meet a lot of people through work. A lot, a lot of people. All kinds of people. None of them are like you. I can't predict anything you're going to say next. You're like a five thousand piece puzzle. In the best way possible.*

Darby's heart glowed as she read. Just a dim light at first, then a deep burn. She couldn't remember the last time someone was this interested in her. Not even in a romantic way, just in a way that made her feel seen. Grammie used to do that, say exactly the right thing to let her know she was loved.

Was it weird that talking to Myles made her miss Grammie with a searing ache?

Maybe a little weird.

She paused for so long, a new message from Myles came under his previous one.

*I can't wait to find out more.*

*I'm really not that interesting. :)*

*That is the only thing you've said in the time we've talked that I completely disagree with. You are very interesting. What do you think about telling me your real name, Emma Stone?*

Darby almost dropped the phone. Day two and they were already moving to the next level. Okay, a baby step next level, but it had to mean something. Yesterday he didn't want to share anything specific and now he was willing to tell her his name.

Didn't that mean something?

It had to.

That made her want to jump up and chicken dance, but still, Darby hesitated to type her name.

If they exchanged names now, the mystery would be over. She would know it was Myles and he would know it was her. That thought made her want to throw up a little bit. She liked the anonymity. It made her feel safer. Like, if she said or did something cringey, which she would, it was only a matter of time, then she could separate herself from it. No one would know it was her, Darby Reynolds, who said or did those things.

Maybe they didn't have to exchange their real names. When she was a kid, Grammie used to call her Rey. It was the start of her last name but sounded completely different so he probably wouldn't make the connection between Rey and Reynolds. She could give that name to Myles. Then he would have a name and she would still have her secret identity.

*How about nicknames? Or middle? I don't think I'm ready for first names.*

*Alright then, you can call me Cole. That's my middle name. No one ever uses it except my sister when she's trying to act like my mom. It's not on any of my stuff so you will never be able to track me down. :)*

*Cole, I like it. You can call me Rey.*

*So you do have the force!*

*Hahaha. I better go. I just got home from work, Cole, talk to you later?*

*I can't wait, Rey.*

* * *

It took Darby a few minutes to transition to real life after talking to Myles—or rather, Cole. She wanted to curl up with a fluffy blanket and daydream about him for hours, but it was only a little after two in the afternoon and she needed to talk to Kenya about the party at the café. She let herself indulge in a thirty-second scene where she and Cole met for the first time in person, then she tucked it away for later and went looking for Kenya.

She sat at the table with an empty plate to the side of the newspaper which was spread out in front of her. Kenya followed the lines with her finger, moving slowly down the column.

"Hey!"

Kenya looked up with a smile. "Hey, girl! How was work today?" She wiggled her eyebrows suggestively.

"No," Darby pointed at her. "Don't distract me, I have to tell you something super important."

"Me too!"

"You too, what?"

Kenya folded her arms over the newspaper. "I have something super important to tell you too."

"Okay," Darby's curiosity made her lose her train of thought. "What's up?"

"I'm going to deactivate my flip phone."

Darby waited. Was that it? That was the super important thing she had to say?

Kenya picked up the paper and used it to smack Darby's arm. "Because it served it's purpose. You're talking to Lover Boy. We don't need it anymore. Mission accomplished."

Okay.

Darby just looked at her.

Kenya sighed. "Well, I thought it was a monumental statement. What do you need to tell me?"

Darby blinked twice, slowly. "I think you're addicted to personal ads. I think I need to stage an intervention."

Kenya wadded up a napkin and flung it at Darby. "Do you really have something to tell me? Or were you just being a brat?"

Darby laughed as the napkin fell harmlessly onto the table near her arm. "I really do have something to talk to you about. Something serious."

"Well." Kenya wiggled her head. "Let me put on my serious face." She tried, but since she didn't really have one, nothing changed. Darby decided to just keep talking.

"Meredith shanghaied me in the bathroom today-"

"Which one is Meredith, again?"

"You know, the one who hits on every male that walks through the door."

"Right, right. Gotcha, go on."

"Then, she told me Samson wants to throw a party for the café's birthday in a couple of weeks, but no one else wants to do it."

"Understandable."

"I know. But then, I was closing with Gretta, and I realized something really important."

"What's that?"

"She's just human, Kenya. She's got things and stuff and junk. Maybe we don't like the way she does it, but she's doing the best she can to juggle all of that and run the Corner Café. It's tough, owning a business."

Kenya pursed her lips. "You want to throw that Gretta Appreciation Day party for the café's birthday?"

"I do. I want to do it. Even if no one else helps." Darby stopped and thought for a second. "I mean, even if no one else at work helps. Obviously, I can't do it without you. What do you think?"

Kenya stared at Darby for a few minutes, chewing on her lower lip. When she spoke, the words came out slowly.

"I will help, on one condition."

"Anything!" Darby said.

And instantly regretted it. She forgot for a second that anything with Kenya could actually mean anything and there were a lot of things she really didn't want to do.

"Oh good, I'm so glad!" Kenya clapped her hands. "Because I've been making phone calls out the wazoo and I can't find a single caterer who has the sixteenth available."

"What's the sixteenth?" Darby asked.

"The wedding! The last-minute wedding. Remember?" Kenya shook her head. "I need you, Darby. I need your sweet, sweet cooking skills to plan and execute a menu for five hundred of the bride and groom's closest friends and family. That's my condition. You do the food for the wedding, and I'll help you with the café's birthday party. Deal?"

Darby leaned into the hard steel chair back and felt the opposite of support. Just the thought of cooking again did something weird to her fingertips. They were all tingly and numb. Cooking for that many people, for the start of a couple's life together.

What if she messed it up?

That tingle transformed into a raging fire that coursed through her arms and settled in her belly.

"Can we make a different deal? Can I help you with something else?"

Kenya's face was full of sympathy, but she shook her head. "I really need your help with the wedding."

In the moments of silence that followed, Darby seriously considered how she would plan and prepare the café's birthday party on her own, without Kenya's help.

It didn't go so well.

Kenya was right, she would end up texting out an invitation and serving cake that turned people's lips purple.

She wanted it to be good. A really, really good party. For Gretta's sake.

But cooking, again, and for a wedding? So many people to witness her awful, terrible, no good, very bad luck.

She just didn't see how she could do that.

Kenya placed a hand on her arm. "I know you're shook up, Darbs. I also know you can do this. I believe in you."

"How?"

"How what?"

Darby clicked her nail on the table a couple of times. "How can you believe in me? How can you know I can do this?"

Kenya pressed her lips together and looked at the ceiling. "I googled you."

"What?"

What did that even mean?

"And your restaurant."

"But—

Darby didn't remember telling Kenya the name of her restaurant.

"When I googled you, the restaurant came up. I read all about it.

The beginning to the end."

That meant she also read the article from Jackson Wilcox. It was linked to everything about Darby and her restaurant that showed up online. She hated that. Her name linked to Jackson Wilcox.

And there was the clench.

Right on schedule.

"Jackson Wilcox is kind of a hottie." Kenya pressed her lips to hide a smile.

"You did not just say that!"

"No, really, he looks like a young Harrison Ford, without the seventies hair cut. Hot."

"Oh my gosh, I might actually throw up right now." Part of the reason was because she'd thought the same thing when she'd researched him before he came to critique her restaurant. He wasn't good-looking anymore, though. Everytime she saw a picture of him she mentally added crossed eyes, a scraggly beard and horns.

"Okay, okay, sorry." Kenya waved her hands. "Just kidding! Don't blow your cookies on my table. I'll stop. Seriously, Darby, your restaurant was amazing! I read through all the reviews. The people who rated it low never said a thing about the food. The food was always five stars! You got chops."

"But—"

"And besides all that, I can feel it in my bones: you are the caterer this wedding needs."

"Kenya—"

"I'll help you. I'll be there the whole time. We can plan the menu together, cook together, all of it. Will you help me? Please? Please? Pretty please?"

Kenya was the master of pathetic puppy dog eyes.

How was Darby supposed to say no to that?

"Hey." Kenya tapped Darby's arm until she looked up. "Didn't Grammie always say, 'When life bucks you off, you jump right back on that thing and ride it into the ground'?"

Darby squinted at Kenya. "It's super unfair that you use Grammie's saying against me."

Kenya laughed. "It's necessary, trust me. You pay more attention to

Grammie than you do to anyone else. Darby, look at me. I see the way you gaze longingly at my pantry. I know you want to cook. You can ignore it forever, or you can embrace it now."

"I don't gaze longingly at the pantry."

Kenya shook her head. "You do, too. Listen, if you ignore this part of you that wants to create amazing food, that part of you is going to die forever. If you embrace it, try again, even though it's hard, you're going to get that old confidence back. You'll be unstoppable!"

More of those positive affirmations.

Instead of being obnoxious, though, Darby wanted them to be true.

She desperately wanted it.

Kenya was right.

Darby had ignored the call to create for so many months, and it was calling less and less. She hadn't even realized it until Kenya said the words. That part of her was fading and now that she knew it, she was terrified that it would stop calling entirely.

And then, she wouldn't have anything left.

Even with that in mind, Darby couldn't get herself to say yes to Kenya. The word hovered there, in the back of her throat, without budging.

"Can I think about it?" She said, finally, her voice low and tired.

"You act like I'm asking you to give me a kidney."

Darby sighed heavily and rolled her eyes.

"Sure." Kenya sat back with her hands in the air. "Fine, if you need to think about it, do that. Take your sweet, lollygagging time. Except I need to know by tomorrow so I can keep trying to find someone else to do it if you won't."

"Wow, Kenya," Darby said, rising from the table. "Just, wow."

She grabbed her phone out of her purse and tucked it into her back pocket.

"Where are you going?" Kenya asked.

"For a walk. I'll be back in a bit." Darby needed someone to talk this out with someone who would understand where she was coming from. Someone who wouldn't judge her or coerce her or have an agenda.

She needed to talk to Grammie.

# Chapter Eight

*Lonely College Student (LCS) Just Looking for Someone to Talk to Who Listens and Tries to Understand. Glad to Return the Favor.*

Darby tapped her thumbs against the phone. She'd taken her walk and had her talk with Grammie but that unsettled feeling was still there, waiting to crush her. She realized on her way back to Kenya's house that what she really wanted to do was talk this through with Cole. He knew food but he didn't know her. He could be totally and completely objective. The first thing she did when she got back to Kenya's house, besides flop on the bed, was text Cole.

Before she could talk herself out of it.

*Hey, are you around?*

While she waited for a return text, she stared at the ceiling, her thoughts heavy enough to crush a beetle. Logically she always knew she was going to have to start cooking again. She couldn't really open a restaurant and not cook. Okay, she technically could, like if she was just going to manage the restaurant and not cook for it. But the food was her passion, the universal language. No matter who you talked to, anywhere in the world, they could relate to a discussion about food. That's what made her want to open a restaurant in the first place.

The business end of owning a restaurant was not her strength. If she'd learned nothing else, she'd learned that. Especially since she started working on her business degree.

Business sucked the fun out of everything.

Seriously.

*I am, what's up?*

Oh, thank goodness!

*I need to talk something through with an objective third party. Do you have a few minutes? Okay, more like an hour?*

*Sure I do. Though, it might be easier to actually talk this out than to type it. Do you want to call me?*

Whoa!

Darby almost dropped the phone on her face. She caught it before it crashed into her nose.

Call him?

Such a simple concept, but the ramifications were huge. If she called him, he'd have her real phone number. He could totally track down who she was.

Her eyes skirted around her room in agitation. She needed to do something with her hands while she thought about this. There was a package of socks still sitting on the desk. Everything else, she'd put away in drawers. Bless her tendency to procrastinate. Socks were exactly what she needed right now.

She rose from the bed and ripped open the package. She started matching socks like her life depended on it. The rambunctious thoughts settled as her hands worked to press and fold. Something about the mundane task let her think more clearly.

Myles was right. No, Cole was right. If she didn't start thinking of him that way, she was going to accidentally call him Myles in one of their chats and give the whole thing away. So, Cole.

Cole was right: calling made more sense. It would be a righteous pain in the rear to type everything in her brain.

She took an armful of matched sock balls to the dresser and shoved them into the top drawer. As she leaned in with her shoulder to shut the drawer all the way, the dresser rocked and something dropped to the floor.

The flip phone.

Oh, duh!

The flip phone!

It was terrible for texting, but for talking it would work just fine. Then she didn't have to give Cole her real phone number!

It's just like Grammie always said, when in doubt, organize a closet. Darby hadn't done the closet thing, exactly, but the principle was the same. Most solutions to hideous problems came while doing routine chores.

Oh, wait! Kenya was going to deactivate it. Shoot. Darby flipped it open and felt relief slide down her back when it lit up. Thank goodness Kenya was too busy to get to things right away.

Darby dashed back to her bed and picked up her phone. Cole had sent a bunch of texts while she was mildly freaking out.

*Are you there?*

*Rey?*

. . .

*I'm going to assume you're having technical difficulties.*

*I think what really happened is I scared you off.*

*Did I?*

Darby typed as fast as her fingers could go.

*No! I mean, yes, you did freak me out, but I thought of a solution. Do you want to call me on the number from the personal ad? Do you still have it?*

*Yeah, I still have it. Give me just a sec.*

Almost one second later, the flip phone vibrated in Darby's hand. She took a quick breath and let it out in a rush.

This was it.

She flipped the cover with her thumb, then held the phone to her ear.

"Hey."

"Rey?"

Oh, heavens!

His voice was luscious over the phone. Even more so than in person. This was so much better than chatting over the counter at the café.

Darby sat on the edge of her bed. "Hey, Cole."

"You really are a woman."

Darby pressed her lips into a smile. "Maybe I just sound really feminine."

"Naw, I can tell everything about you from your voice. You're female, young, and super hot."

A laugh sprung from Darby's lips without any warning. "Whatever, you can't tell any of that from my voice!"

"Are you saying I'm wrong?"

Darby considered the words.

Female, young, super hot.

"Two out of three."

"As long as one of those is female, I'm good."

Darby stood up and started pacing. There was a ton of backed up adrenaline in her legs, making them all twitchy. "So, as long as I'm a woman, you don't mind if I'm hunchbacked and as old as the hills?"

"Which hills?"

Darby pressed her lips into a smile. "The old ones."

"Nope." Cole rumbled a chuckle that gave Darby goosebumps. "I don't care what you look like. I'm just glad we're talking. It's good to hear your voice."

Darby couldn't agree more.

"And this is so much easier than texting. I got a thumb cramp last time."

"Seriously?"

"Yeah, it's real. Super painful. I almost called in sick to work."

Darby couldn't tell if he was joking or not, but she didn't care. She could totally listen to him talk all day long and never get sick of it. It didn't even matter what he said.

"So, what do you need to talk about?" Cole paused. "Actually, first I need you to tell me what you want from me."

"What do I want from you?" Darby said the words slowly, like that would help her understand the meaning better.

"Yeah, you know, how much you want me to say."

"Wait, you want me to tell you what you should say?"

"Yeah, you know, the woman thing?"

Darby had no idea what he was talking about. "Woman thing?"

Cole sighed heavily. "I knew it. There's not a woman thing is there?"

Darby laughed, despite her confusion. "I honestly have no idea what you're talking about."

"My sister," Cole said, "told me that men need to ask what women want when they talk. Sometimes women want a listening ear, sometimes they want men to solve the problem, and sometimes they want to vent and be told they're pretty. Really, none of this sounds familiar? It's not a thing?"

"No." Darby's shoulders shook from laughing. "But your sister is a total genius to tell you that."

There was a long moment of silence before Cole responded, sounding resigned. "I've got to hand it to her, she totally had me convinced that was an unspoken code with women. Now I'm wondering what else she's told me that's completely untrue."

"Well, it's not completely untrue," Darby said. "She's right that sometimes I want advice and sometimes I want to vent and sometimes I want comfort. She didn't lead you totally astray."

In fact, the world would be a happier place if everyone defined what they needed at the start of a conversation, no matter who they were talking to. Parent to child, friend to friend, boss to employee. Darby had a feeling there would be a lot fewer miscommunications if people took the time to sort out individual needs and wants from the beginning.

"No?"

"No. I mean, it's not a thing, I don't think, but it is a very considerate way to start a conversation with someone."

"Yeah?"

"I think so."

"That's good enough for me." There was another brief pause. "So, then, what do you need from me, Rey?"

Darby hesitated as she plopped onto the bedspread.

Okay, now that they were down to it, she felt extremely weird telling him what she wanted the conversation to look like.

Bossy, or something.

"I guess, I mean, it would be nice if you listened while I get all the details out, cause it's hard to stay focused when I'm interrupted, but then I really want to hear your interpretation of the situation. So, yeah."

"Listen with my mouth shut, then give advice, got it, go!"

Darby laughed nervously. "Okay, um, I'm not sure where to start."

"Wherever you want."

It would probably help to start with the present, then ease into the past. "My friend asked me to help her with a wedding reception. She wants me to cater the event for something like five hundred people." Darby paused, not sure how to go from that to the inner workings of her deepest insecurities.

A very long pause followed.

So long, in fact, that Darby started to wonder if Cole was still there. "Hello?"

"Hi, I'm here," Cole said. "I'm listening with my mouth shut. I thought this part would last longer. Are you ready for advice already?"

This whole thing felt ludicrous. "Okay, forget what I said before, I just want to talk this out. I can't process all this stuff in my head, inside my head. And when I talk to my friend, she's great, but she does have an agenda, you know? I need to talk to someone who doesn't have any part in it and can help me figure out why I feel the way I do. So, you."

She honestly wasn't sure what she wanted anymore. And what she needed? That was even more confusing. Part of her wished she'd never brought this up in the first place, even though she was loving the sound of Cole's voice in her ear.

"Got it. So, your friend asked you to cater a big event. Do you want to?"

Did she want to?

"I don't know."

"Okay, no worries. Let's break it down. Do you like wedding receptions?"

"Like, in general?"

"Yeah, do you like them? Are they fun? Is it cool to see someone commit to someone else for the rest of their life or is it super depressing and stupid?"

Darby tapped her fingers against a pillow. It didn't make a satisfying noise, as the top of a desk or table would, but it made her feel better all the same. "I like them. I've never been to one where I don't know the couple, so that might be kind of weird, but in general, Yes, I like wedding receptions. How about you?" She tacked on that question so she didn't feel like this was a completely one-sided conversation.

"Do I like wedding receptions?"

"Yeah."

"I love them! I think they're a blast and the food is always superb."

That clench was back, squeezing Darby's belly into jelly.

Yeah, what if it wasn't?

"But it doesn't matter what I think, it's you we're trying to figure out." Cole laughed. "If you don't have a problem with the wedding reception, it's got to be the catering part. Have you ever catered a large event like this?"

"Sort of." She'd fed that many people in one night at the restaurant. It wasn't a specific event though, certainly not one so important, and she'd never fed people off location before. "Well, no. I guess. I've never catered an event at all. I've made large quantities of food for a lot of people, but it was all in my restaurant and spread throughout an entire day."

Oh, shoot.

She didn't mean to say her restaurant. She meant to say a restaurant.

"Your restaurant?"

"I mean, the restaurant I worked at before. That's all. I cooked for a lot of people there."

"What restaurant was it?"

Darby shook her head. "That's classified information. If I told you that, this flip phone would self-destruct." Her flippant tone helped ease that rotten clench.

"Well, then, by all means, don't tell me," Cole said, a smile in his voice. "So, you've fed a lot of people, you don't hate wedding receptions . . . is it something about the two of them together?"

Darby chewed her lower lip. "Maybe? I hate to think I'd mess up someone's big date with crappy food."

"Do you make crappy food?"

Flashes from that stupid article Jackson Wilcox wrote came to Darby's mind. They still stung, even though it'd been over a year.

"No, I don't make crappy food." Darby said firmly.

Well, she didn't used to. It'd also been over a year since she cooked anything more complicated than a bowl of ramen in the microwave. Maybe she made crappy food now.

"At least, I don't think I do."

"I have a great idea," Cole said. "You should invite me over and cook for me. Then I can tell you if your food is crappy or not." His laugh confirmed to Darby that his commentary wouldn't be helpful at all. He was way too nice of a person to tell her to her face that she was a crappy cook.

Plus, cooking for him meant meeting him.

Officially.

And she was so not ready for that.

"Haha," Darby said. "I just, I haven't cooked in such a long time. I'm not sure if I can do it anymore. Plus," She paused to prepare herself for his reaction, "I have the worst luck in the world. Things just don't work for me. How am I supposed to make a beautiful, amazing menu for a wedding reception? I would end up seriously destroying the whole thing. At their fiftieth wedding anniversary, they'll be talking about their perfect wedding, well, except for the reception food, that was the worst."

"You think they'll still be together in fifty years."

"Sure, why not?" That was a weird question. Totally off topic.

Cole laughed again. "Did you know that you're actually an optimist? All this talk of bad luck is just a cover. If you think people can stay married for fifty years, you can believe in anything."

Darby didn't really get how those things related to each other.

"The other good news is, I think I found your why." Cole went on.

"What's my why?"

"It's the real reason you don't want to tell your friend you'll do this catering gig."

He knew that? When she didn't? That was impressive. "Why?"

"You're afraid of failing."

Wow.

Wow.

As painful as it was to hear those letters strung together to form those words, it was also a strange kind of relief.

"You're right. I am. Is that a terrible reason to not do something?" That was a rhetorical question. Darby was already pretty sure it was. "I'm super selfish, huh?"

Cole laughed. "No, Rey. That's actually the opposite of selfishness.

If you were selfish, you wouldn't care at all if the food stank. You also wouldn't have such a dilemma about helping out your friend. Obviously, you care a lot about doing things well because you care a lot about other people."

His words felt like balm on a hot stinging wound.

"Is that what you think?"

"It is." He paused for a moment. "Do you ever cook for yourself?"

"No."

"Why?"

It was a good question. If she cooked for herself there would be no one to let down. It shouldn't be a problem.

Darby stared at the carpet, specifically the spot where someone spilled nail polish at some point. The bright blue against the taupe color was a horrible eyesore.

"I just can't," Darby said in a small voice.

There wasn't anything more to say. It was both simple, and so dang complicated at the same time.

"Okay." Cole's voice was bright. "No worries. You can't cook."

That actually made her flinch, as though Cole pitched the words at her head.

"But what if you could?"

Darby shook her head. "I can't, though." The words choked.

"I know, but, what if you could? Obviously, doing no cooking, then catering a huge reception is crazy talk so we're not going there. But what if you just considered boiling water for spaghetti noodles? That's pretty basic, right? I think I did that when I was six or seven."

Yeah, Darby did too.

"Okay ... I...."

"Okay?" His voice jumped with enthusiasm. "Awesome! Now, close your eyes. Are they closed?"

"Yes."

"Picture yourself walking to the kitchen, getting a big pot out of the cupboard, filling it with water, placing it on the stove, turning the stove on, adding salt to the pot, and covering it with a lid."

Darby felt stupid, but she did all the things Cole said, as he said them. When she mentally clanged the lid on the pot to let it heat to boil, there was an unexpected tingle in her fingertips.

"Did you do it?"

"Yes," Darby said slowly.

"And? How do you feel?"

It was kind of hard to get the words out. "I . . . I want to cook."

"Yeah?" Cole almost yelled into her ear, "That's awesome! Let's go do it!"

"Wait, what?"

"I'm serious, right now, let's do what you just imagined. I'll be right here the whole time. Ready?"

Darby rose to her feet, but couldn't make one move in front of the other. "I don't know, Cole."

"That's okay, you don't have to know. I know. I know that the only way you are ever going to start cooking again is to start cooking again. Right now. You saw how easy it was to imagine water boiling. Let's just go do it."

She took a step. "But, what about the sauce?"

"We're not making sauce right now, all we're doing is boiling water for spaghetti noodles. Let's go. Are you going?"

Another step.

"I guess I could just butter the noodles and put some parmesan cheese on them. That's easy."

"Sure. Classic and delicious. Are you in the kitchen yet?"

No, but she was in the hall.

"What if my roommate is in the kitchen?"

"I don't know—what if? Is that bad?"

"No, I mean, not really. Kenya would be excited and supportive. I guess it's me I'm afraid of. Like, if I do this one time, I'll have to do it all the time and. . . ." a realization hit Darby so strongly, she gasped out loud. "I'm scared I stink at it."

"It's okay to be scared," Cole said, gently.

Yeah, but was it?

"It's silly to be scared of cooking."

"If you think so."

"You don't think so?"

"No," Cole said. "I don't think it's silly to be scared of anything. Feelings are real. That's why they have actual words for all those phobias, like hippopotomonstrosesquippedaliophobia."

"You seriously just made that up!"

"I swear I didn't!" Cole said. "It's real! The fear of long words."

Darby placed a hand on her hip. "They have a long word to describe the fear of long words? That is seriously messed up."

Darby listened to him laugh for a while, silently, then found herself laughing along with him. Her stomach muscles turned to goo, and she had to bend in half to support her torso on her knees.

Every time she'd start to catch her breath, Cole would repeat another phobia word and she'd start laughing all over again. She'd given up holding herself in place and now sat in the middle of the hall, holding her belly 'cause it really hurt.

"Stop! You have to stop doing that! I seriously can't breathe!" She wiped tears from the corners of her eyes.

"I'm done, I'm done talking," Cole choked.

They spent the next few minutes breathing deeply and thinking of the most boring thing in the world, like political debates. At least, that's what Darby was doing. She couldn't tell from the intermittent long exhales over the phone what Cole was thinking of. And she really wanted to know.

Using the wall to support herself, Darby rose to her feet and walked the rest of the way to the kitchen. Kenya was gone, only the dirty dishes in the sink were there to testify that she'd been in the kitchen at all. Without letting herself think about it for one second, she opened the cupboard next to the stove and pulled out a large stockpot.

"Wait, what are you doing? Where are you?" Cole said, his voice almost completely back to normal. "I hear running water."

"I'm in the kitchen." Darby let a smile spread across her face as the pot slowly filled.

"Are you filling a pot with water?"

"I am!" It was so stupid, but she felt like she did the first time she broke down a chicken properly. All she was doing was boiling water. Like Cole said, a kindergartener could do what she was doing.

It still felt amazing.

Darby hefted the pot to the stove and set it down carefully so no water spilled onto the burner. Then she leaned over and turned the burner to high.

"What are you doing? Tell me everything!" Cole said, impatiently.

Darby walked him through the next couple of steps.

"I salted the water with two handfuls of sea salt, then covered the pot. Now I'm walking to the pantry to pick out a package of pasta."

"Do you have something other than spaghetti?"

Honestly, Darby didn't know. She held the phone against her ear and shoulder, then opened the pantry doors with both hands. It was dark in there, so she fumbled around for the light switch until she found it.

Oh!

Wow, Kenya's pantry really was beautiful. There were rows of labeled containers, boxes, and cans of food arranged by type. So many ingredients that could be combined to create something amazing. It was exactly the type of pantry that Darby was in love with. Exactly the type she'd had at her restaurant.

Okay, Darby was not crying over the state of the pantry.

She wasn't.

"What's going on over there? What are you doing? Did you pick a pasta?"

Darby' blinked to clear her vision as her eyes wandered to the section of pasta. There were so many things to look at, it was hard to focus.

"Oh, sweet, she has campanelle."

"Yeah? That would be fantastic with your cheese and butter."

"It would." Darby removed the box and hugged it to her chest.

No, she didn't kiss it.

But, she thought about it.

"Hey, Rey?" Cole's voice flowed through the series of mind bombs Darby was having.

"Yeah?"

"I just looked at the time. I have a Zoom meeting in ten minutes, but—"

Darby could tell from the tone of his voice that he was about to offer to reschedule his meeting so he could be here for her.

He really was such a nice guy.

"No, it's good, I'm good, you can go. I mean. . . ." Darby took a deep breath. "Thank you, Cole."

"I really didn't do anything, you did. You're the one bossing that boiling water in the kitchen. Seriously, way to go you!"

Darby shook her head. She couldn't find the words to tell him what it meant to her that he stuck there with her, talked out her weird issues, asked hard questions and made her want to try again. It was the nicest thing anyone had ever done for her. Not because of the step-by-step actions, but because of the result. Cole hadn't just talked her through her fear, he'd done something so much more powerful.

He'd reintroduced her to hope.

# Chapter Nine

*Love of Life Wanted (LoLW) For Girl Next Door*
*Tired of Playing Games, Ready For the Real Thing*

Darby smiled as she pulled into the parking lot of the Corner Café the next morning. Kenya still wasn't home from her event when Darby left for work, but she'd put together a plate of pasta, covered in plastic wrap, and set it front and center in the fridge where Kenya would see it as soon as she opened the door.

Also, she wrote a note that said, 'I'll do it'.

She'd been riding that wave the whole morning.

Even though it was only pasta with butter and cheese, she felt like she'd made a five-course meal with a palate cleanser. She'd just conquered something, and it was the best feeling in the world. Like she could hike Mount Everest, swim with sharks, and yes, cater a wedding reception.

Her mind was already buzzing with ideas for the menu. Obviously, all that would depend on what the happy couple wanted, but the fact that she could think about dainty finger foods without shutting down was too huge to fully appreciate at the moment. She got out of the car and tied on her apron, then skipped all the way to the front door.

Yes, she really did skip.

The old man walking by looked at her strangely, but the college girls coming out of the café held the door for her, then linked arms and skipped down the sidewalk, giggling.

That was a win, Darby was pretty sure.

"Good morning!" She called out for whoever was there. It ended up being a lot more people than she was used to because it was Wednesday, her late morning. The café was almost full.

Myles turned around with a huge grin. "Good morning!" he called back, setting off a chorus of good mornings from everyone else in the café. As she made her way to the counter, Darby felt like the whole building and everyone in it was filled with sunshine and lemon drops.

Gretta scowled from her desk in the corner.

But Darby was convinced it was way less scowly than usual. Like, a scowl with a twinkle. Gretta was just used to being grumpy so she had to pretend to be grumpy all the time. It wasn't really how she felt or who she was.

Myles's eyes were fixed on Darby as she took her place behind the counter. "I was wondering if you were coming in today."

"Of course! I come in every day except Sunday and that's because we're closed!" She let out a jolly Saint Nicholaus laugh that was completely cheesy but felt wonderful deep down in her belly. "We each get a morning where we don't have to help with opening and Wednesday is mine."

"That's a pretty great gig." Myles smiled.

"What can I get for you?" Darby pulled the notepad out of her waistband. It was way easier not to stare at Myles when she had something to do. She was so grateful for all his help last night, it took everything she had not to launch herself at him and give him a squeeze that would make his eyes pop. "Or, did you already order?" She almost forgot she was later than usual. For all she knew, Myles could be done with his breakfast and about to skedaddle when she showed up.

"No, I didn't. I was waiting for you."

"Really?"

For more than half a second, she let herself get lost in the clear blue of his eyes. It was probably the closest she would ever come to flying without an airplane. Soaring, really. All the way through the clouds in the blue, blue, blue.

She'd stared at Myles so much in the last year, it was easy to take things about him for granted, that masterful lock of hair in his eyes, for one. But she had never, ever once gotten over how blue his eyes were. And now, with him staring right back at her, like he really saw her, it just took the whole experience to the next level.

"Really, really. I want a surprise breakfast this morning and I don't trust anyone else around here to know what I want."

"You think I know what you want?" Darby lowered her eyes.

"Oh, I know you know what I want."

Darby shifted from foot to foot. Her face was flaming too much to look at him comfortably, but she forced herself to do it anyway.

His perfect lips were turned up in a smile that made her insides turn to Play-Doh. Everything was squishing together so much, she almost didn't hear the second throat clearing from Gretta.

"Okey dokey, C—" She sucked in the word Cole and spit it back out as Myles. It sounded clunky, but that was no big deal. "How much time do you have?"

"All morning. I don't have anywhere to be until two."

"Then you hang onto your toenails because I am about to blow your mind."

Myles half-smiled in a way that was totally flirty.

At her!

Did he mean to be flirty with her or was it some weird flukey thing?

Darby glanced at Gretta, who was watching her with narrowed eyes, and then gave Myles an enormous grin. "I'll be right back."

"Table three needs a refill," Gretta called.

"I'll let Meredith know!" Darby said over her shoulder. She stopped outside the double doors into the kitchen and took a deep breath, then she pushed them open and stepped inside.

Meredith was in there, of course, trying to hit on the newest busboy who was at least five years younger. Darby let her know about the refill, then went to stand by Samson. Her mind was working so fast, her mouth hadn't had a chance to string it all together yet.

"It creeps me out when people hover over my shoulder like that," Samson said in his gruff, old-man voice.

"Sorry." Darby took a step back, suddenly unsure about what the heck she was doing in there.

"What do you want, little sister?"

Okay, now was her moment, words!

"Uh...."

Oh, brilliant. Nicely done, Darby.

"Spit it out."

"Can I make something?"

Samson turned slowly, his huge metal spatula raised in the air. For a second, Darby forgot he was the nicest human in the world and wondered if he was going to smack her with it. "You want to cook?"

"Um, yes?" Darby stared at his sensible black shoes.

"Look at me."

She did, but it took a lot of neck muscles and determination because her instinct was to slide through the cracks of the tile. She thought of Myles out there, and his encouragement last night, and something inside her started a rolling boil.

"Can I make German Pancakes?"

He squinted at her. It was enough to quell anybody, but Darby would not be quelled today.

"There's this guy, Myles, he comes in every day. I want to make something for him that's not on the menu. It won't take long, they cook extremely fast."

"I know who that boy is, and I know how long a German pancake takes. You don't have to explain all that to me, little sister."

Of course, he knew; he was a chef. And a really good one too. In fact, he was way too good to stick around the tiny Corner Café in a tiny town in Southern Utah. Darby shook her head, shaking her thoughts away so she could focus on what Samson was saying.

"What I want to know is why you want my job, when you have your own job at the counter out there?"

A bunch of responses fluttered through Darby's mind.

Because she wanted to do something awesome for Myles.

Because she wanted to cook with all of her tingly finger tips.

Because she felt amazing.

Because. . . .

"Darby?" Samson leaned over, his bushy eyebrows almost brushed her forehead. "You're thinking too much."

"I know." She sighed. It really was her superpower. "Maybe it's stupid, I just have to cook today, Samson. Do you ever feel that way?"

He studied her for a moment, then his face broke into a huge smile. "Every day, little sister, every day. Tell you what, you go back out there, make sure everyone is taken care of. I'll crank the heat on the bottom oven for you and prep the cast iron. Then you hustle back here and make your German pancakes for that boy."

"You won't tell Gretta?"

Samson's forehead furrowed.

"I mean, not that I'm trying to go behind her back or anything." Except that she totally was. "I just meant, it's not like I'm cooking all the time. She probably doesn't need to know. Right?"

Samson jerked his head toward the café doors. That didn't really answer her question, but Darby wasn't about to push it.

"I'll go check on things and then come right back."

He grunted.

Darby shooed herself back into the café, bright lights and bustling sounds catching her off guard after the atmosphere of the kitchen. It was like waking up from a really realistic dream.

"Check, please!" The couple down at the end of the counter grabbed her attention. After ringing them up and making sure everyone was good on refills, Darby tapped the counter in front of Myles on her way back to the kitchen.

"Almost ready."

"Take your time," He called after her.

Darby borrowed an apron from the supply hanging next to the ovens and hurried to the fridge for a bunch of eggs. When she made German pancakes for the first time with Grammie, she'd beat the eggs and flour until every single lump was gone while Grammie worked on the maple butter. She was so proud of herself until she saw the look on Grammie's face.

Apparently, you're not supposed to beat German pancakes at all. It just needs a few good folds to get everything incorporated. But Grammie went ahead and cooked Darby's version, along with another pan made correctly so that she would see the difference. Darby's was dense and flat, while Grammie's was puffed up impossibly high over the baking dish.

It was like magic.

No wonder Darby loved cooking so much. No wonder all she ever wanted to do was become a chef. Grammie taught her that there actually was magic in real life.

Food was magic.

Darby moved her hand away from the salt and grabbed a quarter cup of sugar instead. Yikes, that would have been bad. She needed to focus on what she was doing.

She poured the barely mixed mixture into the cast iron skillet Samson buttered and warmed for her, then stuck the whole thing into the oven. It was so hot, it sent a wave over her face.

Darby brushed her hands together and stepped back. Samson caught her eye, then saluted. "Well done, little sister, well done."

It was silly, but Darby felt pretty dang proud of herself.

While she waited a few minutes for the pancake to puff, she microwaved some butter and maple syrup, loaded powdered sugar into the sieve, washed a handful of blueberries that were perfectly ripe, and rummaged for some mint leaves.

The timer went off and Darby rushed to the oven. She pulled out the golden brown puff and tried not to cry.

It was so beautiful.

She carried it carefully to the workstation where she'd left all her prepped ingredients and set it on a hot pad. The dishwasher, Harvey, already placed a clean plate in her area, like a blank canvas, ready for her to beautify.

Darby rubbed her hands together and let out a short breath of air.

Okay, she could do this.

And then, the magic happened. Darby never knew how to describe it. It was like her brain turned off one side and turned on the other side. She stopped thinking and started creating. Almost like they had minds of their own, her hands flew across the plate, between the prepped bowls, and back again. At some point, her soul deemed it complete, so she stood back to take it all in.

Wow.

A slice of the German pancake sat in the middle of the shining white plate, like a puffy piece of pie. Maple butter rained down the sides in perfect streams, creating a pool of deliciousness around the base. A few plump blueberries surrounded the pancake and a sprig of mint rested on the puff.

Which was already starting to deflate. She needed to get this out to Myles, like, now.

Except that there was something missing.

Darby squinted, then it hit her.

Whipped cream.

Of course.

She raced to the fridge, hoping Samson kept a bowl of whipped cream at ready.

He did!

Of course, he did.

She quickly took it back to her station, filled a piping bag, and made a large puff in the center, then surrounded it with smaller puffs. On instinct, she moves the mint to the top of the middle puff.

And now, it was finished.

Samson let out a low whistle. "That's too pretty to eat."

Darby froze.

Oh no!

It was pretty, but was it edible? She hadn't tried any of it as she worked. What if it was a feast for the eyes and a disappointment for the stomach?

With shaking fingers, Darby took a fork from the drawer and stuck it in part of the pancake still left in the pan. She dipped that in the remaining maple butter, then stabbed a blueberry, and dabbed whipped cream on the top. With her eyes half closed, her heart pounding, Darby stuck the fork in her mouth.

Her eyes flew open.

Oh, wow.

It was delicious! Like, really, truly, amazingly delicious!

She might have broken down crying, or maybe eaten Myles' plate of food, if Samson hadn't brought her back to reality.

"The counter is filling up, little sister, you better get out there."

"Right. I'll come back when it slows down and clean all this up."

"I know you will."

Darby held the plate of German pancake in her hand so tightly, her knuckles started to ache. She'd never give any thought to whisking plates of food from Samson's window to a waiting customer, now it felt like the plate in Darby's hands was as precious as solid gold. If she dropped it, and Myles never got to try it, she might actually freak out.

Somehow she made it through the double doors, even though she was sure they were going to swing into her back and send her sprawling into the ground. Myles' eyes lit up when he saw her coming, he followed the movement of the plate in her hands until it was set down in front of him.

They both breathed out a sigh. Darby couldn't say what Myles was sighing about, hers was pure relief.

"What's this?" He asked, not looking up.

"German pancake," Darby said, totally out of breath even though all she'd technically done was walk a few steps from the kitchen to the counter. "It's my Grammie's recipe. It's like Dutch babies. I don't know if you've had those before." She was starting to babble. Darby clamped her mouth shut.

"You made this?" Myles' eyes flickered from the plate to Darby.

"I did." She breathed out.

Gretta cleared her throat.

That was three.

When Darby turned around, Gretta nodded to the newcomers at the counter. There was a man holding a newspaper, so she couldn't see his face, and a woman with her young daughter.

"Enjoy," She said to Myles.

It was like pulling herself away from a freezer full of chocolate. All she wanted to do was stand there and stare at Myles as he took each bite. She wanted to see the evolution of expressions on his face and hear him declare her German pancake a culinary masterpiece.

Instead, she pulled out her notepad.

"Hey, what can I get for you?"

The woman looked up with a smile, then nudged her little girl. "Can I please have some pancakes with lots and lots and lots of chocolate chips, please and please?"

As nervous as Darby was about Myles and his breakfast, she couldn't stop the smile. She leaned over the little girl so they were eye to eye.

"Do you love chocolate?"

"Yes, yes, yes!" She bounced in her chair.

"Me, too. But I have a very important question. Do you also like whipped cream on your pancakes?"

"Yes, Yes, YES!" the girl screeched.

A rustle of newspaper moving down let Darby know she had an audience. No worries. She was used to tuning out other people and focusing on the person she was talking to. Otherwise, she'd go bonkers trying to keep track of everyone.

"She does like whipped cream with her pancakes." The mom smiled. "In case you couldn't tell."

"You and me, girlfriend. So, that's chocolate chip pancakes with whipped cream, anything to drink?"

The girl looked at her mom, who shrugged.

"Chocolate milk?" she asked like she thought someone had already told her no.

Darby glanced at the mom, who studied the menu.

That meant yes as far as Darby was concerned. She jotted the rest of the little girl's order onto her notepad, then turned to the mom.

"And how about you?"

Mom placed her order for a spinach artichoke omelet with smoked gouda, instead of cheddar, and another glass of chocolate milk.

Darby decided right then and there, that's the kind of mom she was going to be. The kind who drank chocolate milk for breakfast.

Well, as soon as she found a man.

And got him to propose.

Speaking of which.

She ached to go back to the counter where Myles sat, but she refused to let herself even look at him. Not until she'd done her job, appeased all the customers, and Gretta was satisfied. She took a long step to the side and ended up in front of the newspaper guy, whose brown head was bent over the menu.

"Hey, good morning, welcome to the Corner Café, what can I get for you?"

The man lifted his head.

And Darby almost let loose with a legit swear word.

# Chapter Ten

*Enemies to Lovers (ETL)*
   *Tired of Fighting Babe, Just Want That Happily Ever After*

Jackson Wilcox.
   The guy at the counter.
   He was Jackson Wilcox.
   *The* Jackson Wilcox.

Just sitting there on the peeling bar stool at the Corner Café in Hurricane, Utah.

Darby didn't know whether to die or throw up.

She felt like she was about to do both of them at the same time.

"I'm not sure, what's the best thing on the menu?" His brown eyes searched Darby's face. The color reminded her of that gunk that built up in the rain gutters, and the stuff that grew in the bottom of the refrigerator, and whatever happened under the oven when you finally moved it to clean.

Darby opened her mouth and couldn't get a single word to come out.

"Miss?" He tipped his head to the side, studying her.

"Wha—?" Darby's brain whirled. It wasn't until this moment that she fully understood the notion of fight-or-flight. Standing across from Jackson Wilcox, the wrecker of all her dreams, she suddenly had the urge to simultaneously run out of there as fast as she could and also slap his face so hard the hand print never went away.

Darby looked over her shoulder for Gretta, who was surely having a monstrous cow by now. Darby wasn't following a single one of her customer service rules.

But Gretta was nowhere to be seen. Oh, thank goodness. She didn't need a witness to her agony.

"Never mind, I'll take the—" He glanced over at Myles. "Hold on, what's that guy eating?"

Jackson Wilcox's voice was not quiet.

Myles heard and answered. "It's off-menu."

Darby could have kissed him.

For a number of reasons.

"Is it as good as it looks?"

Myles licked his thumb and stuck it in the air. "Better, man. Way better."

Darby looked at him, her heart melting.

Really? It was good?

"Great." Jackson slapped his hand over the menu. "I'll have that."

No.

No.

Nonononononononononononononono.

Darby couldn't, she wouldn't. She absolutely refused to cook for Jackson Wilcox again. She'd rather lose her job than watch Jackson Wilcox eat something she made. Her heart couldn't take it. She knew it couldn't. One slight grimace, one hint that he disliked it and she would completely fall to pieces. Right there, behind the counter at the Corner Café.

Why was he even here?

This day had been going so well.

She was just barely starting to get her confidence back.

It wasn't fair.

"Miss?" Jackson Wilcox said, again. This time impatience clouded over his words.

Darby nodded, pretended to scribble something down, then walked back to the kitchen like she was in a dream.

No, a horrible nightmare.

The one where everything around her dissolves into a bottomless black hole of no return.

With the door between her and stupid Jackson Wilcox, Darby could finally breathe. She made so much noise, apparently, that Samson peeked around the corner.

"You alright there, little sister?"

She tore off the order for the woman and her daughter and handed it to Samson. He took a look, then slapped it up on his order board.

"Samson?"

"Yeah?" He didn't turn around, but his ear moved just a smidge in her direction.

"What would you do if the one person in the world you hate with all your soul showed up in the café and ordered German pancakes?" Darby knew that didn't make a lick of sense outside her head, but she needed help. She'd just taken an order for something she couldn't possibly serve.

"Come again?"

Darby sighed and walked around the corner so she could see Samson better. "There is a food critic out there, at the counter." Darby said, her voice low. "He ordered German pancakes, but I can't serve them to him."

"I don't see any reason why not, little sister."

"Well, you would, if I told you my story."

Samson perked up, visibly. He'd been trying to get her story out of her since she started working there. Darby hated talking about it almost as much as she liked Samson, so she'd resisted. But now, the only way she was going to get through this was with his help.

"Jackson Wilcox is out there. He's a food critic, the food critic, who trashed my-my restaurant. The restaurant I owned before I came here. I can't believe this is happening." Darby pushed her hair out of her eyes. "I actually chose this place because I was positive Jackson Wilcox would never come to Hurricane. It's too small and out of the way. And yet, there he is. I can't serve him food that I cooked, Samson, I just can't. It will destroy my soul."

Samson turned slowly, eying Darby with an unreadable expression.

"What?" She said once the silence got completely unbearable.

Samson opened his mouth, then closed it. After another long moment of waiting, he nodded. "I can make the boy some German pancakes. You go out there and do your job. I'll do mine."

Relief whooshed out of Darby's mouth. "Really? You'll make them for him, even though they're not on the menu?"

"I will." Samson nodded. "Now scoot on out of here. I have work to do."

Darby wanted to throw her arms around him and squeeze and squeeze until he understood with his whole soul how grateful she was.

Instead, she turned on her heel and hurried out of the kitchen. He was right, she had a job to do, and she was going to do it. Jackson Wilcox had no idea who she was. He wouldn't make the connection between a restaurant owner and a waitress at some random café. That put her at an advantage. Now that she wasn't cooking for him, all she had to do was keep his beverage filled and serve him food.

That was something she could do flawlessly.

She locked her eyes on Myles and went right to him like there was no one else in the café. His plate was empty, which was a good sign, and he read his paper like he didn't have a care in the world.

Also a good sign.

People who could dawdle in the morning were the happiest people.

Darby reached for his empty plate, snapping his attention to her at the same time. "You all done, here?"

"That was so good." He said.

The compliment was tainted by the presence of Jackson Wilcox, just a few stools over. She imagined she heard him snort.

Focus.

Darby balanced the plate in one hand. "Do you want a refill?"

"No," Myles looked down at his mug. "Thanks though. Wow, that was good. I totally thought I'd stumped you, like you couldn't beat the crepes, but you nailed it again. I loved every bite of that, what did you call it, again?"

Darby felt Jackson Wilcox's eyes on them, her neck heated up uncomfortably. "It's a German pancake."

"I've never had one of those before. It was awesome. And that butter stuff. Wow!"

"I'll let the chef know." Darby said, her lips tight.

If stupid Jackson Wilcox wasn't there, she'd tell Myles she made the pancakes. Maybe she'd even tell him who she was. She couldn't tell Myles anything with Jackson Wilcox sitting a few stools over like a fat spider. Didn't he know it was incredibly rude to listen in on other people's conversations?

"Awesome, thanks." Myles handed her his mug. "I guess, I better go. Can I get my check?"

Go?

Myles couldn't go!

What was she supposed to concentrate on when Myles was gone?

"Uh, yeah, of course." Darby set the dishes down and fumbled for her other notepad, the one he could take to the register. "So, I didn't see you here yesterday. Where were you?"

Not her smoothest moment.

But Myles smiled because he was just the nicest guy. "I guess I come way too much, huh? If you notice when I'm not here." He flipped that lock of hair out of his eyes. "My sister, actually, she had a . . . well, a thing, and I needed to take care of it. She's good now. No worries. Back to normal." The crease in between his eyebrows didn't exactly confirm his flippant tone.

Darby wished they were alone and that he could open up to her. She wished it so badly it actually hurt her heart. Darby ripped the receipt off the pad and held it out for Myles. "Well, I'm glad things are better."

"Me too." Myles took the paper and gave her one last grin.

"Order up!"

With a sigh, Darby went to the window without watching Myles leave. His empty dishes were the only sign he'd been there at all. She retrieved the pancakes and omelet for the little girl and her mom. While she was down there, she refilled their chocolate milk and listened to a very entertaining story about a hippo that wanted to learn ballet. She would have stayed there forever, while the little girl chattered between bites of ooey gooey chocolaty goodness, except that Gretta was back now, and watching Darby's every move with exceptionally hawk-like eyes.

"Order up."

Darby hurried to the window. Samson held the plate out and Darby took it. She inspected it closely as she took it to Jackson Wilcox.

Samson was good.

It looked exactly the way she'd put together the plate for Myles. And she'd thought he wasn't paying any attention to what she was doing in there.

Darby set the plate in front of Jackson Wilcox without a single word. She also refilled his water and handed him a stack of napkins without speaking. Likewise, he said nothing as he turned the plate around, taking in every part of it.

Of course, he was.

Because that's what he did as a food critic.

Be critical of food.

What a horrible job. He just spent all his time tearing down the hard work of others. Picking it apart to find something wrong with it. It was so messed up on so many levels.

Gretta made a movement that caught Darby's attention. She leaned forward, her eyes on Jackson Wilcox, like she was just waiting for his first bite.

Did Gretta know he was coming today?

Why didn't she say anything?

Actually, Darby knew why. She hadn't told any of her staff either when Jackson Wilcox came to the restaurant. Mostly because she was too busy freaking out to think that they should probably know.

Well, that would explain why Gretta was in such an exceptionally cantankerous mood today. Like, more than usual. She had probably been stressing about this moment for weeks.

Jackson Wilcox cleared his throat in a very Gretta-ish way. Darby startled, coming out of her thoughts just in time to realize she'd been standing there staring at him while she'd been thinking.

That wasn't awkward at all.

He held a fork at the level of his mouth, and peered over it at Darby, a mocking smirk on his lips.

Oh, how much very, very much she hated him.

Darby flounced to the kitchen to get her bearings and leave him to his stupid breakfast. With her back to the doors, she reminisced about the good old days before Jackson Wilcox came into the café when she used to be able to spend her whole shift at the counter chatting with delightful people.

"Hey, now, Darby?"

"Yeah?" She pushed away from the doors and went to where she could see Samson.

"Don't get mad now, promise?"

Darby's heart, which was already on the verge of racing, picked back up the beats per minute. "What?"

"Well, now, I made a German pancake, but it wasn't as good as yours, so I made that there plate with . . ."

"Don't say it." Darby mumbled.

". . . the stuff you put together for that Myles boy. I just warmed it up in the oven for a few minutes."

Darby groaned and dropped her head into her hands. She stayed there for approximately five deep breaths, then she looked up at Samson.

"I'm going on break. Tell Gretta if she asks."

"Now, Darby—"

She grabbed her coat off the hanger near Gretta's office without responding. On her way to the back door, she took a detour to the dishwashing station to ask Meredith to cover the counter for her for thirty minutes. She was sad to miss saying goodbye to the little girl and her mom, but there was no way in the wide universe that Darby could stay there knowing Jackson Wilcox was eating her food.

No way.

She stepped into the bright sunshine and wrapped her jacket around her shoulders. It was more for comfort than it was for warmth at this point. The day was beautiful, with nice spring weather.

Her cell phone hopped in her uniform pocket.

Kenya.

"Hey," Darby said as she started walking away from the café. Maybe she'd take a little detour to Pioneer Park and visit the swings. There was just something about soaring through the air that made a person forget that Jackson Wilcox was eating Grammie's German pancakes at the Corner Café.

"Wow, you sound chipper!"

"Yeah."

Kenya's voice lowered. "What's wrong?"

"Nothing, why'd you call? Do you need something?"

"Well, I was just going to tell you about the amazing pasta I had for breakfast when I got home from work this morning."

Darby had almost forgotten all about that. It felt like a hundred years ago. "It was just boiled noodles with salt, pepper, and parmesan cheese."

"Oh no." Kenya's voice was shrill. "It was much more than that. It was the start of a new era. The one where you let the past die a quick and painless death while you rise from the ashes to become a Utah-famous chef!"

"No, I can't."

"Darby." Kenya sounded disappointed.

Well, she could join the club. The Disappointed in Darby Club. They could make T-shirts.

"What happened to you? I thought you'd be all excited, after the pasta and your note. I still can't believe you're gonna cater, but I am stinking excited!"

Darby's stomach clenched.

That old familiar clench.

"About that—"

"No, no, no you don't. You committed, and I'm holding you to it. What happened, Darbs? What took you from pasta-making wizard to down in the dumps?"

Darby checked both ways for cars, then crossed the street at a fast walk. "Jackson Wilcox."

"I hate that guy. Who is he, again?"

"The food critic."

"Okay, what about him?"

"He's at the café right now."

## DARBY'S CAFE

"What do you mean? Aren't you at the café right now?"

Darby kicked a rock and had a strange sense of satisfaction as it skipped into the gutter. "No, I took a break when Samson accidentally on purpose served Jackson Wilcox some German pancakes I made for Myles."

"You made German pancakes for Myles?" Kenya squealed.

"Yes."

"Man, I would really love some German pancakes right now," Kenya said dreamily. "And also, just so you know, I am not following at all. What happened that got you all upset?"

Darby took a deep breath and started over, explaining the morning in more detail and in chronological order for clarity. When she was done, Kenya started laughing.

Not just, an amused chuckle. They were deep belly laughs that made her wheeze into the phone.

Darby stopped walking near a flower shop and put her hand on her hips. "What in the world are you laughing about?"

It took Kenya a few minutes to get a hold of herself enough to answer. "Jackson Wilcox is at the Corner Café right now eating your German pancakes. You don't think that's incredibly hilarious?"

"No, I really don't. I can't believe you do."

"Well, I can't believe you aren't at the café right now, waiting to hear what he thinks about them! You know he's going to love them. Everybody loves Grammie's German pancakes. It's practically a law. This would be so good for you. He'll praise the crap out of them, then you get your confidence back."

"Yeah, except for a couple problems. I'm not going back to that café until he leaves and also, Jackson Wilcox is a jerkwad and I don't actually care what he thinks about my pancakes."

Which wasn't exactly true. Darcy did care. She cared way too much.

What she didn't know was why.

There had been a ton of people who left rotten reviews on Yelp or Google. Tons. She'd already decided that was fine, she didn't like every restaurant she went to either. They just weren't her people.

But then, Jackson Wilcox showed up. With his power suit and his perfect hair and his stupid phone where he kept recording voice notes about everything from the ambiance to the plating.

Darby didn't know why she cared what he thought. She hated that she cared what he thought. No, she just hated him.

"Darby?" Kenya said. "Are you still there?"

"Yes."

She was still there, and she was standing in the middle of a parking lot while people were trying to park.

Just awesome.

Darby waved and moved her booty to the sidewalk as fast as she could.

"I won't give you a hard time about it anymore. I'm sorry."

"Thank you."

"But I am totally going to the café right now because I have to know what he thinks about those pancakes. Okay? Okay, byeeeeeee!"

## Chapter Eleven

*Back in the Saddle (BitS) Lovelorn Female Ready to Try This Dating Thing Again*

Now all Darby could think about was Kenya showing up at the café in a huge floral hat and sunglasses, trying to spy on Jackson Wilcox behind a menu. Gretta already had a short fuse, something like that just might push her over the edge.

Darby flipped herself around and started jogging back to the café. If she was lucky—*haha, that was hilarious*—she'd beat Kenya and talk her out of whatever she was thinking before she had a chance to make a spectacle.

Unfortunately, her waitress uniform wasn't really meant for sprinting. She had to stop numerous times to pull the skirt down. Her cue was a catcall from a passing vehicle. It was better if she didn't think about the potential number of people in Hurricane that now knew what color underwear she wore.

As Darby approached the café, she knew her mad dash had been completely pointless. She couldn't see Kenya's car, but she was very familiar with how long it took to get from Kenya's house to the café. There was no possible way she'd made it there before Kenya.

She went through the back door, into the kitchen, and tiptoed to the double doors. They were too high to see through the window without standing on something. Darby didn't want to risk pushing the door too hard and falling on her face where everyone could see her, because that would totally happen to her. She turned around and sneaked over to Samson. When he moved to the fridge to get something, she took his place, peering through the order window into the café.

Jackson Wilcox still sat at the counter, doing something on his phone. His plate was empty. Darby couldn't deal with all the thoughts swarming her mind, so she turned her attention to the people around him. The mom and little girl were gone, their place needed to be cleared, and new customers were seated along the counter, waiting for Meredith to stop flirting with Brad Callaghan, the local sportscaster, and take care of them. Why was Gretta nowhere to be seen when Meredith was slacking off?

"What are you doing?"

Darby whirled around to face Samson, who was holding a carton of eggs with a confused look on his face.

"Um, recon."

"Hmm."

She stepped out of his way so he could get to his station. "I just wanted to know what was what before I stepped back into the thick of it."

"Sure." He cracked eggs, one-handed, at lightning speed. Even on her best day, Darby had never been that skilled.

"I'll go now."

"You do that." He glanced over his shoulder. "Make sure you say hi to your friend for me."

Her friend?

Kenya!

Darby got so distracted by Jackson Wilcox, she completely forgot to look for Kenya.

"Okay, yeah, I will."

Samson pressed his lips together in a way that made it look like he was hiding a smile. "Tell her I love the hat."

Oh, no.

Darby nodded and trudged out of the kitchen with her shoulders rounded like they carried the weight of the café. She pushed the double doors with one hand and scanned the room for Kenya.

She was in one of the booths, with the menu pulled up to her nose, staring at Jackson Wilcox through huge black sunglasses. And she was, in fact, wearing a flowery straw hat that had such a wide brim, it would have been difficult for someone to sit next to her in the booth.

Oh, Kenya.

Darby hurried to take care of the new customers, and to clear the dishes of those who had already left. When everyone was settled, she eyeballed Jackson Wilcox like he was something disgusting and hairy crawling on the counter.

She knew her job, she'd been doing it for over a year, she knew what she had to do. Except she really didn't want to talk to Jackson Wilcox again.

*Really* didn't want to talk to him.

Darby told herself to be a big girl, and take his dishes, then give him the bill. That's all she had to do and he would be gone. Hopefully forever. The sooner she did this, the sooner she could go talk to Kenya and find out what in the world the girl was thinking. Hurricane was not a big town. Everyone knew it was her. The only thing she was doing in that getup was drawing attention.

Okay.

Okay, okay, okay.

Go time.

"Can I get you anything else?" Darby asked, trying not to fidget with her hands while she waited for Jackson Wilcox to look up.

It took him a minute, but when he did, his eyes were sort of glazed over. "Hm?"

"Would you like anything else? A refill? Or something more to eat?" Darby was proud of how normal her voice sounded.

"No, I'm through." He went back to his phone.

Darby tried not to be annoyed. That sort of interaction was exactly what she wanted, wasn't it? Just a minimal, take care of business kind of conversation. So, then, why did she feel frustrated that he didn't say more?

Was Kenya right, again?

Did Darby actually *want* to know what he thought of the German pancakes? She was annoyed that he didn't say anything. But she was totally on edge, waiting for him to speak.

She didn't want to know.

But she did.

But she didn't.

This was ridiculous. Darby shook her head and gathered the last of the dishes. All the way to the dishwasher and back, she chided herself for being so stupid.

She was still giving herself a stern mental talking to when Jackson Wilcox called her over.

"Yes?" She clasped her hands behind her back so he couldn't see them tremble.

"Can you give a message to the chef?"

Gretta's chair creaked, which it only did when she got up, sat down, or leaned forward. Darby imagined she was leaning so far forward, her nose was skimming the ground.

"Sure, uh, yes."

Jackson Wilcox looked at her like he wasn't sure she could. Darby squared her shoulders and looked him in the eye, trying not to blink or look away. There, see, she was competent. She was fully capable of giving a message to the chef.

Oh, wait, the chef was her.

Jackson Wilcox tapped his thumb against the counter a couple of times. "Tell the chef that was the best German pancake I've ever had. Maple butter and blueberries were a fantastic choice."

Darby's brain had frozen.

She honestly couldn't process his words.

Did Jackson Wilcox just say her pancakes were the best he'd ever had? He loved the maple butter and blueberries?

Jackson Wilcox?

That couldn't be right. He hated her food so much that he wrote an entire article about it. Maybe she was having some kind of episode where her brain filtered negative words and turned them positive to keep her from having a breakdown.

Was that a thing?

"Did you get that?" Jackson Wilcox watched her with uncertainty.

"Yes." The word came out too quietly. She had to clear her throat and try again. "Yes, I got that. Best ever, fantastic choice."

"Great, thank you." He stood up, finally about to leave, and Darby had the strangest urge to pull him back. She wanted to know more. Why was it the best German pancake? Because it was fluffy? Or because she added sugar to the dough, which most people didn't do? What did he like most? The crunchiness or the airiness? The golden brown color?

Darby actually reached out a hand as he put his jacket on. Luckily, she realized what she was doing before she made a complete fool of herself. She pretended to flick an imaginary fuzzy onto the floor, then tucked her hands away where they couldn't do anything else weird.

Jackson Wilcox looked over at Gretta and gave her a smile. "Walk me out?"

She was off her chair and by his side in record time.

Darby watched them go. The moment the door was closed behind them, she dropped her notepad on the counter and hurried to Kenya's booth. She collapsed on the seat across from Kenya, dropping her head into her arms.

"He loved it!" Kenya said as quietly as she could. "He loved it, he loved it, he loved it! What do you have to say about that? Ms. Nothing Good Ever Happens to Me! What's your luck like now?"

Darby just shook her head. All that adrenaline was wearing off, leaving her head as heavy as a fifty-pound dumbell. She needed sugar, stat.

Kenya poked Darby's arm numerous times.

"Come out of there, we have to celebrate! I'm gonna order you chocolate waffles with strawberries!"

"I can't," Darby spoke into her arms, so she wasn't sure how much Kenya heard.

"Where's your notepad, so I can write it down? I want German pancakes, you want waffles. Where'd you put that thing?"

Darby finally got her head to move enough that she could see Kenya, just barely, over her arms. "It's on the counter."

"Okay, well, you can remember that, right? Celebration breakfast. The turning of the tide. From now on, your luck is amazing!"

"I can't."

"You can't what?" Kenya took off her hat and fluffed her hair. "This thing totally itches after a while. Remind me of that the next time I think I want to wear it to Sand Hollow."

"I can't celebrate with you. I already took my break. I probably have about twenty seconds before Gretta gets back in here and clears her throat at me."

"Oh boo." Kenya's lower lip jutted. "Okay, we'll just celebrate when you get home tonight. After I take a nap." A yawn broke through her words. "Actually, cancel my order. I am wrecked. I'm going to go home and sleep, then you and I will paint the town! You choose where we eat, I'll provide the entertainment. Wow, that hit me hard. I'm out. See you this afternoon!"

Kenya was gone by the time Darby pulled her booty out of the booth. As she walked back to the counter, Gretta entered the café. From the smile on her face, Darby was going to make a guess that the review coming out in the Food and Entertainment section was going to be a good one.

Despite everything, she was glad.

Someone deserved to have their dreams come true.

Darby dragged her feet around, clearing and wiping and taking orders for the rest of the morning. It had only been two hours and it felt like an entire week. It sounded amazing to go home and take a nap.

Kenya had the right idea.

Towards the end of her shift, just an hour before the café was about to close, Gretta left her desk for a fifteen minute break. Meredith seized that opportunity, and Darby's arm, pulling Darby into the kitchen where all the staff and servers gathered.

"What's going on?" Darby asked, trying to get clues from the faces around her.

"We need to talk about this party thing," Meredith inspected a fingernail. "Are we or aren't we? People need to know."

Darby knew what Samson thought, so she directed her attention to him. Just as she expected, he nodded. "I say, yes."

"I say no," Meredith finally looked up. "That makes us even. Who else?"

The word no got a lot of traction in the next few minutes. Darby doubted it had ever been said so vehemently in such a short amount of time, ever. Even if she hadn't already decided they were throwing the party, she would probably vote yes right now. There was something about all the negativity that brought out her contrary.

"Hey," Darby raised a hand to get attention. There was a lot of noise and she didn't have a super loud voice. When mostly everyone was looking at her, she lowered her hand. "I'm throwing the party, with or without you people. My friend, Kenya, is a party planner and she already agreed to help me out, for free. So, we're doing it. Now I guess you just need to decide if you want in or not."

Samson's smile made Darby feel like she was a rock star. He was usually so gruff, and kinda cranky, it was awesome so see such a genuinely happy smile on his face.

Meredith dropped her head to the side. "Are you serious?"

"Yes."

"Why? Gretta is the worst! Especially to you. Why in the world do you want to throw a party for her?"

There were a few reasons, but she didn't think Meredith would go for any of them. Mostly, it was because she found that connection between herself and Gretta. Somehow, that made Gretta's pickiness, and critical eye, and habit of yelling, way more understandable. Maybe Darby wouldn't handle the stress of owning a café the same way, but she certainly understood the temptation. It was hard to be the boss. It was hard to be in food service. It was hard all around.

"I think Gretta deserves to know that she's appreciated for all the hard work she does."

"She deserves something." One of the dishwashers, a burly guy who got a lot of flack from Gretta because he stunk at removing grease, grumbled to his buddy.

"I'm not going to try and talk anyone into this," Darby said. She'd been away from the counter for long enough. She could practically feel the mugs and water glasses emptying. "I'm doing the party either way. I'd love your help, but I understand if you don't want to. It's totally up to you. Just let me know by the end of today so we can start planning. Okay?"

Without waiting for a response, or anymore backtalk, Darby turned and left the kitchen. Just as she thought, there were a bunch of people ready for her. She took care of all of them as quickly as she could. By the time Gretta got back, the café was quiet and organized.

Gretta disappeared to the kitchen, to check on the staff, and Meredith grabbed Darby's arm as she passed. "You gotta take my closing shift today."

"Why?"

"Cause I covered for you while you were cooking with Samson. Fair's fair."

Covered for her! That was funny. What Meredith did was flirt with all the eligible men in the vicinity.

Whatever, it wasn't worth arguing over.

Darby smiled, trying to make it genuine, and shrugged. "Sure, I can do that."

"Great." Meredith gave her a weird look and then went to clear the corner booth.

When the last of the patrons had paid their bills and the last of the staff had cleared out of the café, Darby locked the front door and went looking for Gretta. She'd never come out from the kitchen.

She was back there with Samson, in deep conversation. Darby instantly wished she could retrace her steps and leave them to it.

"Yes?" Gretta said.

"Yeah, I was just wondering what you want me to do and what you want to do." Her words were coming out all jumbled. "I mean, for closing? Do you have a preference?"

"I thought Meredith was closing today."

"I'm taking her shift." No need to explain why.

Gretta glanced at Samson, then shrugged. "Sure, you can start on the booths and counters again. That seemed to work well last time we closed together."

It did, didn't it?

Darby went to work. Her mind wandered as she methodically cleaned salt and pepper shakers and condiment bottles. She was so in the zone, she didn't even register the first couple of times Gretta called her name.

"Darby!"

"Yes?" She jumped to her feet, almost smacking her head on the top of the booth. "Sorry, what is it?"

Gretta shook her head, but looked more amused than annoyed. "Are you about done over there?"

"Yes, just one more ketchup bottle."

"When you're finished, come see me at the register."

Darby's curiosity spurred her through the rest of the task. She threw away the sanitizing towels and stopped next to Gretta.

"You know how to close out a register?"

Darby blinked. Of all the things she expected Gretta to say, that was not one of them. "I do."

"Yeah?"

Darby nodded.

Gretta stared at her for a minute, then reached for a rubber band to wrap around the stack of bills in her hand. "Where'd you learn how to close a register?"

Darby was going to stop analyzing everything and just answer the question. It would be way less stressful.

"I worked at a restaurant before this."

Gretta nodded but didn't say anything. It was like she was waiting.

For what though? Gretta knew Darby's past, she saw her resume when Darby filled out an application.

Maybe she just wanted to hear more?

But why?

Darby shook her head. Be present! Stop trying to see where everything is going before you have to get there!

"I uh, actually I owned a restaurant in Salt Lake, up until about a year ago."

"Oh?" Gretta sounded surprised. Maybe she *didn't* read through all those resumes. "That makes a lot of sense."

"What does?" Darby asked.

"The way you handle things around here. I knew there was something different about you, but now I know why. You know what it's like to be the owner."

Darby's heart stalled for just a moment. She didn't realize it was obvious. Did that mean she was too overbearing, bossy? Had she overstepped?

Gretta smiled, placing a hand on Darby's arm. "You look scared to death. I guess that's partly my fault. I know I'm hard to work with sometimes. Most of the time." She laughed. It was such a rare sound, it threw Darby for a loop.

Had she actually ever heard Gretta laugh before?

Wait, she had, that day they talked about Phantom of the Opera.

It was true Gretta was hard to work with sometimes, but that wasn't the whole story. Gretta was also extremely observant and generous. Like when she met homeless people behind the café to give them breakfast, and when she helped the elderly patrons through the door. People were more than just one thing.

Gretta laughed. "It's okay, I know I'm ornery. I'm . . ." She shifted. "I'm sorry if I've been hard on you."

Darby shook her head. "It stinks to be the one in charge of everything sometimes."

"It does." Gretta looked down. "But that's no excuse. I know I'm harsh and demand perfection and I know everyone hates me. I just get into the zone. I forget that everyone else is dealing with stuff too."

Darby wasn't sure what to say. It was like she was speaking with an entirely different person.

"Samson told me you defended me when the others were going at it." Gretta lifted her eyes to Darby. "That means a lot, really, thank you."

Was that what they were talking about in the kitchen? Darby didn't know whether to be mortified or glad. She was glad she'd defended Gretta, but kind of mortified Samson mentioned it. Especially because Darby had totally done her fair share of griping to Kenya after work.

"Anyway, I didn't mean to make this weird. I just wanted you to know I'm grateful. So, thank you."

Darby smiled. "You're welcome."

# Chapter Twelve

*Anybody Out There (AOT)*
*Happy, cute and fun seeks more of the same. Please respond. It's ridiculously hard to meet people.*

Kenya was still asleep when Darby got back to the apartment. That was okay, Darby didn't really feel like painting the town anyway. Not only was that an extremely strange saying—like, what did that even mean?—but she was also bone tired. Not sleepy tired, done tired. She pulled out her phone and flopped on the couch with the Voxer app already opened. Talking to Cole was fast becoming her favorite way to relax at the end of her day.

There was a text from him waiting for her there like a gift.

*Hey, how was your day?*

*Good*

. . .

That was all she got typed before the flip phone vibrated from the end table next to her head. She must have left it there the last time they talked. Darby reached for it and barely had the chance to say hello before Cole was there, in her ear.

"You had a good day?"

"Yeah." Darby hesitated, she suddenly felt shy. "I cooked at work today. We even served it to a customer."

"You are kidding me! Really?"

Cole's enthusiasm was completely contagious.

"Yeah," Darby laughed. "It's your fault! You got in my head and now I can't stop thinking about making food. It's crazy! And it gets crazier, there was a food critic in the café at the same time. He saw what the customer ordered and wanted it too."

"What, are you serious? A food critic? Is that even a real job?"

Darby laughed. "It is a real job, unfortunately, and you know what else? This food critic was the same one who wrote the review that trashed my restaurant. He's the reason I had to close."

There was a long pause. "Are you serious?"

"Yes! This guy is a major influencer. When he doesn't like a place it tanks. Sort of the opposite of what happens to people who end up featured on Diners, Drive-ins and Dives. Seriously, Cole, it was the worst! I was so tempted to put his tie in the coffee grinder."

"Of all the things you could do, that's what you thought of?"

"Well, the tie looked way expensive. I thought that might be a major blow."

Cole laughed. "Okay, so big scary food critic ate your food, wait, what did you make?"

"Um, can't tell you."

If she told him now that would be the same as telling him who she was. Already she was skirting the line. Any second she expected Cole to ask her if she was the waitress at the Corner Café.

"Why?"

"Too much information," She said.

"Okay, then, what did he think about this mysterious dish you cooked? Did he say?"

Darby smiled to herself at the memory. He liked it. She couldn't believe it, but it was true. She shuffled her shoulders to get more comfortable with the fluffy pillow behind her head and let herself relive that moment.

"Rey?"

"Yeah, sorry, my brain took a tangent. I'm here. What were we talking about?"

Cole laughed. "We were talking about that food critic and what he said about your food. Did he like it?"

"He did. He said it was the best he ever had!"

Cole whooped. "Are you kidding me? That's awesome! It's also torture! You're not going to tell me what you made? Don't you know my screen name is FoodieC for a reason?"

Darby laughed. "I will . . . I'll tell you sometime. Just not right now."

"Okay, fine, I'll try to deal with the disappointment." Cole's voice teased. "So, what's next? Are you ready to open up that five star restaurant now?"

Darby waited for the clench. It always came when someone brought up her restaurant. Or a restaurant. Anything about restaurants. She expected it to be there so thoroughly that her stomach muscles hardened until they ached.

But the clench didn't come.

She let out a whoosh of air.

There was no clench.

Nothing.

She even poked her belly just to make sure.

"You know what?" Darby said the words, slowly, still waiting for the clench. Was it gone for good? Had she conquered the clench? "I just might."

"If you did, what kind of restaurant would it be?"

Darby chewed her lip for a minute. Not random this time, specific. Maybe she'd open a breakfast place. Those German pancakes were such a hit and she had a fantastic waffle recipe. It was like eating clouds smothered in caramel syrup.

"Maybe a café? But just for breakfast. I really like the thought of closing early and having tons of time to chill and prep for the next day."

That had been her other mistake before, serving breakfast, lunch, and dinner. All day, every day.

Burnout was real.

"Have I ever told you breakfast is my favorite meal of the day?"

"No." Darby smiled. "What do you love the most for breakfast?"

"Oh, no, don't make me choose. It's really not fair."

"Okay, top three."

"That's better, I can totally do that. Crepes, Eggs Benedict, and German Pancakes."

Darby's stomach did a little flutter. She opened her mouth to comment, hopefully flippantly, but nothing came out. It was probably better that way. She wasn't sure she could be flippant after that revelation anyway.

"How about you?"

"My favorite breakfast foods?"

"Well, yeah, it *is* the most important meal of the day."

"Right, that would be muffins."

"Muffins?"

"Yes, I love muffins! Fluffy and piping hot, right out of the oven, drenched in butter. Muffins are the best food in the world. But they have to be homemade. Those things from the store are not the same. Did you know, once I got a big package from Costco and froze them because it was going to take like a month for me to finish them off all by myself, and they never froze? Never."

Cole gasped.

"You mock, but that is not natural. That means they are stuffed with artificial guck. Just think about what that's doing to your insides."

"I can't, too scary."

Darby laughed again. "Well, I thought it was disgusting. I had to give them away because I couldn't eat them after that. I'd rather make muffins myself. I mean, I used to rather. I haven't baked anything in a . . . while."

Cole said, slowly. "I have this sudden urge to make you visualize turning on an oven, then mixing muffin batter, putting it in the tins, and setting the timer. Look what happened with the pasta. We could do the same thing with baking, you know? Overcome all the fears."

Darby stretched her arm over her head. "If I visualize, do I have to actually do it?"

"You don't actually have to do anything except for breathe, you're an adult."

Darby laughed. "Then, let's put a pin in that. My brain is mush."

"Okay, no baking visualizations today. I think that might be a better activity for us to do together, anyway. Like in person. On a date. So, what are your favorite kinds?"

"Of dates?" Darby's mind was officially blown. He was talking about meeting, dating, and baking. Together.

What?

"No," Cole laughed. "Sorry! I was all over the place. I meant, what are your favorite kinds of muffins?"

Okay, she was actually super disappointed he moved the subject around so quickly. She really wanted to hear more about this date idea.

Was that a sign that it didn't freak her out?

Was it time to meet?

"Rey?"

"Yes, yeah, yes, I'm here. I love blueberry muffins the most, of course."

"Classic."

"Banana with nuts are amazing too. And pumpkin chocolate chip, Oh, I really love triple berry. My Grammie has a recipe that makes all the other recipes in the world wish they were that good."

Cole laughed. "Nuh-uh!"

"Yeah, for real, no joke. It is phenomenal."

"Well, now I need to try these best muffins in the world."

"Universe."

"The best muffins in the universe. Can I get your grammie's number? She'd make them for me, right?"

Darby's smile drooped. "She would, for sure, except that she passed away almost two years ago."

Before the restaurant tanked, thank goodness. That would have made everything so much harder if Grammie had been here to see her failure.

Well, technically, Grammie did see her failure, from the other side, but that didn't count because Darby didn't have to witness the disappointment on her face.

"Oh, shoot. I'm so sorry." Cole's words rushed together. "That was stupid. I'm sorry."

"You didn't know." Darby said. "And it's okay. Grammie was the best person in the world, and I miss her like crazy pretty much all the time, but she was lonely for Grandpa. It makes me happy to know she's happy with him."

"That's a great way of looking at it." He paused. "Hey, just so I don't stick my foot in it again, what's the status of the rest of your family?"

"That's it."

"Grammie? That's all your family?"

"As far as I know." Darby said. "Grammie raised me. She was, is, my family." Darby pushed her hair behind her ear. "And Grammie was more than enough. I never felt like I missed out on anything."

"No, yeah, I get that. But, what about your parents?"

"Um, I don't really know. Grammie didn't like to talk about them. I've figured out stuff over the years. I think I was a teen pregnancy, or at least an unwed one. My dad didn't stick around and my mom's health was never good. She passed away a few months after I was born."

"Wow, Rey, I'm so sorry."

"It's really okay, like I said, Grammie was more than enough for me. She loved me fiercely."

"That I can get behind."

"What?" Darby asked, her face wrinkling up in confusion.

"Loving you fiercely."

Wow, her heart might have actually stopped. "What does that mean?" She said with a laugh. Better to downplay what he said, then to get her hopes up.

"It just means you're the type of person who people can love fiercely."

"How so?" Darby was proud she didn't stammer on the words.

There was a long silence where Darby started to regret her question. She was about to tell him to forget it when Cole spoke again. "I haven't known you that long, but I feel like I have. It's like I'm getting concentrated Rey the way we do this. Maybe it's because we talk so often without seeing each other, it takes away all the normal barriers, you know? You don't have to hide who you are because there's no risk. So, I think I know you better than anyone else in the world right now and from what I know, I can say without hesitation that you are easy to love."

How did a person respond to something like that?

Darby couldn't snatch the right words. Thank you sounded so dumb. He'd just given her the most beautiful compliment in probably her entire life. There were no words.

And now her cheeks were about to set off the fire alarm. The only thing she could think to do was change the subject. "How-how about you? What's your family like?"

Cole answered like it wasn't weird or awkward that she didn't acknowledge what he'd said. She was beyond grateful. It was going to take her about a week of processing to get that all worked out in her mind.

"We have the dad thing in common, unfortunately. My dad bailed when I was three. It was just me, my sister, and my mom. Mostly me and my sister. She's nine years older than me, so she pretty much bossed me around constantly. Still does, actually. All the time."

"You don't make that sound like a bad thing."

"Yeah," Cole chuckled. "No, I guess I do sort of love it. It's annoying sometimes. But I have to admit, it's super nice to have someone who cares so much about you that they are a supreme pain in the you know what."

Darby grinned. "Yeah, I can see that."

There was a long, comfortable pause. Darby breathed into a smile as she stared at the ceiling. It was also super nice and that was having someone you could just be silent with.

Cole cleared his throat. "Yeah, so, anyway, what else is going on with you?"

There was something else she wanted to talk to him about. She was glad he gave her the chance to remember. "The place where I work is coming up on the tenth year anniversary. Ke-"

Whew, she caught herself just in time. Cole would certainly make the connection between Kenya and the café. What with all the wild costumes Kenya always wore and the fact that the two of them were always together at the café, he would figure it out for sure.

"My friend is a party planner and she's going to help me throw an amazing party for my boss."

"What? That's awesome! Do you really like your boss, then?"

Darby pursed her lips and pushed them to the side of her face. That was also a tricky question. She wasn't sure how to answer honestly because she wasn't sure where they were at with that. The friendship, or understanding, thing was still really new.

"I really respect her. I think she's awesome for doing everything she does and I think she deserves a party."

"That makes you a very, very nice person."

Did it? Darby's cheeks flushed. "Thank you."

"If you need some help, let me know?"

"I will." She nodded, and then felt silly. It's not like he could see her. "We've spent this whole time talking about me. How was your day?"

"I like talking about you."

"So do I, apparently."

Cole's laugh was delicious. "My day was good. I got up early, went for a run with my sister's dog who almost killed me three times, then I had an amazing breakfast at this tiny little café."

Darby's heart leaped.

"After that, I came home and worked with the city on building permits. I'm trying to open a restaurant."

"In Hurricane?"

"Yes, I mean, I'd like to. This is a great community, I'm really starting to love it."

"How long have you lived here?"

Cole was silent for a moment, probably doing math. That always made Darby quiet too. "So, aside from the four years I spent here in high school, I've been back for about ten months. I'm living with my sister and my mom while my sister works through some stuff. It's a long story."

"That's okay, you don't have to tell me."

"It's just complicated, honestly. I'll spare you the details. So, yeah, that's what brought me here."

"And are you happy to be here?"

"I am now," Cole said.

Darby almost swallowed her tongue. There were butterflies having butterflies in her stomach. "What's your favorite thing about Hurricane?"

"I'm a fan of Pioneer Park. I spent a lot of time on the swings when I lived here before."

"In high school?"

"Yeah, why do you say that like it's a weird thing? I think the second you get too old to swing, you might as well eat prunes and listen to Billy Holiday."

"Who?" Darby laughed.

"Exactly my point."

"That was a joke. I'm the girl who grew up with her Grammie as her only parent, remember? I know Billy. Me and Billy are like this." She intertwined her first two fingers even though Cole couldn't see them.

"And I'm the guy living in his mother's basement. You still want to talk to me?"

"Actually, I do." Darby surprised herself. "Talking to you is pretty much the highlight of my day."

"I feel exactly the same way."

Darby rubbed her cheeks, glad again that he couldn't see her. "So, what do you do exactly? Something with business?"

"Yeah, I don't think you want to know."

"Why?"

"Because it might make you feel bad."

"Try me."

"You're sure?"

"Yes, please."

"Okay, you asked for it." Cole took a deep breath. "Because I own restaurants."

"Restaurants?" She put emphasis on the s, drawing it out.

"Yeah," he paused. "Many restaurants."

"How many is many?"

"You really don't want to know."

"I actually really do." And she meant it. "You can tell me. It won't make me feel bad, I promise."

"Okay," he let out a long breath. "I have seven, total. Three in Utah, one in Arizona, two in California and . . . oh, wait. I just sold the one in New York because it was way hard to run cross country. So, actually six. The Hurricane restaurant would be my lucky number seven. See, you didn't want to know that."

"Yes, I did! That's awesome! Good for you!" She really was glad for him. Sincerely. Did that mean she was evolving? A few months ago, the clench in her belly would have gone nuts listening to him talk about his numerous successful restaurants.

This was big.

"Okay, before you get too impressed, I just own them. They stay alive because of the amazing managers and chefs I have on staff. I don't do much except pay the bills these days."

"Is that what you've always wanted to do? Own restaurants?"

"Um, no, not exactly. I've only really been in the restaurant game for a couple of years, but I do like it."

"What did you do before?"

A thump down the hall caught Darby's attention. Kenya stumbled into the kitchen just a few moments later.

"What day is it?"

Darby grinned at Kenya, who was rubbing her eyes like she was a little kid. "Hey, Cole, I'm sorry, I have to go. Can I call you tomorrow?"

"Absolutely you can."

"Awesome, thanks, bye!"

"Bye, Rey."

She was really starting to love that name.

# Chapter Thirteen

*Gorgeous Tall Brunette (GTB) seeks her alpha male.*

It was a fluke that Darby checked Voxer before she went to work the next morning. Her thumb brushed it as she put her phone in her purse. It lit up with a message from Cole.

*Call me when you get a chance!*

Darby had a few minutes. She went to the living room and got the flip phone off the coffee table where she'd left it the day before. She opened it up, clicked on his name and held the phone to her ear.

Cole picked up on the second ring. "Hey, Rey!"

"Hey! What's up?"

"What? No talk about the weather, how'd you sleep, what are you eating for breakfast. Straight to business, huh?"

Darby cleared her throat. "Oh, yeah, that was such a bad oversight.

Excuse me. Cole, how are you? Can you believe this weather? So weathery, right? Did you eat breakfast well last night? What are you sleeping this morning?"

Cole's belly laugh rumbled through the phone. "That was awesome."

"Thank you." Darby bowed her head slightly. "I have ten minutes before I have to leave for work, so no more time to waste. Also, I haven't had breakfast yet, so I'm going to eat cereal in your ear while you tell me what's going on."

"Sounds fun."

Darby grabbed her shoes off the floor so she wouldn't forget where she left them and swung them by her side as she walked to the kitchen. Kenya was nowhere to be seen, she'd done a Quinceneara the night before. Those were definitely party all night kinds of things.

"So, why did you want me to call you first thing this morning?"

Silence.

"Cole?"

"Yes," Cole said in a low voice, and then there was more silence.

"Cole?" Darby tried again.

Cole laughed. "Sorry, my sister is on the phone with our mom and I'm trying to eavesdrop."

Darby grabbed a bowl from the cupboard and set it on the counter while she searched the pantry for something tasty. She had to admit she was really going to miss Kenya's cereal supply, not to mention her pantry, when it was time to move back into her apartment.

She chose a cereal that was fruity but not too sweet, then poured it into the bowl. She grabbed the milk from the fridge on her way to the table. It would be pressing her luck to fill the bowl ahead of time. For sure it would slosh all over the tile. She set the bowl on the table with the spoon sticking over the side at a jaunty angle while she twisted the cap on the milk. "I can call you on my break."

Cole let out a gust of air. "No, it's all good. Everything is fine. They're talking about shoes. For a second, I thought it might be something important."

"Shoes are important."

"Of course they are," Cole said. "Okay, to business. After we were done talking last night I kept thinking about you."

Darby stopped with the loaded spoon right in front of her mouth. "Really?"

"Yes, it's not that surprising. I think about you a lot. Why did you stop cooking and baking?"

Darby had to make a concerted effort to answer the question instead of swooning about the other thing he said. Luckily it was an easy question. "I stopped cooking because a food critic destroyed my restaurant. I couldn't cook or bake anything without thinking about that horrible experience and getting angry, or sad." Which was the worse emotion of the two by far. "It was just painful."

"A food critic?" Cole let the words drag like there were more coming. Darby took a deep breath and let it out slowly, waiting. She didn't want to talk about Jackson Wilcox. Getting ticked off was a terrible way to start the day.

Thankfully, Cole went on like he hadn't asked the question at all. "Would you say you were good at cooking and baking?"

Up until yesterday she would say she used to be. "I don't know, I haven't done it in so long. It's hard to feel like you're good at something that you don't ever do."

"That's fair. But you could just try again and then you'd know."

"But what if I stink at it?"

"Would you say you are a good waitress?"

The subject switch made Darby pause for a moment. She certainly wasn't a bad waitress. She was friendly and kind and took care of people when they were at the counter. The only way she could be better was if she didn't do stupid things because of her rotten luck, there wasn't really anything she could do about that.

And where the heck was he going with all this?

"Sure."

"Were you a good waitress when you first started working as one?"

"I made a bunch of mistakes, but it was okay. I figured it out."

Wait a second.

Darby saw what he did there. "Okay, fine. You might have a point."

"I have a great point."

"Okay, okay, okay. You got me." She dropped her spoon in the bowl and carried it to the sink. "Go ahead and gloat."

"I'm not a gloater, but thanks for the offer."

Darby laughed.

"Okay, so, this is how it went down. I was thinking about my sister. When we were little she loved telling me stories that she made up. She was really good at it too, then she took a creative writing class in high school and the teacher was a writer that couldn't get published. He'd been trying for years. The guy was so critical, he totally crushed my sister. Instead of coming out of that class pumped to chase her dream, she gave it up. Never wrote again. Never told another story. She was totally broken."

"That's terrible."

"It is, but it's also instructive. I had a similar thing happen when I was first starting out in my career. I don't want you to give up, Rey. We're going to conquer this cooking and baking thing. You and me."

You and me.

Darby dried her hands on a towel and started for the door where her purse hung. "I hate to say this, but I really need to get to work."

"Yeah, I know. Sorry, I'll let you go. I just wanted to tell you not to give up. We can do this."

Darby balanced on one foot while she pulled on a shoe. "Cole?"

"Yeah?"

"Why do you care? I mean, what does it matter if I conquer my fear of all things kitchen-y? It just seems like a silly thing to keep you up at night."

"I think you know the answer to that, Rey." Cole's voice was low and serious.

Darby didn't know what to say.

"Hey . . ." Cole let the word dissolve in the silence before he picked it back up again. "Hey, will you think about something?"

"Sure." Darby could honestly say she would. She thought about a lot of things.

Oh wait, he meant specifically.

"How about we . . . uh, meet?"

Meet?

Like in person?

Meet?

Darby couldn't understand the word or the concept. It might as well be Vietnamese he was speaking. She didn't know what to say. Her brain gave off a low buzz to compensate for the emptiness.

"Did I freak you out?" Cole asked.

Yeah, kind of.

"No, I mean. . . ." Darby stumbled over her words. "I just. . . . There's just a lot going on right now, with the party, and that wedding reception coming up. I can't really wrap my head around meeting right now, you know? It feels like a lot."

"Yeah, of course, I get it." Cole sucked in a breath of air. "No problem."

Darby pulled on her jacket. "Did I just make things super awkward?"

"No, I did." Cole laughed. "It's fine though. We're going to move forward like I never said anything okay? I won't bring it up again. When you feel like you're ready, you let me know. I am ready to meet in person when you are. Deal?"

"That sounds perfect." She swung her purse over her shoulder. "And now I really have to go."

"Okay, it was good to talk to you this morning."

"It was." Darby smiled.

It was always good to talk to Cole.

\* \* \*

Gretta smiled when Darby walked through the door.

Actually smiled.

She even lifted her hand into a half wave.

It blew Darby's mind.

She was always a believer that kindness went the farthest, Grammie drilled that into her every morning before breakfast. You throw a rock, it can only go so far and it can only hit one person. You throw kindness and it breaks apart when it hits someone, spreading to every person they meet and every person that person meets and so on.

It was just cool to see it happen right before her eyes.

When Meredith stopped clearing tables to flirt with some guy that was already with another woman, Gretta just rolled her eyes. But then, when Meredith walked by, Gretta quietly asked her to keep it professional. When one of the table bussers dropped a plate on the floor that shattered into a thousand pieces, Gretta just marked it in her liabilities book and handed the girl a broom. She didn't once clear her throat, not even when Kenya came in, dressed in a cinderella ball gown that took up three barstools.

Kindness spread.

Kenya left Darby with a list of assignments for the party, then flounced her way out of the café. She only got her dress stuck in the door for a couple of minutes before a Good Samaritan helped her wiggle it free, so that was good.

How in the world did Kenya fit behind the wheel of her car in that thing? Darby was enjoying a really cheesy thought tangent about someone carting Kenya around in a truck bed when Myles came into the café.

He was a little later that morning, but Darby was expecting that. Their conversation that morning would obviously put him a few minutes behind his usual schedule. He took his seat at the counter, set the newspaper down, and ran his hand through his hair.

It was mesmerizing.

Darby hurried over to take his order. "Good morning, sir. What can I get for you this morning?"

He scanned the menu, even though he must have it memorized by now, then looked up. "What would you order?"

Darby pursed her lips. It was risky, but the truth often was. "The blueberry muffins. Nothing beats Samson's blueberry muffins, and I happen to know he has a batch coming out of the oven in a few minutes."

Myles narrowed his eyes as he looked at her. They roamed all over her face, almost like they were searching for something. "That sounds awesome. I'll take three blueberry muffins."

Myles' eyes stayed on Darby the entire time she jotted down his order. She could feel them there like rays of sunshine, lighting her cheeks and forehead.

"Alright, I'll get this in." She slapped the order into Samson's window.

"Thank you, Darby." He said, still watching her.

The way he said her name gave her goosebumps. She rubbed her arms to make it less obvious. "You're welcome."

Things got busy then. Darby didn't get a chance to stare at Myles or consider their future life together one single time the entire morning. She did notice when he left though. The room was so much emptier without him sitting on the stool at the counter.

After the noon rush died down, Gretta left to take her lunch break. As she slipped on her jacket, she told them she was meeting her brother and asked if she could bring something back for anyone. This was more personal information than Darby had ever heard her volunteer. It dumbfounded most of the kitchen staff, but not enough to keep them from asking Gretta to bring back a gyro and tzatziki fries.

Darby seized her chance the moment Gretta disappeared around the corner.

"Hey, guys, come here. We have business to discuss."

The waiters, waitresses, cooks, and bussers gathered in the kitchen where Darby could see them all. Meredith stationed herself by the window to watch for Gretta's return and make sure the patrons stayed happy.

Darby looked down at the notes she and Kenya made earlier that morning before Kenya had to leave to extricate herself from her corset. "We're going to have the party for Gretta and the café next Saturday. Those of us who are scheduled just come to work normally, those who are not scheduled, and would like to help out, come at noon. Someone will take Gretta to lunch, then make sure she's here again at one. The café will be all decorated and snazzy when she gets back and filled with regulars. How does that sound so far?"

There was a general chorus of 'greats', 'fines', and 'cools'. Nothing super enthusiastic, but Darby wasn't expecting enthusiastic so it was fine.

"Is there anyone who won't be able to make it?"

No one said anything.

Frankly, Darby was surprised after how vehemently Meredith opposed the party in the beginning. For sure she thought at least a few people would bow out. She glanced at Samson, who gave a short nod.

"Everyone will be here," He said in his croaky voice.

Darby needed to make assignments before Gretta came back, but she really wanted to hear how he got everyone on board. She kept envisioning Samson wearing a mafia suit and hat, cracking his knuckles, threatening to toilet paper the house of anyone who refused to participate.

The image made her smile.

"Great! So, I'll read off what we need to do and then we'll go back through and make assignments. Be thinking about what you want to do."

No one objected, which was the same camp as agreement, so off Darby went.

"Okay, we need someone to take Gretta out to lunch, Samson, I thought maybe you? You know her the best so it might be less weird coming from you."

"I can do that."

"And I can manage the kitchen while you're gone." Darby let out a breath. This was the only part of the plan that made her incredibly uncomfortable. "It's just an hour and most of that will be people helping us get ready for the party. I don't think we'll have any orders."

At least, she hoped not.

"Then, we'll need people to help decorate, my friend Kenya will be in charge of that, and people to help clean up afterwards."

"Everyone will pitch in," Samson said without looking around. No one argued though. It was like they were all robots controlled by a central computer. In this case, Samson.

That was perfectly alright with Darby.

"Great! So, the last thing we need to do is the menu and decide if we want to do any party games. I don't know, what do you think Gretta would like best?"

People glanced up from their shoes, then looked away the second they caught someone else's eyes.

Yeah, Darby could relate. She didn't know Gretta well enough to know which she would prefer either. "Samson?"

"I think a couple games to keep things moving would be good. Low key things people can do if they want but don't have to."

Darby thought of the Baby Shower Kenya did a couple months ago. "So, things like a café word scramble and Guess How Many Customers the Café Had on the Opening Day. Stuff like that?"

Kenya would have a multitude of ideas they could use for simple party games.

"That sounds great." Samson said.

"Okay, so, menu. What does Gretta like to eat?"

There was a very uncomfortable pause.

"Gyros?" one of the waiters suggested.

A very good guess considering her lunch choice that day.

But there was probably more to it than that.

"She always snitches the bacon when it's crispy." One of Samson's assistants said.

"Yeah, and she likes lemonade. She refills her cup all day long."

Now they were getting somewhere!

"I overheard her telling someone that she'll eat anything with sugar and butter in it."

"She likes nuts."

"Last Christmas she destroyed the cheese ball."

Darby wrote as fast as she could, hoping it would be legible later. "So, maybe we do a bunch of finger foods and appetizers? Heavy on the sweets?"

"That sounds good." Meredith said, glancing out the window. "I'm going to run and refill that gentleman's drink real quick." She grabbed a pitcher and disappeared through the swinging doors.

"Samson?" Darby raised her eyebrows.

"You get specifics and I'll buy the ingredients. We can make everything together."

Meredith plunged back into the kitchen, her hair flying wildly. "Gretta's coming back! I just saw her turn the corner."

"That was a fast lunch." Darby said. When she looked up from the notepad to see what the others were doing, she found herself completely alone. Everyone scattered so fast it was like they were never there at all.

Darby hustled back to her own position at the counter and busied herself with refilling salt and pepper shakers so she'd look busy when Gretta walked through the door.

The bell chimed, and Darby looked up to smile a greeting.

The smile died before it even had a chance to form.

Gretta stepped into the café, holding a number of paper bags. Close behind her, laughing at something she'd said, was Jackson Wilcox.

Darby started to feel a little light headed, at some point she might have forgotten how to breathe. She sucked in a bunch of air and then let it out, to remind herself.

"That was crazy," Gretta said, setting her purse on the counter. "I'm going to take these to the back and then we can eat." She disappeared into the kitchen, leaving Darby alone with Jackson Wilcox.

She ducked under the counter and starting stacking cups for some unknown reason. They were already stacked. It's not like they needed her to pull them apart and put hem back together again. She just had to do something with her hands so she didn't explode all over the café. The noise would make it impossible to talk and she didn't have to look at him from down there, that was also good.

Jackson Wilcox leaned over the counter and peered down at her. "I don't think we've met."

Darby pretended she couldn't hear him, but that was increasingly hard as he continued to stay there and stare. Finally, she gave up. She pressed her hands into the counter to support herself and rose to her feet.

Jackson Wilcox leaned back, so he wasn't in her space, and smiled. "I'm Jackson Wilcox, and you are?"

Darby couldn't remember her name. What was it with this guy that made her brain stop firing? Just in time, she remembered she had a name tag clipped to the left side of her uniform. She looked at his ear instead of his stupid face and pointed to her tag.

"Darby?"

She nodded.

Jackson Wilcox held out his hand. "Well, it's really nice to meet you, Darby."

Darby looked at his hand, hovering in the space between them. She wouldn't take it. She couldn't shake hands with Jackson Wilcox! That went against everything she believed in.

Gretta saved her by coming back at that moment. "Okay, they are all set. I'm starving. Do you want to eat at a booth, or the counter?"

Jackson Wilcox dropped his hand. "The counter's fine."

No it was not!

Gretta took the stool next to him and pulled a paper bag in front of her. That's when she noticed Darby. "Hey, sweetie, did you want a gyro?"

Darby shook her head.

"You're sure? I'm happy to share." Gretta pulled out a package wrapped in thin white plastic wrap.

"I'm good." Darby cleared her throat. "I ate not too long ago, but thanks."

Gretta nodded, then glanced over at Jackson Wilcox. "Have I introduced the two of you?"

Darby refused to look at him. She kept her eyes on Gretta but could see Jackson Wilcox shake his head in her peripheral.

"I'm sorry! Jackson, this is Darby Reynolds, one of the best waitresses this café has ever had. Darby, this is Jackson Wilcox. My brother."

# Chapter Fourteen

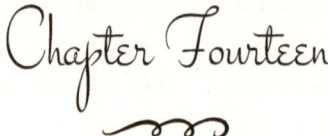

*Successful Young Woman (SYW) is wiser than Yoda, as kind as Mother Theresa and more loveable than gummy bears. You know you want to call.*

The second Darby walked through the front door of Kenya's house, she opened the Voxer app and brought up her chat with FoodieC.

*You will never believe who came into my work today.*

*Who?*

*Jackson Wilcox!*

*Jackson Wilcox? What? That's crazy! Who is he again?*

Darby stalled. They'd talked about this, hadn't they? She ran back through her memories of previous conversations and only came up with the term 'food critic'. So, okay, maybe they hadn't specifically talked about Jackson Wilcox.

*He's the food critic we were talking about.*

*Gotcha, yeah, the guy with a fake job. What is it with him, anyway?*

*I don't know, I was wondering the same thing. And guess what else?*

*No, there's more?*

*Uh, yeah, he's the brother of my boss.*

*The cranky lady?*

*She's really not that grumpy anymore, actually. I don't know what happened. All of a sudden, she's so nice. She even brought lunch for some of the staff today.*

*You happened, Rey.*

*I can't tell if that's a good thing or a bad thing.*

*Good, sheesh. You treated her like a human, that does things to people. And you're throwing this party for her. Kindness spreads.*

*Wait, what?*

*Kindness spreads!*

Darby couldn't remember if she'd told him that particular phrase of Grammie's. It seemed like too much of a coincidence to be a coincidence. Rather than overthink it, she tucked it away for later, like she did everything that reminded her of Grammie.

*But, she doesn't know about the party so that's not why she changed.*

*You really can't take a compliment, can you? Okay, let's do logic. When you think a certain way about a person, they can sense it and they treat you according to what they sense. You changed how you feel about your boss, so she changed how she treats you. See? That's how you happened.*

*That's sounds like hooey.*

*No, Rey, it's psychology.*

*Whoa, are you a shrink in disguise?*

*Haha, no. Though, I did take my fair share of human development classes in college. Good thing, too. I think I use what I learned in psych 101 more than I use my actual business degree.*

*Okay, then, shrink me. What do I do about Jackson Wilcox? I don't think he's going away.*

*Are you asking what I think you should do or what I would do?*

*Either, both, I guess.*

*I would make peace with him. He can't be all bad.*

*You mean, like, be his friend? I don't think I can do that.*

*Right, yeah, that would be a big jump. How about make peace with the fact that he's your boss's brother so you'll see him occasionally. You know? That way you don't have to feel all the feelings every time you see him.*

*Okay, I'm not saying that's a good idea, but . . . :)*

*Whatever, it's a great idea.*

*Give me another option. If that's what you would do, what do you think I should do?*

*I can't tell you that.*

*Why? State secret?*

*No, because I'm not you. You are the only one who knows what you should do.*

*Now you sound like a motivational slogan.*

*Just do it! You're in good hands! Like a good neighbor! Eat Fresh!*

*Okay, smart guy, what do I do if I don't know what I should do?*

*You know, you do. You just don't want to do it.*

Darby hated that that made sense. Maybe she did know, deep down. It was worth giving it a second of thought at least, right?

Okay, so if she knew what to do. . . . She closed her eyes and made her thoughts go away for a minute.

Cole was right, she didn't want to hear it.

*So, I guess I'm going to have to make peace with seeing him at work sometimes, then?*

*Is that what you think, or are you regurgitating what I told you I would do?*

*That's what I think. But I kind of hate it.*

*Would it really be that bad?*

So, no, okay. Maybe it wasn't the worst thing to make peace with seeing him regularly, but it was not going to be easy either. Darby couldn't imagine a reality where she would be in the same room with Jackson Wilcox and not have the clench squeezing her belly to smithereens the entire time.

*I don't know.*

*Maybe he's not so bad, you know? What if he ends up being the nicest guy in the whole world? He might surprise you. Haha*

*Haha is right.*

*You don't think so? Are you one of those leopards and spots kind of people?*

*No, I think people can change. I change all the time. I just don't think there's more to Jackson Wilcox than what I already know about him.*

*And what do you already know?*

*That the only kind of person who becomes a critic is the kind of person who thinks their opinion matters more than anyone else's opinion. He's someone who can spend thirty seconds with a person's hard work, that took hours, and tear it to pieces using a few poignant sentences.*

*Is that what he did to you? Tore your dream apart in a few poignant sentences?*

That was exactly what he did.

*It's just stupid. With all his influence, he could do so much good. You know? What if he was less critical? He could build people up, help them succeed instead of destroying them.*

*You make good points.*

Darby took a deep breath, her fingers flying over the key buttons. *After his article came out, my business died overnight. People really care what Jackson Wilcox thinks. With a bad review from him, my business hopped a sled down a mountain of failure.*

*There's an image! I suppose you still won't tell me the name of your restaurant? I'm really curious to read that article.*

Darby's heart thudded against her ribs. *Not yet. Sorry. Too soon.*

*It's okay, I get it. Like I said, I'm just curious and curiosity didn't kill the Cole. Not yet, anyway.*

*Thank you for listening, Cole. Or, reading, or whatever. I appreciate it. This is just crazy. When I left Salt Lake, I thought I'd never have to deal with Jackson Wilcox again.*

*Not even when you open your new restaurant? After you finish business school? Won't there always be food critics wanting to eat and critique?*

Oh shoot.

Darby almost dropped the phone.

She hadn't even thought of that.

How had she never thought of that?

Suddenly her whole plan to get a business degree and start over with a new restaurant was in the corner with a cone shaped hat on its head.

A cap that said, stupid.

*Rey, are you there?*

*I think I just had a mind bomb.*

*Why?*

*Because, you're right. What am I thinking? I can't open another restaurant! I thought if I had some business know-how behind me I could do it again and avoid what happened with Jackson Wilcox, but the truth is, there's always going to be a Jackson Wilcox, isn't there? I can't please everyone. I'm just going to get another horrible review and lose everything all over again.*

*Whoa, slow down, of course you can do it! That's not what I meant at all. You're fully capable of opening a restaurant and making it work this time. You're just going to have to find a happy place with critics, that's all I was saying. You can do that! Because, you're right, you can't please everyone. Someone is always going to hate on your hard work. That's a fact. So, the question is do you try anyway? Or do you fail upfront because you never try?*

What the heck?

*That's really insightful, Cole.*

*I thought you'd figured that out by now. I'm a super insightful guy. As wise as Yoda.*

*Hey, that's from a personal ad! I read it in the newspaper.*

*I saw it too, cracked me up.*

Me too!

*Rey?*

Yes?

*You can do this. You should do this. If only to prove to yourself that you can.*

But what if I can't?

*But what if you can?*

Darby was ready to type her question all over again, when the screen lit up with an incoming call.

*Shoot, sorry, I'm getting a call. I have to take this. Talk to you later?*

Please.

Darby stared at the word for approximately one second, that's all the time she had to soak in all the happy feelings before she pressed the talk button on her phone.

"Hello?"

"Darby Reynolds?"

"Speaking."

"This is Al, your building superintendent."

"Right, hi, Al."

"Hi, I'm just calling all the tenants to let you know the fumigation went well and we're going to let things air out here for another couple days, then give it another couple days to make sure none of those critters come back. You should be able to move back into your space by next Saturday at the latest."

Sadness rose in Darby's belly like a souffle. She didn't realize until this moment how much she really loved living with Kenya. The thought of going back to her small studio all by herself already felt lonely.

"Oh, thank you, so much. I appreciate the update."

"No problem, you take care now."

Darby said thank you again, then hung up. Saturday was the party for Gretta. After that, she could move home. A bunch of conflicting emotions vied for top spot in Darby's chest. It was a little suffocating to tell the truth. She stood up, looking around for something to do.

In the past when she felt like this, she'd cook or bake. There was something so soothing about combining ingredients to create something new. She shook out her hands as she walked to the pantry and opened the door.

Her eyes went straight to the pasta shelf, but she didn't want to make pasta again. She itched to try something different.

But easy.

That's when her eyes landed on the ramen noodles.

Without letting herself think about it too much, Darby grabbed a couple packages and set them on the counter. Then she went on a rummage through the fridge and cupboards. When she was done, she'd collected fish sauce, coconut aminos, ginger, garlic, red pepper flakes, broccoli, brussel sprouts, snap peas, carrots, mushrooms, egg, and honey.

Back to the pantry for chicken stock and she was ready to roll.

For the next hour or so, Darby let her mind wander as she took her sweet time boiling water, chopping vegetables, heating pans, sauteeing those very same vegetables, and mixing a delectable sauce that made her heart sing.

When Kenya stumbled down the hall, sniffing dramatically, Darby was just putting the finishing touches on two bowls of ramen. Cilantro and green onion with a spattering of sesame seeds.

"Is this a dream?" Kenya plopped onto a stool at the island, rubbing her eyes.

"Oh no, all real." Darby slid the bowl to Kenya. She caught her breath and held it. There was no way she'd be able to eat a bite of her own food until she knew if Kenya thought it was any good.

Kenya used a fork and a spoon to twirl noodles into her mouth, and then sip the sauce. She swallowed slowly and looked at Darby. "This is incredible."

"Yeah?"

"Yeah! Wow, I wish we could do ramen for the wedding reception, this would knock their socks off!"

Darby picked up her own spoon, blew on the broth, then slurped it off the spoon. It wasn't as rich as a bone broth she could make herself, but the flavor was there. So tangy, and the perfect amount of salty. Kenya wasn't lying, it was incredible.

Darby carried her bowl around the island to sit next to Kenya and the following minutes were full of the sounds of slurping and clanging utensils. Every so often Kenya would make a nom nom noise and close her eyes.

Darby forgot how good it felt to feed people food that made them nom.

When her belly was stuffed with just enough room left to breathe, Darby pushed her bowl away and let her chin drop to her arms. "That was yummy."

"It was." Kenya lifted her bowl and drank the rest of the broth out of the bottom. "It really was. Light bulb! I just had the best idea. You should cook dinner every night. It would be good practice and I'm tired of eating cereal."

Darby ignored her thoughts and spoke from her soul. "Okay."

"Okay?" Kenya sounded way too surprised.

"Yeah, okay. I'll do it."

Kenya squealed and wiggled all over the stool. If she wasn't careful, she was going to slip right off and hit the tile. Darby just smiled and shook her head.

"Shake your head all you want, I am so excited! Not only do I get an amazing dinner after the longest night ever, but you get to get your cooking mojo back, girl! This is the best case of win-win I have ever heard of!"

That gave Darby the perfect opening to change the subject. "How are you holding up? This week has been bananas for you."

Kenya stopped her impromptu happy dance. It was comical to see her features droop like they were all hooked to a string that an invisible someone kept pulling downward.

"Darby, no lie, I am completely exhausted. I don't know what I was thinking, scheduling all this stuff back to back. If today wasn't Friday, I think I'd run away to Mexico. Let the people plan their own dang parties."

Darby bit back a giggle. "You need a break."

"I really do." Kenya dropped her cheek to her hand, making it pooch out like she was storing acorns for winter. "It's fine. After the Mabens' anniversary tomorrow, I don't have anything on the schedule until the café party. That's a full week to recuperate."

Darby's guilt flared up something fierce. "Hey, so I made the assignments with the staff today, I really think we can do this party without you, if you need to take a break."

Kenya shot into the air, her hand slapping the counter. "What? I'm fine! What are you talking about? I'm totally doing this party!"

Darby gave her a skeptical look.

"I'm just slumpy. Everyone is allowed a slump. I'll be fine by Monday and ready to plan. But right now, I need to make rice krispies and coconut cookies for the chocolate fountain." She pushed away from the table and started pulling things from the cabinets.

Darby watched the counter fill with ingredients like magic in front of her eyes. "Do you need some help?"

Kenya paused, her eyes flickering all over Darby's face. "Yes, I do. Are you offering?"

"I am."

Kenya smiled and handed Darby a spatula. "That's my girl."

# Chapter Fifteen

*Trail Blazing Blond (TBB)*
*With All Her Teeth Seeks a Compatible Companion With All of His.*

Darby stared at her phone, trying to decide.

It was Saturday afternoon, with just a little bit of time left before she was going to leave to help Kenya with the Maben's anniversary party. She'd been messaging off and on with Cole for two hours, two blissful hours, and now his question had her stumped.

*What do you have going on today?*

On its own it didn't look like a stumpy question, it was pretty straight forward, but it brought on a pretty hardcore dilemma. If she told him she was helping with the Mabens' anniversary . . . well, it wasn't a huge community. Cole went to high school here and the Maben's had lived most of their lives here too. Practically the whole of Hurricane and most of the surrounding areas were invited to the party.

If she told him she was helping with it, and he came, he would know who she was.

Which was why she still sat there, minutes after the question blinked into existence, drumming her thumbs on the phone, trying to think of a way to word the answer.

*Did I lose you?*

*No, I'm still here.*

*Oh, good. Thought I scared you away with that penetrating question.*

*I know, you're so invasive.*

*Haha. Wait, really?*

*No, not really, I'm just trying to figure out how to answer you.*

*Right, I get it. You don't want to tell me what you're doing because it's more of that super secret Jedi stuff you've got going on, huh?*

There it was—the perfect deflection. She could joke about her Jedi training and that was that. Off the hook. The only problem was, she kind of wanted to tell him what she was doing that evening.

It would be such a passive-aggressive way to reveal who she was. And passive-agressive was totally Darby's jam.

"Darby?" Kenya called from the other room.

"Yeah?"

"I'm going to start loading up, I wanna get there early."

Darby looked at the clock on her phone. How did it get so late so fast?

"Be right there!"

Okay, it was now or never.

Darby took a deep breath and let it out slowly.

*I actually gotta run, I'm helping my friend with an event tonight. It's a fiftieth wedding anniversary party.*

Whew.

She meant to tell him the name of the couple the party was for, but she couldn't muster the courage. That's okay, what she said was riddled with clues. Cole would get it unless he was super dim.

And Darby already knew he wasn't.

*Go save the world then. :) Talk to you later?*

*Absolutely!*

Darby tucked her phone away. She'd done what she'd done. Now she could go help Kenya with a clear conscience. Just see what happened. Really, it could be nothing. Nothing could happen. There was a chance he didn't know the Mabens, or couldn't make it to the party for some reason of his own.

So, better to just concentrate on helping Kenya.

Darby grabbed a box from the kitchen table and went out the front door. Kenya had her Tahoe door open and ready for boxes. She was smart to buy such a big car. If she had Darby's car, she'd have to make four trips with all this stuff.

"There you are! How's Lover Boy?"

"Fine, he's fine."

"Is he coming tonight?"

"I don't know, I didn't ask. But I did tell him I would be there, so that's something."

"Hold that thought." Kenya disappeared into the house and returned with the chocolate fountain box. "There's one more and we're ready."

"I'll get it." Darby needed to grab her purse anyway. She locked the front door and dropped the box of gold dohickeys into the back seat. Kenya had already started the car and was checking her eye makeup.

"Ready?"

"Yeah." Darby wiped her sweaty hands on her black pants. That was only a partial truth. She was ready, but she was also crazy scared. She slipped in the passenger side and buckled the seat belt. Now that she didn't have Cole to distract her, all the nasty fear mongering voices she'd been ignoring were back and raging.

"Yay!" Kenya said absently as she checked over her shoulder to start backing out of the driveway. "Did I tell you thank you, by the way? I am so excited you're going to party with me tonight."

"About that," Darby's hands shook slightly in her lap. "I'm kinda afraid I'm going to mess something up, like I did at the Sock Hop. What if I knock over the chocolate fountain, or. . . ." She couldn't think of anything worse than that, actually. Knocking over the fountain was totally the worst case scenario.

"Pshhhh." Kenya flung her hand in the air.

"No, really. You know about my luck."

"No, I don't. I thought we agreed that wasn't a thing? It's going to be fine."

Yeah, but would Kenya still think that if Darby wrecked the party Kenya had been working on all week? Would the Mabens think it wasn't a big deal? Fifty years of successful marriage accumulated into one big mess of a party.

Darby felt sick. "Maybe I should go home. If you pull over, I can walk back."

"No way. We're doing this. If only to show you you can do it. You make your own luck, Darbs."

Darby tucked her hands into her side and tried to think positive thoughts. Kenya's inspirational board was in her head now, so it was easy to come up with thoughts.

What was hard was believing them.

"So, tell me more about your talk with Lover Boy. You guys were chatting forever! So, you told him you're going to be at the party?"

"I did." Darby squeezed her arms into her belly, it helped with the nerves.

Well, it kind of helped with the nerves.

"That's big, Darbs! Really big. You've come such a long way. I'm so proud of you." Kenya wiped an invisible tear and sniffed a couple of times.

Darby rolled her eyes. "Wow. Just . . . wow."

"In all seriousness, tonight is going to be amazing, I can feel it!"

All Darby could feel was the rolling of whatever she ate for lunch. "Do you ever get nervous, planning these events?" Darby didn't understand how Kenya could keep doing it if she did. This was worse than the night her restaurant opened.

"Naw." Kenya flipped her hair out of her eyes. "I mean, sometimes. But this is easy. A moderate guest list, the venue is already beautiful, it's the perfect party. It's just fun."

"You don't worry about screwing it up for people?"

Kenya glanced over. "Why would I worry about that?"

"I don't know, because something could go wrong and then it's ruined. This special night goes kablooey because of you."

"Wow," Kenya said. "That's a bunch of depressing thoughts."

"But they're possible thoughts."

"Maybe." Kenya shrugged. "If something goes wrong, I'll handle it then. In the meantime, I'm gonna have fun. Let's get this party started right!" She cranked up the radio and started moving with the beat.

Darby watched her with a slight smile. It was impossible not to smile at Kenya jamming out to the Backstreet Boys, even with all those butterflies swarming Darby's belly.

"Dancing is mandatory in this vehicle." Kenya jabbed a finger into

Darby's side and kept poking until Darby wiggled her hips. Then tapped her toes. From there, she was a goner. Hands in the air like she just did not care, head bobbing, shoulders swaying. Darby car-danced her worries into oblivion.

They pulled into the parking lot of a resort in St. George and waited to be directed to the back door of one of the ball rooms. Kenya parked and jumped out of the car.

"Come on! This is going to be so fun!"

They unloaded all the boxes into the ballroom and then got to work decorating. Without the pop music and silly moves to distract her, the nerves came back in full force. At first, Darby had to double-check everything she did with Kenya, to make sure she was doing it right. After a couple of flippant replies, Darby got into a groove and could cover a chair and arrange a center-piece like she'd been doing it all her life.

They did the chocolate fountain last. When it started flowing like a waterfall of fudge, Darby suddenly understood why Kenya loved her job so much.

Seriously satisfying.

They took the extra food into the small prep room off the ballroom and arranged it so everything would be easy to grab when it was time to refill.

And there they waited.

Darby checked her email, then the Canvas app to make sure her professor's didn't post anything on her classes. After about five minutes, she was out of things to do. When she looked up, Kenya was shifting things around.

"What do you do with all the down time?"

"Oh," Kenya shrugged one shoulder. "It only lasts for a few minutes, then we'll be running back and forth for the rest of the night. Enjoy it while you can."

Darby tapped her fingers against her leg.

Kenya glanced over. "You can go make sure the hotel staff set out the water pitchers if you want."

Darby jumped to her feet, ignoring Kenya's smile. The ballroom was still empty, except for a middle-aged lady and a teen girl. They looked up when Darby entered the room.

"Hello, are you Kenya?" The woman stepped forward with her hand extended.

"No," Darby shook the woman's hand and her own head at the same time. "I'm Darby, I'm helping Kenya out."

"Well, it looks fantastic here. I couldn't be happier."

"I'll make sure Kenya knows," Darby said with a smile. She went to check the refreshment table. There wasn't a water pitcher anywhere she could see, so she had to flag down a hotel worker and ask him about it. When the table was heavily laden with three pitchers and Darby's task was done, the room began to fill with people.

Most of them crowded around the happy couple instead of the food tables, so there still wasn't much to do. Darby tugged on this thing and adjusted that thing, trying to keep busy. She wished people would start eating, then she could be doing something that actually needed to be done.

She'd learned a long time ago that it only took one person to start in on the food and everyone else would follow. Darby looked around the room for the most likely candidate. An elderly man sat by himself at a table near the refreshments.

Perfect!

Darby went over to him. "Sir, have you seen the chocolate fountain?"

He looked her way, his eyes half closed. "Heh?"

"The chocolate fountain." This time she extended one arm toward the fountain to help him figure out what she was talking about. "It's really fun. There's lots of stuff to dip in it."

The man stared at the table for a moment, then leaned heavily on the back of his chair to stand up. "Don't know what I'm doing sitting on my duff when there's chocolate to be had."

Darby didn't know either, but she just smiled.

As soon as he picked up a small plastic plate, a number of other people made their way to the refreshment table. Darby celebrated with a mental fist pump. She did that! She started the food line.

Maybe she wasn't a complete disaster.

After that, the time passed in a blur. Kenya and Darby moved from room to room in a graceful dance, trying to keep up on the refreshments. About halfway through the party, they had to add more chocolate to the fountain. The sight of it flowing thick once more inspired everyone to go back for seconds, or thirds.

It was then that Darby realized she'd gone the entire time without tripping herself, or someone else, knocking anything over, or breaking anything.

It was a fiftieth wedding anniversary party miracle.

Now she just had to keep that up for the second half of the night. She found an empty wall and stood against it, with her hands tucked behind her back, and one eye on the refreshments.

Kenya joined her a moment later. "The macarons are a hit, we're almost out."

Darby didn't know if that was good or disgusting. She'd seen how many of those things Kenya made.

"Everyone looks so happy."

"They do, don't they." Kenya leaned into the wall, too, a content look on her face.

This was why Darby loved food so much. It was so universal. It had a way of bridging gaps and making people feel good. It never got old, watching people enjoy food she'd helped create. That was her favorite thing about owning her restaurant.

Darby waited for the clench that always came when she thought about her restaurant, or Jackson Wilcox.

But it didn't come.

There was just a light feeling of nostalgia. It was so foreign, Darby didn't know what to do with it so she turned her attention to the crowd.

And then she stared.

No way.

Darby groaned.

"What?" Kenya whispered.

"Jackson Wilcox, ten o'clock," She hissed.

He was just entering the room so he hadn't looked their way yet. A few people greeted him as he made his way to Mr. and Mrs. Maben. There was a lot of hand shaking and hugs.

Darby tried not to stare, but she couldn't help it. She didn't know why. It was like that need to look at the mess after she squashed a bug. It was disgusting and fascinating at the same time.

Jackson Wilcox laughed loudly and slapped Mr. Maben on the back. His brown hair caught what dim light there was so it looked golden and glowy. Like there was a halo around his head. Now that she knew he was Gretta's brother, she could see the traits they shared. A round face with a semi pointed chin and dimples in both cheeks. His eyes were closer together than Gretta's though and when he smiled it did something weird to Darby's insides.

It just threw her off, that was all. In her mind he was a giant beast with horns and things that oozed. He never smiled when she thought about him. Seeing him in real life brought out his humanity.

And she didn't like it one bit.

She snapped her head away from him and tried to be fascinated with the pattern of diamonds on the carpet.

"He's coming over here." Kenya said out of the corner of her mouth.

Darby refused to look up.

Not until his fancy black shoes were blocking her view of the carpet and she had to.

And then she refused to smile.

Jackson Wilcox smiled, though, all big and friendly. It ticked Darby off that he appeared like he was a nice person. She knew the truth.

"Mrs. Maben tells me you're the ladies in charge of this party. Well done, both of you."

"Thank you," Kenya said, placing a hand over her heart. "That's so nice of you to say."

Darby scowled. Her and Kenya needed to have a talk about ignoring compliments from jerkwads.

There was a long silence in which Darby felt both of them staring at her. With a deep sigh, she lifted her head and grimaced her way into a smile.

"Oh, hey, I know you." Jackson Wilcox pointed at her.

Darby didn't help him out, she just stared at him and waited.

"Corner Café, right? You're the waitress."

Kenya elbowed her in the side, so she responded this time.

But she didn't have to like it.

"Yep."

"Remind me your name?"

Of course he didn't remember it.

"Darby."

"I'm—"

"Jackson Wilcox, I know." Darby folded her arms.

"Good memory." Jackson Wilcox dropped his hand back down to his side. "So, waitress by day, party planner by night?"

"I'm just helping out a friend. I think we're low on strawberries. Excuse me." Darby slid along the wall and disappeared into the prep room, where she could finally breathe.

Jackson Wilcox.

Ugh!

What was he doing there?

Not supporting the Mabens, surely. He couldn't possibly know anything about friendship. He either came for the free food or to check out some lady.

Okay, maybe not that.

The ladies in this room were over the age of seventy, and/or married.

Unless that was his thing.

Darby wouldn't put it past him.

Just to make sure she wasn't a liar, Darby grabbed a container of washed strawberries and carried them to the refreshment table.

See! The strawberries *were* almost out, she wasn't making excuses. Jackson Wilcox caught her eye and started towards her. For once, luck was on her side. There were so many people milling around, he had to be polite and wait for an opening, or for them to move entirely. And while he did that, Darby darted through a gap in the elbows to hide in the prep room.

Why was he trying to talk to her?

He was probably coming over to tell her what was wrong with the aesthetic of the refreshment table or complain about the quality of the fruit.

Well, she wasn't going to let him.

From that moment on, Darby transformed into an amateur ninja spy. She made avoiding Jackson Wilcox an artform. Seriously. If she'd been in all black and could have done a tuck and roll without injuring herself, she would have a pro.

It was tricky to keep a constant eye on Jackson Wilcox, but it had to be done so she could make sure she was always as far away from him as possible.

"Girl, what are you doing?" Kenya eyed Darby with confusion

"I'll explain later." She would have explained then, but Jackson Wilcox was about to turn around and she had to squat behind a chair so he wouldn't see her.

"Okay." Kenya shook her head and went to refill the crackers.

Darby was feeling pretty awesome about herself, overall. She'd managed to do her job, not wreck anything, and avoid Jackson Wilcox for most of the night. There was only like fifteen minutes until the party was scheduled to end.

Oh shoot!

Jackson Wilcox moved suddenly. Darby jostled the refreshment table in her rush to get out of his line of sight and then darted for the prep room.

That's when she heard the crash.

Darby poked her head around the corner and almost said a word Grammie would have washed her mouth out for.

The chocolate fountain was on its side, oozing brown goodness onto the surrounding food, and the floor. The unfortunate people who had been nearby, wiped chocolate off their faces with dirty sleeves.

Darby's heart sank.

With no thought other than fixing her tremendous blunder, Darby hurried to Kenya's side. They righted the chocolate fountain, got rid of the food that was now ruined, and did their best to clean the floor. It was going to need a solid mopping.

When they were back in the prep room, Darby couldn't hold it in any longer.

"I told you! I ruined everything! Kenya, I am SO sorry!"

Kenya just stared at her. "For what?"

What did she mean for what? "For the fountain. The mess. The disaster. I told you! I shouldn't be allowed in public. Me and my luck."

The words had the hardest time coming out. Her throat just wanted to close around them.

"You didn't do anything." Kenya squeezed her arm. "Darby, that wasn't your fault. Really."

There was no way Darby believed that. "Then why was the fountain horizontal?"

Kenya let out a snort.

Wait.

Was she laughing?

Darby peered into her friend's face. Her cheeks were red, her eyes were watery. It looked like she was about to cry.

Except that her shoulders were shaking and she had to cover her mouth to muffle the noise of a total crack up.

"What happened?" Darby crossed her arms over her chest. "What did I miss?"

Kenya took a minute to get a hold of herself. "One of the grandkids, sorry, sorry, one of the grandkids climbed on the table to put their face in the fountain." Kenya lost it again, bending over to laugh into her lap.

Darby still didn't believe her. There were a billion adults in that room, someone would have stopped that from happening. It was Darby's fault, she knew it was. She bumped the table or something when she was dodging stupid Jackson Wilcox.

Kenya sat up, wiping her eyes. "Everytime I set that fountain up, I have the biggest urge to stick my face in it. I just can't believe someone finally did it!"

"Wait, you're serious?"

It wasn't Darby's fault?

"Yes! Didn't you see that kid all covered?"

No, Darby had been too overcome with her own shame spiral to notice anything.

"Well, it was hilarious!"

"You're not upset?" Darby was still trying to transition. "I didn't ruin the party?"

"No, weirdo. Even if it had been your fault, which it wasn't, the party is almost over anyway. No biggie." Kenya slapped her hands on her thighs and stood up. "Let's start packing up. It'd be nice to get out of here in time to watch a movie tonight, yeah?"

Darby nodded, trance-like, as she followed Kenya out of the room.

She hadn't knocked over the chocolate fountain.

No worst case scenario.

It wasn't her fault.

It was fine.

# Chapter Sixteen

*Upright Young Lady (UYL) Seeks Warm Hearth, Clergyman Preferred*

Kenya swore there was a party planning time warp that made time blur between parties. Darby always thought she was a nut for saying so, until the next week passed in a blink. Seriously, there and gone. Before Darby knew what was happening, it was Saturday morning.

The morning of the café birthday party.

When Darby tried to think about the flurry of buying ingredients with Samson, making cheese balls and cutting vegetables, helping him bake, and shopping for decorations with Kenya, not to mention working her shifts at the café and going to her business classes every night except Wednesday, all she saw was a bunch of colorful blurs. She seriously had no idea where the time went.

Kenya dropped a box of crepe paper and garland on the café counter and looked around. "Alright people, we don't have a lot of time before Gretta gets back from lunch." Then she proceeded to boss everyone around with the efficiency of a drill sergeant.

Darby stayed a moment longer to make sure everyone was listening to Kenya. She didn't need to worry. Half of the waiters and kitchen staff were following Kenya around like puppies, jumping to do whatever she commanded.

Yeah, Kenya had this handled just fine.

Darby went to the kitchen to help Samson bring out all the food. Originally, he was going to be the one to take Gretta to lunch, but on Tuesday he called Darby into the kitchen to explain he'd been thinking about it and was concerned it would make Gretta suspicious. They'd never done lunch before and Samson was the one cook. The one to rule them all. If he left the kitchen it might actually implode.

So he asked Gretta's brother, the infamous Jackson Wilcox to be the one to take her out. Whatever. As long as Jackson Wilcox didn't mess everything up by bringing Gretta to the café early, before they'd finished preparing, it would be fine.

It might be fine.

Darby grabbed a huge tray of deviled eggs from the fridge and carried them to the folding table the others had set up against the wall. There were two actually, sweet and savory. Kenya had the brilliant idea to bring in folding tables to create a buffet flow.

Darby didn't know what buffet flow was until that moment. Which was just another reason that Darby was glad Kenya was in charge.

"Oh, crackers," Darby said to herself, then hurried back to the kitchen for the boxes of rice crackers to put around the cheese ball. If she didn't do it right that moment, she would totally forget.

She saw Samson coming with the beautiful cheesecake he'd made at home the day before. Since both his hands were full, she pushed the door and held it open until he went through.

"Thanks, little sister." He winked as he went by.

Darby nodded, then repeated the word crackers a couple more times, under her breath. There were at least a million things in her brain, the reminder was necessary.

While she was in the kitchen, with the cracker package tucked firmly under her arm, Darby snagged one of the vegetable trays to take with her. Once that was placed on the table, with ranch beautifully centered, and the crackers were arranged artistically around the cheese ball, all that was left to do was bring out the cookies, cupcakes, and cream puffs.

On Thursday Kenya had the brilliant idea to make sugar cookies that spelled out 'HAPPY BIRTHDAY CORNER CAFÉ' instead of making a banner. Darby and Kenya had a wild Friday night making tons of cookie letters, in case some didn't turn out, and decorating them with royal icing.

Samson already got the cupcakes and was on his way back for the cream puffs, so Darby took the first tray of cookies to the counter and began propping the cookies into a standing position. Using marshmallows, thanks to Kenya's brilliant party planning brain.

When she finished, she stood back to admire.

Okay, that seriously looked cool.

"I love it!" Kenya clapped near Darby's ear. "We did good!"

Darby linked her arm through Kenya's elbow and squeezed. "You are amazing. Gretta is going to love this."

"I know, right?"

Darby poked her side and then let Kenya go so she would harass one of the servers about his garland alignment.

That sounded like a personal problem.

"Hey, y'all." Samson's voice boomed. "I have a text from Jackson, they'll be here in ten minutes."

That sent Kenya into a last minute decorating tornado. Whether people were on the decorating team or regular patrons there to eat, they were suddenly roped into setting out paper plates and folding napkins to look like birthday hats.

With eight minutes gone and two to go, they had just enough time to hide behind the counters before Gretta and Jackson Wilcox walked into the café.

"Why is it dark in here?" Gretta's voice sounded strained as she fumbled for the lights. When the café was flooded, everyone jumped out and yelled.

"Surprise!"

Gretta froze, her mouth dropping into a perfect oval shape.

Jackson Wilcox grabbed her shoulders and shook her slightly. "This is for you Gretta. They've been planning it for weeks."

Gretta still didn't say anything. Her lower lip trembled as tears gushed from her eyes.

Like, really gushed.

There was no slow trickle here. One minute her face was dry and the next, tears were sliding to the floor like duo leaky faucets. Gretta brought both hands to her mouth.

Jackson Wilcox slid his arm across her shoulders and leaned over to whisper something Darby couldn't hear.

Samson was the first to make a move. He crossed the room in a couple long strides and lifted Gretta into a bone crushing hug. "We love you, Ms. Gretta."

When he set her down, the tears were still going strong, but they had to find new paths around her ginormous grin.

One by one the patrons and staff formed a line to shake Gretta's hand or give her a hug. Darby listened unabashedly to the many expressions of gratitude for her service to the community, for her kindness to someone or another. The best moment came when Meredith went to shake her hand and got roped into a hug instead. When they pulled apart, both of them were sobbing.

An arm snaked around Darby's shoulder, pulling her close. She smelled Kenya's pineapple body spray before she had a chance to get weirded out.

"You are pretty amazing, my friend."

"And so are you."

"No, really, look at this," Kenya waved her free hand around the room. "All these people, all together, crying and laughing. It's beautiful and it's because of you."

"You did most of the work."

"But you had the idea. I'm really starting to think Grammie had it right about the sugar and the salt."

There was nothing surprising about that. Grammie was the wisest person who ever lived.

Darby rested her head on Kenya's shoulder for a moment. "Thanks for your help."

"Are you kidding me, thank you for letting me help."

They watched people move through the line to talk to Gretta in a deeply contented silence.

"You know," Kenya breathed. "This is why I became a party planner. My mama thought I was a loony. She tried to talk me out of it for months. I know it sounds silly, a party is frivolous really, in the grand scheme of things. It's not like becoming a doctor and saving lives, but it called to me. The first time I did a party, it was a little girl's sixth birthday and I actually thought the parents were stupid for spending that much money on a kid's party." Kenya paused to wipe her cheek. "Then I found out that little girl had a birth defect, something to do with her heart, and her birthdays were numbered. It clicked for me then, this is what life is about, you know? These little moments, all together, with people connecting. It is so worth it."

"You never told me that story."

"Yeah, because I can't talk about it without crying like a big old baby." Kenya laughed and ran her face along her sleeve. "Anyway, I love this so much, girl. Thank you for letting me be a part of it." They shared a smile, then Kenya went into bossy mode. "Now, stop messing around and go refill the cream puffs, those things are disappearing fast."

"On it." Darby hustled to the kitchen where Samson had two more covered trays of cream puffs. She forgot the tongs and had to go back for them, then back to the café to cut in line and refill the cream puffs. While she was that close to the food tables, she took a moment to assess everything else. They were going to need a refill on the ranch dressing soon.

"Hey, Darby?"

Darby turned slowly, her heart thudding against her chest. Jackson Wilcox stood in front of her with a huge smile on his face. It still weirded her out. She did a lot of internet stalking on him before he trashed her restaurant and the first time she'd seen him smile was at the Maben's anniversary. His pictures were always so stern and, well, critical.

Smiling made him look like a real person.

Jackson Wilcox couldn't be a real, relatable person. He was the one who crushed her dreams. If he was something other than who she thought he was, she'd have to stop hating him until the day she saw Grammie again.

"Yes." She clutched the cream puff tray so tightly the tips of her fingers stung.

Jackson Wilcox didn't seem put off by her less than friendly greeting. He swung his shiny smile around the room and then turned it back on her. "I heard you're the brains behind this party today. I just wanted to tell you thank you."

"Oh, no problem." Darby glanced toward the kitchen doors, wondering if she could dash for them without making a scene.

"No, really. Gretta has had a really rough year or so. She really needed this. I can't thank you enough."

"It's really no problem."

Jackson Wilcox's smile fell about an inch. He tipped his head to the side and let out a short laugh. "I—uh, sort of get the impression you would rather be at the dentist than right here talking to me."

That stumped Darby for a minute. Really, how was she supposed to respond to that? 'You're right. I would rather have a root canal without anesthesia than have a conversation with you.'

She couldn't say that. Not even to Jackson Wilcox, who pretty much deserved whatever he got. So she just stared at him. Her mind was completely blank except for images of drills and that weird cotton stuff they put in your cheeks.

"I'm sorry, I didn't mean to corner you. I just wanted you to know I'm grateful." He gave a small smile and turned away.

Darby let out a long breath, then disappeared into the kitchen as fast as her legs would go.

She thought she could do this. When she was talking to Cole it didn't seem that hard. Just get used to seeing Jackson Wilcox at the café, no big deal.

Well, it wouldn't be except he kept trying to talk to her.

She was not prepared for conversation with Jackson Wilcox. That was too much. Especially this, thanking her, acting like a normal human when she already knew he was a heartless jabberwocky.

It was messing with her mind.

Darby yanked open the fridge and pulled out the ranch dressing to go refill it. They would probably need that other cheese ball soon too.

For the next hour, Darby kept herself in a constant state of busy. She didn't even take the time to greet Gretta. Especially because Jackson Wilcox stayed glued to her side most of the time. The food was beginning to disappear for good, a sure sign that the party was running down.

Ten minutes before the café was scheduled to close, Gretta called for attention.

With a quivering voice, she thanked everyone for being there, for showing up every day, for helping out and for caring. She lost her voice numerous times and Jackson Wilcox had to squeeze her hand to get her going again.

Darby watched the whole scene with an increasingly leaden heart. All she wanted to do was go home, put on her pajamas and hunker down with a gallon of ice cream and a cheesy romcom. Instead she had to wait for Gretta to finish her acceptance speech so they could start cleaning up.

"And to show my appreciation, I'm going to close the café tomorrow, on the actual ten year anniversary, to give my amazing staff a well-deserved day off."

As soon as the hugs and cheers died away, Darby started transferring the leftovers into take-home trays. She set those on the café tables for people to grab on their way out.

Kenya was waiting in the kitchen on Darby's next trip. "Are you okay?"

"I'm fine, why?"

"You look seriously ticked. Are you sure you're okay?"

"I'm fine."

It was fine.

Everything was fine.

Fine fine fine fine fine.

"You sure?"

"Yes, I need to put the rest of these vegetables out."

Kenya's face didn't lose the worry lines, but she did move out of the way, so that was something. Darby rushed to add vegetables to the disposable containers.

The decorations came down.

The tablecloths were bundled to go home with Kenya and get washed.

The cookies were packed up for Gretta to take home.

The extra folding tables were taken down and stacked against the wall.

In and out people went, moving boxes of things to Kenya's car. The café was almost back to normal. Even the kitchen was spotless, thanks to Samson. He disappeared about halfway through the party to get a headstart.

Darby went to get a wet rag to wipe everything down, and when she returned, everyone was gone. Either on their way somewhere else or standing on the sidewalk outside, laughing and talking just a little bit longer.

Everyone, that is, except Jackson Wilcox.

Darby stopped short when she saw him and was already halfway turned around when he spoke.

"Darby?"

She continued the turn so her back was to him.

Jackson Wilcox let out a long breath. "I'm not sure what I did to offend you, but I'd like to make it right. What can I do?"

A hurling ball of rage appeared out of nowhere. It coursed through Darby's body, consuming all rational thought. She whipped around to face him. "Are you kidding me right now?"

"I'm sorry?" Jackson Wilcox blinked.

Oh no he did not just pretend he didn't know what she was talking about. He had to know. Darby couldn't stand the thought that he could ruin her life and not even remember doing it.

"My name is Darby Reynolds, does that mean anything to you?" Darby slapped the wet rag on the counter, half of it slid away, dripping onto the tile, but she didn't care. "How about The Purple Penguin? Does that ring a bell?"

Jackson Wilcox's face stayed blank, but Darby had a feeling it was on purpose this time. He did remember. She chose the name of her restaurant on purpose to stand out, to be memorable. He made no move to answer her questions, so Darby went on.

"Well, I know who you are, Jackson Wilcox, food critic and influencer. I also know that exactly sixteen months, one week and four hours ago, you came to my restaurant, the Purple Penguin, and wrote an article." Darby hated that her eyes stung, she blinked rapidly to get them to stop, but it didn't work. Tears wormed their way through the blinks and coursed down her cheeks.

"After your article came out, demeaning my restaurant from name to food, people stopped coming. I had to close. You destroyed my dream, Jackson Wilcox. So, yes, I have a problem with you. I have a big problem. And you're not going to be able to fix it with any amount of gratitude or apologies."

Darby couldn't talk anymore, the words choked her throat like built up sawdust.

"Darby, I—"

"Don't say anything." Darby held up her palm. She had to swallow multiple times to clear a way for words to come through. "I don't want to hear it. In fact, I would very much appreciate it if you never spoke to me again."

Jackson Wilcox stared at her for a couple of long moments. Darby could feel his eyes on her, even though she refused to look at him. Every breath she took rattled her chest like it was composed of razor blades instead of air. Just when she thought she would spontaneously combust, Jackson Wilcox slowly turned.

And walked away.

\* \* \*

Darby was too numb to feel Gretta's arms around her, when she came back inside to get her purse. "You poor thing, you must be exhausted, let me get your friend, there she is. Kenya, can you take Darby home? She looks like she needs a good nap."

Kenya laughed and led Darby to the car.

Once inside and buckled up, Darby leaned her head against the cool glass and stared out the window without seeing anything. Kenya kept up a constant stream of chatter which was both comforting and grating. She told Darby to go right inside instead of helping bring the leftover party decorations.

Darby did just that.

And she didn't even feel bad.

She snuggled up with her favorite zebra striped blanket that was soft enough to make most things all better and willed herself to fall asleep.

Thankfully, it didn't take long.

\*\*\*

When Darby woke up, she had no idea where she was. The darkness surrounding her was really disarming. She fumbled across the top of the nightstand until her fingers found the lamp and flipped it on.

She rubbed her eyes with a groan.

What time was it?

What day?

What planet was she on?

She found her phone in her purse by the side of the bed where she'd dropped it earlier.

It was three in the morning.

Fabulous.

At least it was Saturday and the café was closed so she didn't have to go to work. That was good because there was no way in the world she would be able to go back to sleep now.

Darby opened her Voxer app. She really wanted to talk to Cole right, but she wasn't mean enough to wake him up this early in the morning. Instead she put the phone away. It would be better to talk to him about it when she wasn't sleep deprived.

If only she could sleep.

Rolled over and snuggled the extra pillow for approximately three seconds before she realized that was so not happening. Sleep was so not happening. Everything ached and her mouth felt like she'd fallen asleep with one of her socks in her mouth. She just had to get out of bed. It was unbearable to lay there not sleeping.

Darby swung her legs over the side and rose to her feet slowly. She'd never had even a sip of alcohol in her life—Grammie always said fools and alcohol were conjoined twins—and the image was enough to take away any allure for Darby. But she imagined this was what a hangover probably felt like.

Her head pounded.

Her legs felt like jelly.

When she finally got all the way upright, she swayed for a few awkward moments before she got her balance.

Her eyes were raw and squinty which made walking really interesting. Her depth perception was so off she almost tripped three times in the couple steps she took from her bed to her door.

When she made it out to the hall, the door to Kenya's room slammed open and Kenya jumped into the hall with a baseball bat.

Darby screamed.

Kenya screamed.

And then they both collapsed onto the floor, laughing their heads off.

"What . . . in the world . . . are you . . . doing awake right now?" Kenya gasped for breath between hysterical giggles.

"I couldn't sleep . . . what are . . . you doing with . . . the baseball bat?"

"I thought you were . . . a burglar!"

And then more laughing.

Darby's belly hurt so much she vowed to stop doing crunches and watch comedy instead. Her abs had never had a workout like this. Kenya leaned her head against the wall and shook it back and forth.

"Look at us! Is this what we've come to?"

"I'm super thirsty," Darby said.

And her mouth tasted gross.

"There's water in the sink."

"Ugh, what else do we have?"

"Milk?"

That sounded even worse. "Ew, no."

"I think that's it. Unless you want to eat an orange and pretend you're drinking the juice?"

"Pass." Darby thought for a minute. "Let's do something bonkers. Let's drive to Maverick and get some drinks."

"At three in the morning?"

Darby nodded.

"You want to go get drinks at three in the morning? What would Grammie say?"

Darby smacked Kenya's arm. "Not those kinds of drinks, you weirdo. Juice and chocolate milk and gatorade and. . . ."

"Wow."

"I'm thirsty, okay? Everything sounds good. Come with me?"

It would be way more fun to go with Kenya then alone. Well, that and she was actually kind of scared to go out this late, or rather, this early. Hurricane was such a small town it shut down off-hours. Something about it made Darby feel like she was in an Alfred Hitchock episode. One of the ones where a person discovers everyone else on earth was abducted by aliens and they are now all alone on the planet.

Kenya studied Darby for a moment longer, chewing on her lip. Then she grinned. "Let's do it! Adventure adventure adventure!" She grabbed Darby's wrist and dragged them both to their feet. They didn't bother getting dressed, just slipped on shoes and tucked money into their pajama pockets.

"This is bananas," Kenya said, grinning as they walked to the car. "But also, kind of amazing. I feel like I've been missing out on something my whole life. It's so liberating!"

"What are you talking about?" Darby rolled her eyes. "You're up at this time all the time, cleaning up from parties. You're such a goof!"

"Well, it feels different doing it voluntarily." Kenya sniffed, opening the doors with her car clicker. "Maverik, ho!"

Darby got in and buckled. She had to admit Kenya was right. It felt amazingly awesome to do something so totally outside the routine. And Hurricane, creepy and deserted as it was this early in the morning, was also kind of cool.

Maybe it wouldn't be the worst thing in the world to be the only person left on the planet.

She might be able to get used to it.

Especially because there were no other cars triggering the traffic lights so they had a green every time they came to an intersection.

Darby could definitely get used to that.

Kenya pulled into the Maverick parking lot, completely empty except for one car, and grinned at Darby.

"Let's go!"

They shuffled through the doors, greeted the completely zombified clerk, and went straight to the section with sports drinks. Darby grabbed a snapple, a chocolate milk, an apple juice, a berry naked juice and then she ran out of hands. Kenya had to carry the two flavors of gatorade and the strawberry lemonade for her.

"We're going to need a second mortgage on the house to cover your drinking problem." Kenya said, her voice echoing in the empty store.

The clerk didn't even acknowledge that someone had spoken. He might have actually been asleep standing there.

Kenya chose a gatorade for herself, then they stumbled to the counter, trying not to drop anything.

The clerk moved into motion when he saw the drinks through slinty eyes, but he didn't say a word to either Darby or Kenya. When he read off the total in a monotone voice and held out his hand for the money, Darby changed her opinion of him. He wasn't a zombie, asleep, or a mannequin.

He was a robot.

And so realistic looking.

As they left the Maverick store, Darby looked back over her shoulder. The clerk was in the same position, like they'd never even been there.

Darby was too thirsty to wait until they got home. She popped open the bottle of Snapple and chugged until she was no longer thirsty.

Okay, she chugged the whole bottle.

And then half of the chocolate milk.

And a quarter of the strawberry lemonade.

By that time she was so full, there was a constant sloshing in her stomach. But there were so many other drinks waiting unopened she felt bad not at least trying them.

One glug of each and then she was done.

Kenya sipped her gatorade and watched the whole thing with an amused expression. "Are you ready to tell me what happened yesterday?"

"Yesterday?" Seriously, after that weird night sleep and all that sugar, Darby couldn't remember what day it was again.

"At the party." Kenya sipped. "For the café."

Oh, that yesterday.

Darby twisted the lid on her gatorade off, and then back on again. "Jackson Wilcox talked to me."

"Gasp," Kenya said with a smirk.

Darby glared. "You know how I feel about that guy!"

"I do."

"So you know him talking to me is pretty much the equivalent of him stealing my puppy or keying my car?"

"I do know that too."

"So, just keep your little gaspy gasp to yourself then." Darby twirled a finger through the air around Kenya, and then dropped her arm to the seat. "I told him off."

"What?" Kenya's smile morphed into shock. "You what?"

"I told him off. I told him why I hate him, and I will never forgive him. I told him to never talk to me again."

"Girl."

Darby turned her head to face Kenya. "It felt so amazing. And then . . ." She looked back at the ceiling. ". . .it didn't."

"What do you mean?"

Darby shrugged. "I've dreamed about telling Jackson Wilcox off pretty much constantly for the last sixteen months. Well, telling him off and opening a new restaurant that blows his mind so much he has to issue a retraction for what he said about me before. I had this great memorized speech in case I ever saw him in real life I'd know what to say to him."

"Really?" A smile played around the corner of Kenya's mouth. "You thought that would fix everything?"

It sounded stupid when she said it like that. "No, not really. I just wanted a chance to counter his dumb article, you know? Like I got my say in too."

"Okay, so, you got to do it. You told him off. Do you feel better now?"

"No." Darby shook her head against the headrest. "No, Kenya, obviously. I feel a billion times worse. It's not fair. I shouldn't have to feel bad about anything I say to Jackson Wilcox after what he did to me. What's that about anyway?"

Kenya was silent for a moment, then she poked Darby. "What would Grammie tell you right now?"

Darby didn't want to answer that. She'd been specifically ignoring everything she thought Grammie would say so it wouldn't make her feel even worse. No matter the justification, imagined or real, Grammie was never a fan of telling someone off.

Darby sighed deeply.

"Okay, never mind. Don't think about Grammie. Let's play the fun game where I'm a contrarian."

"Say what, now?"

"My brother does this to me all the time. He says the opposite of what I want to hear to make me think harder about what I want. It totally works. Just go with it."

Darby didn't say no, which was the same as saying yes.

"So, getting that all off your chest should have made you feel better, right? You should have dropped the mic and walked out of that room with fireworks going off behind you."

That sounded awesome. "Right?"

"So, why do you think it didn't work?"

Darby closed her eyes, then popped them open when Jackson Wilcox's face materialized behind her lids. "He looked upset."

"Isn't that good? He should be after what he did."

"Yeah, except, he looked like I really hurt his feelings."

"No, he doesn't have feelings."

Yeah, but he did.

"And if he does, so what? You care, why?"

Darby didn't know. She thought she *wanted* to hurt his feelings. She thought she wanted him to feel how she felt when her business died. But the thing was, it felt awful to want someone else to feel awful.

That was what Grammie had been trying to tell her for years. When you tried to hurt someone else, you got hurt too.

Darby understood now.

Boy did she get it.

Kenya's face softened. She put a hand on Darby's arm. "What are you going to do, Darbs?"

"I don't know."

"He's Gretta's brother. It sounds like he lives here now. You're probably going to see him often, you know?"

Oh, Darby knew. She knew that all too well.

"Maybe you should tell Lover Boy and have him beat that Jackson Cole up."

Darby burst out laughing. It made all the liquid in her belly slosh around but it felt so good to laugh that she didn't care. So, beating up Jackson Wilcox probably wasn't the best idea, but telling Cole about it was. Talking it out with a guy might give her some perspective on how to move forward.

Too bad it was so early or she'd call him right then and there.

"You know," Kenya said slowly. "You could always quit the café and come work for me full time."

Darby smiled at the thought. "Tempting."

"No, actually, I'm being partially serious." Kenya gripped Darby's arm. "How about you take a vacation from the café this week? We could concentrate all our juju on the wedding reception and then, when you go back, there would have been some time since you told Jackson Wilcox off. He might not even remember it anymore. Yeah?"

"You think?" Darby wasn't so sure. The look in his eyes came back to her now, making her squirm.

"It would be nice to have your full time help with the reception. It is kind of huge."

That was true. For some reason it made Darby's brain jump to the phone call from her superintendent.

"Oh," Darby said. "I almost forgot to tell you. My apartment is all cleaned out. I can move back in now."

Kenya's face froze into a Halloween mask of horror. "No!"

It seriously cracked Darby up. Maybe things were just funnier early in the morning, hopped up on sugar, with small amounts of sleep. She couldn't stop laughing.

"Stop! No! I'm serious! Don't move out!" Kenya grabbed Darby's forearm and shook it gently. "At least, not until the reception is over. It will be so much easier if we're in the same house."

Darby took a deep breath, making the giggles fizzle. Mostly. At least enough that she thought she could get words out around them.

"Please!" Kenya wiggled Darby's arm some more. "Please, please, please! Stay and help me. I need help!"

A bubble of laughter threatened to burst out again, but Darby swallowed it. She was more than happy to comply. The thought of going back to her tiny apartment alone wasn't all that appealing anymore.

"Okay, yeah, let's do it."

"Yeah?"

"Yeah, I'm going to call Gretta right now and ask for the next six days off for vacation." Darby pulled her phone out of her hoodie pocket and started to open it.

"Don't do that." Kenya put her hand over Darby's phone.

"What? I have to ask. Not everyone is their own boss and can just do whatever they want, you know."

"Duh, I know that." Kenya rolled her eyes. "I mean don't call her now. You do realize the sun hasn't even come up yet? You can't call Gretta until it's normal human waking hours"

"Oh, right." Darby said, tucking her phone away.

\* \* \*

Gretta had no problem with Darby taking the week off. She was still so touched with the café birthday party, she probably would have given Darby her car and her first born child too if Darby asked for them. This gave her hours and days of free time in which to help Kenya plan the wedding reception.

She was in the middle of making centerpieces one night with the flip phone near her elbow when Cole called.

"Hey!" Darby said. She'd texted him earlier that day to see if he had a sec to talk. Even though she'd been practically too busy to breathe all day, she couldn't get that thing with Jackson Wilcox out of her head. "I'm glad you called!"

"Yeah, me too. Sorry it took so long. What's up? What are you doing?"

At that precise moment, Darby was taping artificial flower stems together so they would fit in vases. "Helping my friend get ready for a wedding reception this weekend."

"Big job."

Yeah, it totally was.

Darby filled him in on the details, just talking to cover the silence while she gathered her thoughts. She really wanted Cole's perspective on how she handled the thing with Jackson Wilcox, but she didn't want to sound like a big jerk either. It was a fine balance.

"Wait, wait, wait. Are you seriously telling me that you and your friend are doing a wedding reception completely by yourselves?"

"Yes. . . ." Darby had to pause to bring her thoughts back around. That was what she'd told him but she couldn't figure out why he sounded so appalled.

"Can I help?"

"What?" Darby blinked.

"Can I help? Seriously? How are you guys doing that with only two people?"

Well, mostly they were working late into the night and eating a lot of chocolate. So far it was working fine.

Of course, it was only Monday.

"No, we're good. My friend is crazy organized." And kind of a perfectionist, actually. Kenya liked doing things her way, which made sense now why she usually worked alone. Darby was a good soldier though. They made a really great team.

There was a long silence.

"Cole?"

"I'm here, I'm just wondering how much I should insist."

Darby tipped her head to the side. "What do you mean?"

"I mean, I want to respect what you want, but I also think it's insane that you two are doing that all alone. I can help. I could bring my sister and my niece and nephew. Four more people is less crazy. What do you think?"

Darby thought she maybe stopped breathing there for a minute. "We're really okay." That was true, but also, she didn't want to meet Cole for the first time when they were crazy busy working at a wedding reception.

That wasn't very romantic.

"You're sure?" Cole didn't sound like he liked that plan very much.

"Yeah, yes, I am."

"I'm not convinced."

Darby laughed. "Tell you what, if anything changes, you will be the first person I call. Deal?"

"Promise?"

"Promise."

"I'm satisfied. Okay, now, what did you want to talk to me about? I'm ready to be wise and practically omniscient."

Darby laughed again. "Well, good, because I have a pretty good dilemma."

"Hit me, baby."

Darby had been reliving the experience since it happened and rehearsing it in her mind for hours, it was easy to relay the information to Cole. When she got it all out, she breathed in deep. "Do you think I was too hard on him?"

"Do *you* think you were too hard on him?"

Darby set aside a flower bouquet and let her hands rest on the table. "Yes." She paused. "And that makes me really mad."

Cole chuckled. "It should feel good to put a big, bad food critic in his place, huh?"

"It really should!" Darby protested. "Don't joke. It's not fair that I feel bad. I should feel so good right now."

"Except that it never feels good to make someone else feel bad."

"That sounds like something Grammie would say."

"Thank you." Cole said. "I think that was probably the biggest compliment anyone has ever given me."

"Believe it!" Darby said, and then sighed. "So, what do I do now?"

"What do you mean?"

"I mean, do I apologize to him? Or do I just forget about it? Just let it go, or whatever?"

"Can you forget about it?"

"No." Darby picked at a piece of clear tape that was stuck to the table top. "I feel awful."

"Can you apologize to that guy, what was his name again?"

"Jackson Wilcox." Darby groaned. "I mean, technically I can. I am capable of saying I'm sorry. I just really don't want to."

Cole was quiet for a long time before he spoke again. "How do you feel about second chances?"

"I'm a huge fan." That's what she was working for, in fact, a second chance at running a restaurant. One that didn't fail.

"Do you think people can change?"

A flick of suspicion went up Darby's back. "Sometimes."

"What if this guy, Jackson Wilcox. . . ."

"Nope!" Darby cut him off. "Maybe some people deserve a second chance and maybe people can change, but we're not talking about people. We're talking about Jackson Wilcox. He is the worst!"

"Right, I forgot. Totally the worst, that guy. So we just need to figure out something you can do to take away your guilt without inviting any kind of a relationship with the food critic. Is that what you're thinking?"

No, right now she was thinking that putting the word relationship anywhere near the word food critic was super nauseating.

"Maybe. . . ." Cole stopped, leaving Darby hanging in the worst possible way.

"What?"

"Maybe, if it's too much to, you know, apologize to his face, you could write him a note or something."

Hmmm.

That wasn't a terrible idea.

Maybe she could do that.

It would be a billion times better than seeing him, or talking to him, and it would probably get rid of this guilt bubble in her chest.

"I'll think about that." Darby said slowly.

"If you need help, let me know." Cole laughed. "I'm crazy good at apologies. Don't ask for details. You don't want to know."

The front door opened with a bang and Kenya clambered into the house with her arms full.

"Oh, shoot, I have to go. Sorry, see ya, Cole." Darby hung up and was out of her chair in an instant. She caught a box just as it slipped out of Kenya's arm. They shuffled to the table and started unloading. It was completely impossible how much stuff Kenya fit in her arms.

From that moment until the day before the reception, Kenya kept Darby too busy to think about writing a letter to Jackson Wilcox or daydreaming about Cole. It was one thing after the other. Right when Darby thought there couldn't possibly be more, there would be.

If she got overly tired or overly whelmed, she gave herself a pep talk for being there. No way could Kenya do all this alone. There was no more talk about Darcy moving back into her apartment. They could figure that out after the crazy died down.

It was funny, though. Darby started the week thinking she might actually take Kenya up on the job offer, real or jest, but by Friday Darby was glad she still had her day job.

Kenya insisted on going over the plan for the next day again and again.

And again.

A few minutes before midnight, Darby interrupted. She wasn't entirely responsible for what came out of her mouth. It was the Sugar Babies and lack of sleep talking.

"Kenya, we need more help."

"What?" Kenya looked up from her paper with whirling swirls instead of eyeballs.

Darby repeated her statement, more emphatically this time.

"There is no more help, Darby, just us."

"I remember." Darby said patiently. "But we need more help."

Kenya slapped her papers on the table. "We have to make this work with us, that's all. I've tried calling in every favor from the last ten years and no one is available this weekend. The temp agency has no one. . . ." Kenya rubbed her eyes. "Mitch is out of town again for his stupid job. There is no one else, Darby. Just us."

Darby spit the words out fast, before her thinking brain could talk her out of it. "I know someone who can help."

"What? Who?"

"Cole."

"Lover boy? How is he going to help?"

"He's been begging to let him do something to help. And he said his sister and his niece and nephew can help too. That's four extra people Kenya, just say yes." Darby's stomach was in knots, but she knew this was the right thing to do.

"Yes." Kenya dropped her head to the table and spoke into the wood. "Yes, yes, and yes. Tell Cole I love him."

Darby laughed. "No way, you're going to have to fill out your own personal ad if you want some of this."

"Seriously, tell him thank you." Kenya raised her head just a little. "Wait a second. This is the first time you guys will meet! Are you really okay with that? I mean, you better be because I really need the help, but, are you?"

Darby nodded, slowly. "I'm ready. I want to meet him." The weirdest thing was, she meant it. Texting and talking over the phone has suddenly become extremely unsatisfying.

"Well, thank you. And thank Cole too. I love you both to the ends of the earth."

"I'll tell him." Darby said. "But not the part about loving him."

At least, not yet.

# Chapter Seventeen

*Well Proportioned Female (WPF)*
*In Search of a Man That Doesn't Care What She Looks Like. Do Those Exist?*

Saturday morning dawned bright and sunny with a wave of butterflies that settled somewhere around Darby's midsection.

Holy chocolate bark, she was going to hurl.

Kenya rapped on her door, propelling her out of bed and onto her feet. "Wake up sleepy head, today's the day!"

And a couple other cliché phrases that were annoying enough when Darcy wasn't already on the verge of a superb freak out.

"Coming!" Darby got dressed in a hurry, it helped that they'd already laid out a slim black skirt and white button down the night before. All of them would be dressed in black bottoms and white tops, like a uniform.

Darby slipped into her shoes and hurried into the kitchen. Instead of piles of stuff covering every square inch, there was nothing.

Kenya already had the car loaded.

Or someone burglarized the house

"How long have you been up?" She said when Kenya came into the room.

"Since four. I couldn't sleep anymore so I went to work. Are you ready?"

Darby slipped her smartphone and the flip phone into her purse in case there was an emergency or something. The flip phone had Cole's number and it was only way he had to actually call her so she wanted to keep that handy.

The drive to the event venue only took a couple of minutes, another benefit of living in a small community. Darby had never been to Litchfield Ponds before, so she stuck her face close to the window as Kenya rounded the curve. This was Kenya's favorite wedding venue. She'd told Darby all about it many times. She was already planning her own wedding there when Mitch finally got the guts to propose.

It did not disappoint.

Darby's mouth hung open as she took in the green grass, the shimmering pond with swans and the gazebo.

Might as well get married in a fairytale.

"Right?" Kenya said, not a little smugly.

"You win. I want to marry this place."

Kenya laughed. "So, we're in the main building, there, and the wedding is at the gazebo." There were already workers setting up a billion chairs. "They should be done with the ceremony around noon and the luncheon is at one. What time is Lover Boy going to be here?"

"At ten and if you call him Lover Boy on accident, or on purpose, to his face, I will throw you into the pond."

Kenya widened her eyes and pretended to shake.

Darby rolled her eyes. "Come on, drama queen, let's go set up your stuff."

They had two hours before Cole and the others were supposed to join them, so they focused on the decorations. Bows on the aisle chairs, billions of chair covers with sashes, the food tables clothed and flowered and centerpieced.

It was a lot of work.

But it was gorgeous when they were done.

Unfortunately, Kenya was too far in the zone to stop and admire anything. "The wedding cake will be here in about an hour. Oh, look, I think that might be Lover Boy."

Darby looked at her phone instead of the car pulling into the venue. She had a sudden attack of nerves all over again.

It was 9:55.

That had to be him.

Other than the wedding cake, there were no other deliveries and it was way too early for guests.

This was it.

The car came to a stop next to Kenya's car and doors started to open. Darby tugged at her shirt and tried to remember the greeting she had rehearsed. She knew exactly what she was going to say and how she would react when Myles realized she was the waitress that took his order almost every day.

She'd planned it all out.

But she hadn't planned on anything else.

See, that's where she went wrong.

It never occurred to Darby that the woman walking towards her and Kenya with a teenager on either side, waving her hand and smiling would be Gretta.

Her boss.

Or that the man strolling just to the right of them with a super stressed out look on his face wouldn't actually be Myles from the café.

He was Jackson Wilcox.

* * *

Darby's stomach dropped to her toes.

"Is that...." Kenya's voice trailed off.

"Jackson Wilcox," Darby said, her voice sounded wrong.

"Is he...." Kenya stared at her.

Darby opened her mouth but nothing came out.

"So, wait, are we saying that your Cole is actually Jackson Wilcox?"

Darby shrugged. It was a simple movement that took monumental effort.

"Did you know?"

Darby could only shake her head.

When they got close enough to exchange words, Jackson Wilcox threw his hands in the air like he was warding off blows. "Let me explain."

Darby's eyes swept over Gretta and the two teens that had her nose and hair color. There were so many things she wanted to say that she couldn't say in front of her boss.

Or young ears.

Kenya stepped forward. "I don't know what is going on, but we don't have time to sort it out. There are five hundred people coming here in two hours that expect a magical experience. Can you put this aside for now and help me out here?"

She included Darby in her questioning gaze.

Darby nodded, her head felt like a bowling ball balanced on a toothpick.

"Of course, we are here to help." Jackson Wilcox said with a smile. His expression switched to worry when it landed on Darby's face.

She turned away and started for the reception hall.

As far as she was concerned Jackson Wilcox, or Cole, or whoever the heck he was, did not exist. She would go do her duty, as she promised, and then she was going to go home and drop that stupid flip phone in the toilet.

No good, rotten luck.

She knew this whole thing was too good to be true.

Darby walked through the reception area, already set up with tables and chairs, and stopped for a second to get her bearings. The kitchen would be off this big room somewhere, probably towards the back. Darby headed that way and discovered logic was still alive and well in the world.

It was a shame she was a smoldering wreck. The kitchen was a chef's dream. Gleaming countertops and appliances, tons of space to move around. A couple of islands for prep work. She walked straight to the sink and washed her hands so she was ready when the boxes of ingredients started to appear.

The reception food was going to be served buffet style. They'd made most of it the night before to keep things simple today. All Darby had to do was get the food out there and keep it warm.

Or cold, depending on the dish.

Oh yeah, with Jackson Wilcox hovering over her shoulder, waiting for her to mess up again.

Darby took a deep breath and shook out her hands.

She could do this.

It was fine.

She was fine.

Everything was fine.

One of the teens, the boy, brought in a huge box that had the salad ingredients. Darby planned to premix a caesar salad and then dish it into plastic champagne cups. It was a pretty, elegant way to serve salad that was easy for guests to grab, but she didn't want to do that until about thirty minutes before the start of the luncheon or the croutons would get soggy.

Darby placed that box in the enormous fridge and waited for the next.

Gretta brought the box with cutlery, plates, napkins and cups. That, at least, Darby could do something about. She took it from Gretta without saying anything to Gretta's sympathetic smile, and made her way back out to the big room. Tables were already set up, clothed and ready for food.

Darby placed the cups artistically around the punch and water bowls, then stacked plates and utensils on the first table. Napkins went on last. Kenya had told her that people always forget to grab a napkin at the start, so it makes more sense to put them at the end.

When Darby got back to the kitchen, there were two boxes waiting for her there. One had the basil orzo salad, which also went in champagne cups and needed to wait until the end to put together so it would still be cold when served. That went to the fridge with the caesar salad.

The other box was filled with finger desserts in plastic containers to keep them separate and unsmooshed. Mini cheesecakes, cream puffs and petit fours. Darby was really proud of those desserts. She and Kenya spent the whole week making them and they turned out beautiful.

Darby had just set the desserts to the side when the teens returned with the trays of chicken cordon bleu and bowls of honey mustard sauce. Both would need to be warmed. Darby set the ovens to warm and stacked the trays next to the oven.

Gretta and Kenya appeared next with boxes of the warming cages and candle burners, and french bread. This kept Darby busy setting up the warmers on the buffet table and then slicing bread. It didn't matter if it went a little stale, they were going to toast it right before the luncheon started. Darby smothered the slices with garlic butter and arranged them on baking sheets, ready to go in the oven when the time came.

When Darby finished, the counters were filling up with boxes from Kenya's car. Specifically, the box with basil, balsamic vinegar, tomatoes, mozzarella cheese balls and wooden sticks to make caprese skewers was waiting for her. That she could do right now. Until the box with serving dishes came in, she could stack the skewers on a spare baking sheet. She washed her hands again and went to work assembling skewers with cheese, tomato and basil leaves. She'd have to wait to do the balsamic drizzle until right before serving or it would break the tomatoes down.

She was so in the zone, she didn't notice two more boxes that appeared while she worked on the skewers. Inside one was the serving dishes. Those she set aside. The other had containers with the mini quiches, which all went into the fridge.

The oven beeped that it was ready and Darby checked her watch. It was only ten forty-five, the luncheon was at noon, but she had a horrible fear that the chicken would be cold and Jackson Wilcox would gloat, so she started moving the chicken cordon bleu from the trays onto baking sheets in a single layer. The temperature was so low on the oven, it would be fine in there for an hour, then they could transfer it to the warming tray on the food table.

With all the chicken in the oven, the sauce in a large pot warming, and two more boxes to go through, Darby breathed a sigh of relief. She was just fine when she had stuff to do, it was the lull moments that worried her. Any chance for her brain to stall and think about Cole, or Jackson Wilcox, or Myles, that was a moment Darby wanted to avoid.

For as long as possible.

Darby unpacked the chicken salad and set it in the fridge, then arranged the mini croissants on a tray, ready to slice and fill. She didn't want them to get soggy, so she would wait a little longer to put the salad inside and put them out.

The last box of food to appear had the Italian wedding soup. Kenya thought soup would be too complicated, but Darby insisted. Grammie told her a wedding wasn't a wedding without the creamy meatball soup with kale, sweet potatoes and bowtie noodles. Darby showed Kenya how they could put the soup in a warmer, then let people ladle their own. That way it would stay warm, which was Kenya's biggest concern, and it would be easy to serve.

Darby got the soup warming in a huge stock pot and arranged spoons and fluted glass bowls next to the soup warmer.

Then she looked around.

They were actually in really good shape.

When she went into the kitchen, Kenya was barking orders. The teens were hopping to it and Jackson Wilcox walked in with his arms full of napkins, immediately catching Darby's eye.

"What are you doing with those?"

He stopped walking like someone zapped him with a freeze ray. His eyes shifted to Kenya, who was too busy talking to Gretta to pay any attention. "Kenya asked me to bring them into the kitchen."

"Why?" Darby's voice sounded like a cactus. "I set those up already, with the cutlery."

That's when she noticed the cutlery set in piles on one of the counters. She hurried over to the piles and put her hands on her hips. "Why is this in here? We don't have extra time to be moving things back and forth for no reason."

Jackson Wilcox set the napkins next to the utensils and opened his mouth to answer, but Kenya beat him to it.

She clapped her hands. "Start rolling people, go, go, go, go."

The teens jumped to attention, grabbing a knife, fork and spoon, then rolling them into the napkin like a utensil burrito. They were so efficient, it was obvious Kenya had already told them what to do.

Too bad she hadn't told Darby.

Now Darby got to look stupid and incompetent, again, in front of Jackson Wilcox.

Fabulous.

Darby stalked across the kitchen, as far away from Jackson Wilcox as she could go, and tried to look busy. She'd just stay out of the way and let Kenya be the boss, that's what she obviously wanted.

Gretta sliced croissants so they would be ready to fill when the time came, and started Jackson Wilcox chopping watermelon and sprigging mint to put in the water.

Darby checked the oven to make sure it was actually heating, then helped Kenya with the flower arrangements for the food table. When they'd finished that, they set up an additional table with a fluffy tulle tablecloth for gifts and cards.

Kenya had found a glass box with a slot at the top like a child's bank, to secure cards with money and put the couples name on the front in swoopy vinyl lettering.

"You are really good at this," Gretta said as she walked by with the tray of sandwiches. "I wouldn't have thought of half the details you put together here."

"Yeah, well," Kenya shrugged, "that's why they pay me the big bucks. It's eleven fifteen, let's get the rest of that food out."

Darby followed Kenya to the kitchen. Gretta already had the sandwiches filled and covered with plastic wrap so they wouldn't dry out. She was on her way to the main room as Kenya and Darby entered the kitchen.

"Fabulous, thanks." Kenya patted Gretta's shoulder. "What do you want me to do Darby?"

Darby took a minute to answer. Both because she wasn't used to bossing Kenya around and because she'd just caught Jackson Wilcox's eye. Her confidence was deflating with every breath she took.

Okay, come on, Darby. You can do this.

All she really had to do was mimic Kenya and pretend like she had everything under control.

"Why don't you set out the quiche, cover them like Gretta did, then you can arrange desserts. I'm going to start the orzo and salad cups."

"Perfect." Kenya saluted and went to work.

Darby tried not to look at Jackson Wilcox again, but her eyes were traitors and strayed to his back every time they got the chance. She refused to linger there. Refused to acknowledge his presence, except in the moments where her brain geeked out all over again with this thought.

How in the world was Jackson Wilcox the same guy as Cole?

It just didn't make sense.

Darby took the orzo to the big room so she didn't have to breathe the same air as Jackson Wilcox anymore and filled the glasses there. It was easier anyway, this way she didn't have to worry about making a billion trips back and forth from the kitchen trying to balance everything on a tray.

While she worked, the bakery showed up and began to assemble the cake. It was six layers with a rustic design and edible flowers. It gave Darby a strange ache in her chest to look at it. Like, it was almost too beautiful.

Too perfect.

When the orzo was finished, Darby went back to the kitchen for the caesar salad. She had to mix it with the dressing, so that was annoying, but then she could dash back into the other room to fill more champagne cups with salad and croutons.

It looked fantastic in there.

Eleven forty-five and the only thing left to do was set out the skewers and everything on the warmers. They worked their collective tails off and finished at precisely noon. The wedding party started filling the big room at the same time Darby and company were leaving it.

The teens pulled out their phones while the adults leaned on whatever was closest and tried to catch their breath.

"I can't believe we pulled that off," Kenya said, with a shake of her head. "Darby and I would never have been able to do that without you guys. I can't thank you enough. Really, you have to let me pay you."

Gretta already had her palm in the air. "It is our pleasure. After what the two of you did for me, I still feel like I'm in your debt for life."

Kenya smiled. "That was just fun. This, this was work!"

Darby peeked through the window into the big room. The bride and groom stood behind the food table, talking to the crowd. Darby couldn't hear what they said, but a cheer went up and people stood to get in line.

It was time.

After spending all week making five hundred and fifty chicken cordon bleu rolls, desserts, salads, quiche, and garlic bread. This was it.

Oh shoot!

Darby looked around the kitchen. She didn't remember setting out the garlic bread. She assembled it, but she didn't put it in the oven, or take it out to the food table.

She dashed across the room to the oven and pulled it open.

"What is it?" Kenya asked.

"Where's the garlic bread? I didn't take it out, did you?" Darby peered over her shoulder, purposely focusing on Kenya's face. It was beyond humiliating to have this moment with Jackson Wilcox watching.

"I didn't." Kenya hurried to Darby and opened another oven. "I don't think I put it out there either, did you guys?"

The teens didn't look up from their devices, Gretta shook her head with a worry line between her eyes.

Jackson Wilcox shifted. "I took it out. I hope that's okay. I saw it sitting there and you were both so busy, I just took care of it."

"Oh my gosh, thank you," Kenya said, like the wedding would have been ruined without garlic bread.

Darby let the oven door slam shut and walked back to the window into the big room without saying anything.

Of course, Jackson WIlcox took care of it. Perfect, organized Jackson Wilcox. He would never forget the bread.

Darby wrapped her arms around herself and seethed.

The only thing that would have been able to take her mind off what was happening inside her own head was what was happening in the big room. She carefully scanned the room to see if anyone was spitting food into their napkins or making puke faces.

So far, everyone seemed happy.

That was good.

This should have been a great victory.

So, why did Darby feel so horrendous?

The others chatted behind her, and Darby ignored them all. She told herself she wanted to make sure the people were happy and the food stayed filled, but they had put out all the food, so that wasn't really a thing, and if the people weren't happy, there wasn't anything she could do about it at this point. What was done was done. The real reason she separated herself from the others and stared out that window like it was the most important thing in the world, was that her heart was completely crumbled.

Like an overbaked cookie.

Cole was Jackson Wilcox.

How was that ever going to be okay?

It didn't matter that Cole was amazing, easy to talk to and funny. Because he was Jackson Wilcox, so he couldn't really be any of those things. It was all a sham. Her brain just couldn't negotiate the huge chasm between who he appeared to be and who she knew he was deep down inside.

How could he talk to her about himself without ever fessing up? Joking about a food critic not being a real job. Pretending like he couldn't remember the name of the food critic, his name! It was almost like lying. Worse, actually, because he'd manipulated her.

All of this would have been a lot easier for Darby to swallow if she could ignore one thing. She hadn't realized it for awhile, things happened so gradually, it kind of snuck up on her. And now she was stuck with the knowledge that Cole was Jackson Wilcox and . . .

. . . she was pretty sure she was in love with him.

# Chapter Eighteen

*Athletic Olympian (AO)*
 *Seeking Someone Who Can Keep Up. Is it You?*

Darby spent the rest of the afternoon in a trance-like state. She turned off her brain and her emotions, pasted a smile on her face, and did what she had to do.

When the bride's mom came into the kitchen towards the end of the reception, with an envelope full of money even though they'd already prepaid, and burst into tears because Kenya really came through at the last minute and she couldn't thank them enough, and the food was better than they ever could have hoped and they were all amazing saints and angels.

Darby heard it all in a detached sort of way.

It wasn't even satisfying that her menu was complimented multiple times in front of Jackson Wilcox. That was the strangest thing. She always thought she needed a chance to show him she really could cook and everything would be better. Well, she was here and it wasn't better. It was awful. She just wanted it to be over. In fact, she didn't care anymore what he thought.

She didn't care about him at all.

As they cleaned and packed up and lugged boxes back and forth, Darby slowly and steadily erased every memory of Cole. The sooner she took him out of her heart, the better off she would be.

When the last box was loaded and Kenya was doing a final walk through of the big room and kitchen while the rest of them waited outside, Gretta herded her kids into the car and left Darby standing next to the gazebo with Jackson Wilcox.

Traitors.

Darby wrapped her arms around herself and stared pointedly at the water.

"It went well today," He said, swinging his hands by his side.

She didn't answer.

"So, uh, this was a surprise, huh? I should have told you sooner. I know I should have. I just . . . couldn't do it. Plus, you guys needed the help and there's no way you would have let us come if you knew who I was. You guys really needed help."

Darby let out a breath and shook her head.

"Rey, please—"

Darby whirled on him, her pent up fury rising in her chest. "Don't you dare call me that!"

Jackson Wilcox's eyes widened and he took a step back. "I'm sorry. I-I'm sorry. I messed this up, didn't I?"

Darby glared at him. "You think?"

"Darby, please." He pleaded for understanding with his deep brown eyes. "I didn't know how to tell you. I figured out who you were about a week before Gretta's party just in time to realize you hate my guts. I thought that if you got to know me as Cole, I don't know, you'd—"

"What? Forgive you? Forget everything? Seriously?" Her eyes burned as she looked at him for the first time. "You lied to me this whole time. Is your name even Cole?"

"Yes, it's my middle name. Jackson Cole Wilcox. I didn't lie, Darby, everything I said was true."

She shook her head. "You talked to me about yourself." She barked a laugh. "'Maybe he's not so bad.' You knew and you just—you totally played me. Why would you do that? Never mind." Darby turned away.

"I know why, it's because you're a selfish, critical, horrible person that likes messing with people."

"You're right," He said.

Darby was so surprised she looked at him again, even though she planned on never doing that again for the rest of her life. "What?"

"You're right, Darby. I am all of those things. Sometimes I am selfish, sometimes I am critical and sometimes I really am horrible. But I am also a good listener, a pretend psychologist, and I make you laugh. Do you want to know why I didn't tell you who I am? Really?"

Darby did, but there was no way she was going to admit it to him.

Jackson Wilcox grabbed her hand and tugged so she had to face him. She didn't have to look at him though, instead she stared at the ground, hating that his hand was warm and comforting.

"I didn't tell you because I knew things would change when you discovered who I am. I knew it was inevitable. But I wanted to keep what we had as long as I could. Darby, I am seriously falling for you."

She snatched her hand away from his. "Don't say that."

"It's true."

"No, it's not."

"It is, though. Please, Darby, please hear me out." He was desperate. It wasn't a good look for him. "At first it was just curiosity, I told you that. Your personal ad was quirky and fun, then, the more we talked, the more I saw how kind you are, how passionate and loyal and humble. You made me want to be better, to do more...."

"Stop!" Darby shook her head as she backed away from him. His words were like papercuts. "Nothing you say is true, I know because I know Jackson Wilcox. I read every article about you when I found out you were coming to review my restaurant. I probably know more about you than Gretta does. You don't care about anything but yourself."

Jackson Wilcox sucked in a sharp breath.

"You can't deny it." Darby straightened her shoulders. "That's because you know it's true."

"Darby, do you know what I do for a job now?"

"Business." she laughed without a trace of humor. "So vague. Perfect really. Anything is business."

"I'm not a food critic anymore. Did you know that?"

Darby blinked rapidly, trying to rid herself of the urge to look at him. "Oh, really?" The extra bite in her words was there to cover up the sudden wave of doubt that crashed over her head.

"I quit that job about a year ago. Do you want to know why?"

She refused to answer.

"Because I saw what it did to people. I didn't want to be that person anymore. When I first got into it, I was carried away with the millions of followers and comments and I guess you would call it fame. I did and said things I am not proud of. I built my following by being brutally honest and snarky and as time went on, I hated it all. I quit, Darby. I contacted some of the restaurant owners that I'd built a connection with and invested in their restaurants, then I started buying restaurants for chefs who were talented but lacked the funds to get started. I am not the same Jackson Wilcox you read about."

That sounded so pretty, but it only succeeded in irritating Darby more. He just sounded conceited again, saving these restaurants, funding these chefs. It didn't matter what he said or what he did, Darby knew who he was deep down. And none of that other stuff made up for what he did to her.

"Darby?"

She pulled her arms tighter and shivered.

"Okay, it's fine. You don't have to look at me, or care, but I have to say this and I hope you're listening and not humming show tunes in your head." He paused like he expected her to laugh. Then he sighed and went on. "I'm sorry about your restaurant, I really am. I didn't know that happened. I didn't think what I said was that harsh. I've never had a review actually close a restaurant before, and I feel terrible that happened to you. It's expecting a lot for you to forgive me, but would you? Could you forgive me?"

Darby gritted her teeth.

There was no way.

"If you give me a chance, it might be fun to collaborate. I'm looking for space in Hurricane. What if we opened a new restaurant? Together?"

Seriously?

Darby couldn't believe he had the nerve to say that to her. She couldn't believe she'd actually stood here this long and listened to anything he had to say. Without giving him a second look, Darby walked away.

* * *

She sequestered herself in Kenya's car and locked all the doors. She wished she had the keys so she could crank the radio until the car windows exploded. Instead she pulled out her phone and deleted the Voxer app.

Kenya knocked on the driver's window. Darby leaned over to flip the lock.

"Girl, why are you all hunched in here?"

Darby looked away. "I'm ready to go."

"Well, let's go!" Kenya started the car and turned the car around. Jackson Wilcox and Gretta were gone, which was the only bright spot Darby could find for the last long, miserable hours of her life.

Kenya chatted cheerfully, filling the car with a play-by-play remake of the day. She loved to talk events through to process what went right and what went wrong. Darby knew this, but today it grated. When they got to the first light out of Toquerville, and Kenya started gushing about Jackson Wilcox and the others, Darby snapped.

"Can we talk about something else?"

"Woa." Kenya looked over sharply. "What's up with you?"

"Nothing's up with me, I just don't want to talk about that stupid wedding anymore."

Or the stupid people who helped them pull it off.

Kenya was silent for a long time. The car behind them had to honk twice to get her to move when the light turned green. Kenya stepped on the gas and glanced over at Darby.

"Are you upset that Cole is Jackson Wilcox? Is that what this is about?"

"I couldn't care less."

Kenya tapped the steering wheel with her thumbs and then took a deep breath. "It's understandable if you're mad, but Grammie always used to say that you can tell a tree by its fruit, right? The fruit of this Jackson Wilcox is that he devoted most of his Saturday to help us last minute and totally without pay. I even tried to hide some cash in the leftovers container I gave him, and he caught me. He wouldn't take it."

"He's a saint," Darby grumbled.

Kenya glanced over again. "That's some pretty good fruit, Darbs. I just have to think he's not really a bad guy."

"Are you serious?" Darby's head whipped around to face Kenya. "Are you kidding me right now? You know what he did to me and you think he's a nice person?"

"Darby, when was the last time you actually read that review he gave your restaurant?"

That had nothing to do with nothing.

"Listen, Kenya, if you're going to quote Grammie, you need to understand what she's saying. Fruit: my restaurant closed after Jackson Wilcox reviewed it. Still think he's a good tree?"

"Darbs, I know that was hard for you—"

"You have no idea."

Kenya took a deep breath. "That was hard for you, but do you really want to spend the rest of your life mourning that restaurant? You blame Jackson Wilcox and your rotten luck, but what if it isn't any of that? What if your restaurant was supposed to close?"

Darby's stomach clenched horribly. It was like icy hands reached from the bottom and climbed up her rib cage, trying to get a grip around her heart. Kenya seemed to take Darby's silence as encouragement to go on.

A terrible assumption, really.

"Bad things happen Darbs, all the time, it doesn't do any good to get stuck in them. It just makes you miserable and keeps you from moving forward. You have so much potential, you can do whatever you set your mind to, but if you don't let this thing with your restaurant go, you're always going to be sitting around, blaming other people for your failures."

"Stop the car."

"What?"

"Stop the car, right now."

"Darby?"

"RIGHT NOW!"

The tires squealed as Kenya swerved to the shoulder. The car shuddered to a stop as Darby opened the door and got out.

"What are you doing?"

Darby slammed the door and started walking. She was not going to sit there for one more second.

Kenya waited for a car to pass, then got out and jogged to catch Darby. "Darby, come on, what are you doing?"

Darby couldn't answer. If she unclenched her jaw she knew she was going to say too much. For the sake of their friendship, she had to keep her mouth closed.

"Darby?"

Darby yanked her arm out of Kenya's grasp and broke into a run. She knew Kenya couldn't follow in those high heels.

"Darby!" Already Kenya's voice sounded far away. Darby didn't think she was running that fast, she didn't feel it. Her breath was ragged when she started and her heart started pounding when she was still in the car. It felt better now, like she could finally get air into her lungs.

Like she wasn't trapped.

Darby ran to Pioneer Park but couldn't stop there. Stupid Jackson Wilcox. She took a sharp right and circled around the flower shop. After ten minutes of running aimlessly, she realized she was headed towards her apartment.

Her apartment which was now cockroach-free and ready to move into.

The timing couldn't be better.

Darby stopped running and dug through her purse for her keys. She couldn't remember if she had them, or if they were still at Kenya's house.

She almost cried when her finger brushed her key ring.

Darby gripped the keys in her hand so tightly it hurt and picked back up into a jog. Her apartment rose up when she turned the next corner. There were cars in the spaces, so other people had already moved back in. Darby ran to her duplex and stood there for a minute having a slight out of body experience. It'd been such a long time and really no time at all.

With shaking hands, Darby opened the front door and walked

inside her apartment. It was incredibly clean and bare compared to Kenya's house. It smelled dusty and stuffy. She went around, opening windows to air it out, then inspected every corner of the studio.

It looked the same as always.

Like she never left.

Darby sank into Grammie's old, overstuffed chair and curled into a ball.

And cried.

* * *

Darby had about a billion missed messages when she checked her phone later that night, but she refused to answer any of them. She turned the phone to silent and threw it under a couch cushion. For the next thirty six hours, she binge-watched musicals and ate ice cream that she had delivered from the nearest grocery store.

When she woke up Monday morning, her head felt fuzzy and there were dark circles under her eyes that made her look haggard. She considered calling in sick, she sure felt sick. The thought of working with Jackson Wilcox's sister and probably seeing him at the counter was too much.

Darby was going to have to quit her job.

That's all there was to it. It was a shame, just when Gretta was more bearable and she'd gotten the hang of the café. But there was no way she could stay there.

Two weeks notice, starting today.

She showered and dressed in normal clothes. Her uniform was still at Kenya's house so she'd have to borrow another one from the cafe. That's what she used to do, before... everything. Her house was actually pretty close to work. The morning was bright and birds chirped cheerfully all along the walk.

Darby was indifferent.

When the bell over the door jingled her way into the café, Gretta jumped to her feet.

"You're here. I wasn't sure if you were coming in. You didn't answer your phone. Are you well?"

"I'm fine," Darby said in a monotone.

"Are you sure you're fine?"

"Totally." Darby tried a smile but let it go. It probably looked more like a grimace anyway. "Hey, I wanted to talk to you about something."

"Yes, me too! Oh shoot, I almost forgot! Thank you for reminding me. I was so impressed with that food you made for the wedding reception, Darby, it was incredible. I had no idea you were so talented. Samson works so hard around here, I was thinking it would be really nice for him to have backup. How would you feel about starting in the kitchen today? I can get one of the bussers to do tables and Meredith can take the counter." Gretta spoke fast, like she was expecting Darby to interrupt and start yelling at any moment.

Darby was just trying to keep up. "You want me to cook?"

"Yes, I'd like to move your position to assistant cook. It's a bit of a pay raise, even without the tips, and it would be a great opportunity to use your talent."

Darby itched to ask if this was Jackson Wilcox's idea. It was right on the tip of her tongue, but she couldn't get the words to move. If it was his idea, she wouldn't be able to do it. But this really was a great solution. If she worked in the kitchen with Samson she wouldn't have to see anyone but him all day. That solved everything.

She would keep the job for now, until she came up with a different plan.

"That's great, Gretta, thank you. I accept."

"Fabulous!" Gretta threw her arms around Darby. "Don't worry about a uniform for now, just tie back your hair. We'll get you a chef coat that fits. You'd be swimming in one of Samson's. I'm so happy! I just know you're going to do great things."

Darby smiled and nodded, but her brain wasn't in it. She'd just caught sight of Myles at the counter on his stool, tapping fingers against the newspaper.

"Excuse me, Gretta, I need to talk to someone, and then I'll report to Samson."

"Take your time, sweetie."

Before Darby could talk herself out of it, she hurried to the stool next to Myles and sat. "Have you ever answered one of those personal ads?" Her finger flicked the edge of the newspaper.

Myles looked at her, blinking in surprise. "What?"

Darby repeated her question slowly.

"No." He said.

"Never?"

"No." He scooted slightly away from her.

"Because I distinctly remember a few weeks ago you were reading one of those and you said if you were ever going to answer one, it would be that one."

Myles squinted, his eyes lifting to the ceiling. "Uh, I don't remember saying that. Are you going to take my order?"

"I work in the kitchen now." Darby placed her palm on the newspaper. "I placed a personal ad, sort of as a joke, hoping you would read it and answer it. I thought you did. I've been talking to a guy for weeks and I thought it was you."

"What?"

Darby went on, talking more to herself than Myles now. "He lives with his sister, he loves food, he runs a business. . . . I thought you were him."

"I'm . . . sorry?"

Darby shook her head. "It doesn't matter now. It's just stupid. But I had to know, I had to make sure it wasn't you."

"It wasn't me." His lip twitched. "If I said that, about answering the ad, I was just messing around. I have a girlfriend. I'm, uh, I'm actually thinking about proposing this weekend."

"Congratulations." Darby stood up. "If you need a wedding planner, I know the best one. She's Utah-famous."

"Cool." He turned back to his paper, picking right back up where he left off.

Darby watched him for a minute, then whispered, "Good-bye, Myles."

And walked away.

# Chapter Nineteen

*Beauty seeks Beast. (BSB)*
*Floor to Ceiling Library Necessary*

Darby's life settled into a manageable routine of cooking with Samson, studying for finals, and ignoring calls from Kenya and Jackson Wilcox. She didn't know how Jackson Wilcox got her phone number. Probably from Kenya, which was one more reason not to talk to her anymore.

Both of them, separately, had come into the café at least twice and asked to see her, but she sent one of the tattooed dishwashers to tell them she was too busy. Neither one of them pushed it.

If it wasn't for that, she'd be almost incandescently happy. Working with Samson was a dream. Cooking and creating again, it was magical. If only she could erase that stupid fight with Kenya and make Jackson Wilcox disappear forever. Her life would be absolutely perfect.

On a Wednesday morning, almost two weeks after the fateful wedding reception, Darby donned her chef coat and tucked her hair into a tight bun. "What are we making today, Chef?"

"You're baking biscuits," Samson's gravelly voice said.

"Excuse me?"

"You're baking biscuits," Samson repeated in the exact same way, like someone pressed a button on his back with a prerecorded phrase.

"I heard what you said, but you know I stink at making biscuits." She'd already told the story to Samson, about when she was in high school, the last time she'd made biscuits, and the hockey team ended up using them for practice. Biscuits were probably the one and only thing she hadn't put on her restaurant's menu.

"I don't know that." Samson shook his head. "You just think you can't do it, so you're gonna conquer that fear today, little sister. You're going to bake biscuits, all by your lonesome, until you get it right."

That sounded like a supreme waste of flour.

"What if I never do? What if I'm just bad at it?"

Samson lifted his bushy eyebrows to look at her. It was probably the way an amoeba felt when the microscope zoomed in. "You ain't ever gonna get better if you don't try, so you might as well bake those biscuits."

Darby's hands dropped to her sides. "Are you serious?"

"Know what your problem is? I mean besides that you don't think you can do it?" Samson said.

"Do tell." Darby raised an eyebrow.

"You think too much, little sister. Baking, it's about feeling. You can follow the same recipe in the summer and it turns out perfect, then do it again in the winter and it's too dense. There's a lot happening. Recipes don't matter here, sis, it's how it looks, how it feels here." he wiggled his fingers. "And how it feels here." He tapped his heart.

Darby had no idea what that was supposed to mean.

Samson grunted. "Get to work. You'll figure it out."

"And if I don't?" Darby mumbled as she walked to the station nearest the huge bin of flour.

"Then you won't."

\* \* \*

Darby crossed her fingers as she pulled the tray of biscuits out of the oven. This was her fifth try. The first was too dry, the second too soggy, the third tasted tinny—too much baking powder, and the fourth bunch were doughy in the middle.

And the fifth was burned.

"Crap!" Darby slammed the biscuits on the stove top and glared at the black char on the bottom. "How did that even happen? I set the timer for the same amount of time as all the rest!"

Samson chuckled from his corner, just like he had with every other attempt.

Well, yippee for him.

She was glad he was so amused.

"I give up!" Darby threw her oven mitts on the counter.

Not only was it not working, it was never going to work. Samson needed to face the facts.

"Little sister?"

Darby lowered her head to the counter and groaned. She was so not in the mood for any of his words of wisdom.

"You have a visitor."

Darby's head popped up.

Kenya stood near the island, kneading her hands together. Her brown eyes were enormous.

"Darby." Her lip quivered.

Darby scowled. This was terrible timing on Kenya's part. Darby might have been able to concentrate on forgiveness, because she really did miss Kenya, if she wasn't so consumed with her biscuit failure.

Kenya held out her hands, they were empty, but she kept them there like she was offering Darby a present. "Grammie always said the first step to happiness is forgiveness."

Grammie did always say that. It was one of her most favorite sayings. Either that or she just had to say it a lot because Darby loved her grudges.

Kenya's forehead dissolved into wrinkles. "And that friends are the whipped cream on the cake."

Okay, that was one of Darby's favorite Grammie sayings. Because whipped cream really was the best part.

Darby bit her lip, her arms sagging to her sides.

"And that we have to love people and cook them tasty food. Remember that one?"

"Grammie never said that," Darby said, a smile twitching the corner of her mouth.

"I know. I just thought it sounded like her." Kenya looked so miserable, as miserable as Darby felt. She missed her friend. Darby scooted around the island and wrapped her around Kenya.

Kenya immediately dissolved into sobs. "I'm so sorry, Darby! I'm so sorry! I know that restaurant thing crushed you. I was such a butt. Can you ever forgive me?"

Shame slid down Darby's spine. All this time she'd avoided Kenya because she'd only been thinking about herself. Kenya had suffered too and part of that suffering was Darby's fault for ignoring her for so long.

If anyone was a butt around here, it was Darby.

She pulled away and held onto Kenya's shoulders. "I'm sorry. It was all me. You didn't do anything wrong. In fact," she took a deep breath, "you were right."

It wasn't until she said the words that she realized how true they were. The clench that had been in her stomach since that stupid Saturday, slowly began to unravel.

"I was completely wrapped up in my own disappointment and pain. I just, I handled that so bad. Can you forgive me?"

Kenya swiped her hands together like she was dusting off flour. "Already done."

Darby pulled her back in for a tight hug and then let her go for good. "So, we're alright, you and me?"

"Well, I will be," Kenya bit her lip. "Once you move back in with me. Will you? please? My house is so boring without you. Can you just dump that lame apartment and be my roomie forever?"

"Serious?"

"Please, yes. So serious!"

"I would absolutely love that."

"Yes!" Kenya squealed.

"Yay!" Samson waved his spatula in the air. "Now, get your rear out of this kitchen. It's staff only, missy."

Kenya blew him a kiss and skipped towards the swinging doors. "See you at home!" She waved.

"See you at home." Darby smiled.

"That was touching," Samson grunted. "Now make biscuits."

Darby stuck her tongue out at his back and turned to the mess in front of her. It mocked her with its inedible ness.

Know what, biscuits?

She *was* going to make more. And she was going to make the best dang biscuits anyone had ever seen.

Darby pulled the mixing bowl towards her to try again. By this time, she knew the quantity ratios so well she could probably do it with her eyes closed. She sifted flour, cut in butter and added buttermilk with her hand in the bowl to mix as it poured. When the dough reached a sticky consistency and she could still see flecks of butter, she stopped mixing.

She didn't know how she knew to stop, but she did. She could feel it in her bones. She plopped the dough onto the floured counter and sprinkled more flour on top. She gently flattened the mound with her palm, then grabbed the biscuit cutter. Each plump round went on the baking sheet with parchment to help it cook evenly. When she slipped the tray into the oven, she let out a long breath.

There, what's done was done.

She set the timer for five minutes less than she thought it needed. She could always put it back in if it was still doughy, that's what she'd learned from burning the biscuits. They needed to be golden brown on top was what she'd learned from making them too doughy. Never assume you know a recipe well enough to remember everything was what she learned from forgetting the salt.

So many good lessons in a super short amount of time.

When the timer went off, Darby cracked the oven and peered inside. The biscuits were lightly browned, not pasty white, but not brown enough. It made sense that the browner they were, the more buttery they would taste and the texture would be crunchy on the outside and soft in the middle.

She gently closed the door and set the timer for two more minutes.

The longest two minutes of her life. If it was true that a watched pot never boiled, it was triply true that a watched timer never moved.

And it was tremendously hard not to peek.

As soon as the timer dinged, Darby pulled the oven door open. The rich scent of browned butter filled her nose.

It was heavenly.

She pulled the baking sheet out, keeping her mind purposefully blank. It was no use thinking anything about it until she tried a biscuit and knew what was what. It was also no use waiting for them to cool. She needed to know what it was like, now.

Darby broke a biscuit in half.

It sounds so simple, but it did something to her. The steam wafted into her face, the browned crust crackled beneath her thumbs as they sank into the pillow-soft center.

She didn't even need to try one to know it worked.

It was the perfect biscuit.

She couldn't wait to tell Cole what she did! He would be so proud of her!

Wait.

No.

Not Cole.

Jackson Wilcox.

Darby's heart shuddered as she stuffed the biscuit half in her mouth. She couldn't tell Cole, because Cole didn't exist. Cole was a big fat lie and Jackson Wilcox was a big fat liar.

Anger was way easier to deal with than that crushing despair. That knowledge that she'd lost something infinitely precious. It didn't matter because it was never real in the first place.

Darby flung her shoulders back, and flung her thoughts away with them. She wrapped a biscuit in a paper towel to take over to Samson. He took it with a blank face, as she knew he would, the man was the worst at facial expressions. Meaning, he never used them.

Darby clasped her hands behind her back and rocked onto her toes while Samson chewed. His swallow seemed to take forever. Then, instead of saying something, he took another bite.

Was that a good thing? Because it was so yummy he couldn't resist?

Or was that a bad thing, like he needed another taste to make sure it was as disgusting as he originally thought?

Waiting for that second swallow was excruciating.

"Little sister," Samson slowly raised his fist, "congratulations. You conquered the biscuit."

Darby couldn't stop the smile spreading on her face if she wanted to. It took on a life of its own, stretching her cheeks until they ached. She raised her fist to bump Samson's.

"I did, didn't I?"

"Best dang biscuit I ever had. Bring 'em over here and let's serve 'em up."

"Really?"

"Yeah, really." Samson turned back the eggs he was scrambling. "What'd you think, we'd just stare at them?"

Darby tried not to skip as she brought the tray over. Then she tried not to soar around the room when Samson asked her to whip up another batch. It was hopeless. She did both as she spent the rest of her shift cranking out beautiful browned biscuits.

When the café closed, there were only three biscuits left. Those she wrapped in plastic and stashed in her purse for Kenya. Not only did the girl love her biscuits, but this was proof that Darby could do things she thought she couldn't. For some reason it seemed really important that Kenya knew that.

But first, Darby had a stop to make.

# Chapter Twenty

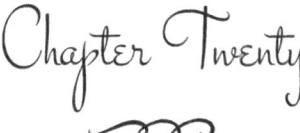

*Brainy College Professor (BCP)*
*Seeks Dumb Blond to Add Balance to Life.*

Darby veered off the sidewalk onto the path that turned into the Hurricane City Cemetery. Her feet knew the way without her brain directing the show. She'd walked this path many, many times since she moved to Hurricane.

Because Grammie was there.

She had been for almost two years.

Darby walked the path through the overhanging trees, just beginning to bud, and turned towards the center. Grammie waited under a modest headstone next to a vase filled with artificial sunflowers.

She sure did love her sunflowers.

Darby sat on the grass in front of Grammie's tombstone and brushed her hand along the top to get rid of the dirt. Grammie didn't mind dirt one bit, but it made Darby feel better to brush it away. Like she was taking care of her. It was only fair, after all those years of Grammie taking care of Darby.

"Hey, Grammie." Darby sighed, then bit her lip. She didn't quite know where to start. "I made biscuits today. And no, I didn't put in a cup of salt." Darby laughed, then sighed again. "It was funny, I started out so angry at Samson for making me keep making biscuits over and over. Failing over and over. It seemed so pointless and wasteful. And then . . . and then, Grammie, it was the weirdest thing. The biscuits turned out great. I didn't do anything different, at least, I didn't think I did, and it just . . . worked. I made a billion tons of them after that, and they were all great. I didn't know I could do that, and then . . . I could."

Darby stared beyond Grammie's headstone, to the rolling green hills dotted with people who slept peacefully. This was the perfect place for Grammie to rest, right next to Gramps, who died before Darby was born. Grammie loved Hurricane. It was where she fell in love and raised her daughter and lost her husband.

It suddenly struck Darby how much of a sacrifice it was for Grammie to move to Salt Lake City with her. Grammie never complained. She was always so focused on Darby and the restaurant, but she must have missed Hurricane every day.

Darby sucked in a shaky breath. She'd messed up so many things in so many different ways. It was overwhelming.

"Grammie, my restaurant failed. I know you know. I know you watched the whole thing. I actually felt you there sometimes, when it was really hard. But I needed to say those words to you. I failed."

Darby slid a lock of hair behind her ear, a stubborn one that kept trying to fly into her mouth. "Remember how you always told me to take responsibility for the stuff on my turf? Well, I haven't been doing that. I've been blaming . . . others for that failure. Okay, Jackson Wilcox. I've been blaming Jackson Wilcox. And my luck. It was just easier that way. If I really had the worst luck, and hated Jackson Wilcox, then I didn't have to take responsibility for all the things I did wrong with my restaurant. It seemed easier. But you know what's weird? It hasn't really been easy to hate him. Especially now."

Darby groaned and leaned forward until her arms rested on Grammie's headstone. Grammie's name, carved so perfectly into the stone, was just under Darby's eyes.

"Grammie, I think I love him." She laughed. "And I hate him." Darby wiped her cheek as a trail of tears made a slow stream to her chin. "What am I going to do? I wish you were here. I know I said I was glad you passed away before my failure, but I'm not. Not really. I can't figure this out on my own. I'm not wise, like you. I just mess everything up."

A breeze took Darby's hair and spun it into the air above her. She let it play, it seemed to be having a good time up there.

Darby closed her eyes and pictured herself kneeling on the carpet of the apartment in Salt Lake that she shared with Grammie, her chin on Grammie's lap. Grammie would stroke her hair while she listened to all of Darby's woes, then she would tell a story that would make Darby laugh, just to lighten the air a little. When the last bit of laughter faded, Grammie would say something incredibly profound that would give Darby courage to get up and face the world again.

Something like...

The only thing you have to fear is boa constrictors, and those don't live in Utah.

Or...

When life gives you lemons, make a sour face and get on with life.

Or...

You are the strongest you I know.

The tears came faster now, making a puddle around Grammie's name. "I don't know what I want anymore, Grammie. I thought I wanted to get my degree, so I would know how to run a business better. But I hate business classes. They suck the life out of me. I thought I wanted to run another restaurant—successfully this time—but then I realized someone is always going to hate on and judge my work. I don't know if I want to put myself out there like that again. I thought I wanted a second chance with Jackson Wilcox, to show him I'm a good cook, and I got it but it didn't make a lick of difference in the way I feel. What do I do, Grammie? What do I want?"

Darby hid her face in her arms. The musty smell of earth and that distinct scent of concrete filled her nose, but she barely noticed. She'd give anything to have Grammie there, with her.

She'd messed that up too. Those last few months of Grammie's life, the restaurant was so busy, she hardly had time to do much more than hug Grammie before she ran out the door. And when she got home, Grammie was already asleep.

Of course, Grammie never complained. She left love notes for

Darby all over the apartment and texted her encouragement throughout the day, but Darby couldn't forget that horrible moment when she realized Grammy wasn't going to be there when she got home.

She'd wasted those last, precious bits of time she had with Grammie. Wasted them.

On a restaurant.

That failed.

"I'm so sorry," Darby sobbed. "Grammie, I'm so sorry." Her heart beat into her throat and choked her so that no sound came out as her shoulders shook.

She could never forgive herself.

Never.

"I love you."

Darby lifted her head slowly and looked around. That was Grammie's voice, she'd bet money on it. But it couldn't be. It had to be someone else talking nearby.

Except that the cemetery was completely empty.

Darby rubbed her sleeve across her nose and sniffed.

"I love you."

No, really, there was no one there.

The breeze wrapped around Darby like a hug, she pulled her arms into her chest and rubbed at the goosebumps forming.

"Grammie?"

Grammie wasn't there.

But she was.

"I told you I love you more than beans, no matter how many stones get mixed in."

The voice wasn't audible, there was no way another person could have heard it if there was anyone else around. It was like Darby heard it with her heart, instead of her ears. It was like Grammie sat right next to her on the grass, except that Darby couldn't see her.

It should have been spooky, but it wasn't.

Instead, there was love, as thick as pancake batter and four times as sweet. It smelled like sugar with just a hint of forgiveness sprinkled in. It was the most loved Darby had felt in a very long time.

"I messed up," Darby said in a small voice.

"I love you. I love you. I love you."

And suddenly Darby remembered something. A moment when she was six years old and tried to make breakfast for Grammie as a surprise. All she succeeded in doing was burning the toast and making a huge mess in the kitchen. When she dissolved into tears, so disappointed, Grammie pulled Darby into her lap and told her something she forgot a long time ago.

"Be proud of yourself, darlin'. I love this mess you made because it means you loved me enough to try. You are really good at trying, my Darby, and I love you for that, too. You never, never, never give up."

Darby gasped as the breeze tickled her ear.

She forgot that some people love you no matter what.

She forgot how to be proud of herself.

She forgot she was good at trying.

She forgot she never gave up.

But she would never forget again.

"I love you, too, Grammie," She said as she rose to her feet. "I'm going to fix this, you just watch."

From now on, she was making her own dang luck.

\* \* \*

Kenya waited for Darby at the kitchen table when she walked through the front door. She sprang to her feet and attacked Darby with a hug.

"You have no idea how happy the sound of that door makes me! How in the heckfire did I live alone for all those years? It's so stinking boring. Plus, there's no one to cook for me. Did you bring back anything good?"

Darby held out her purse and Kenya snatched it like a greedy toddler. She found the biscuits immediately. "You know what I like."

Darby kept quiet while Kenya broke off a piece and put it in her mouth. It was worth it to see Kenya's eyes roll back in her head.

"Oh my sassafras, girl, this is the best biscuit I have ever eaten. Remind me to tell Samson he outdid himself."

"I would, except Samson didn't make those biscuits."

"No?" Kenya chewed faster and swallowed, like she couldn't wait to take another bite. "Wait, was it you?"

Darby grinned. "They're good huh?"

Kenya gave Darby a strange look, one she couldn't identify.

"What's that look for?"

"What look?"

"I don't know, it's like you can't believe I said that the biscuits are good. Am I wrong?"

"No." Kenya stuffed another large piece in her mouth. "You're right. These are so good. So so good. I'm just surprised *you* thought so. Usually you're so worried that what you make isn't good enough."

Yeah.

She did used to feel that way.

But not anymore.

Darby straightened her shoulders. "As my friend Kenya always says, I decided to have my own back."

"Look at you!" Kenya shoved her shoulder. "I've never had someone quote me to me before. I think I like it! I sort of feel like Grammie now."

"Let's not get crazy. Those are super shoes to fill." Darby grinned. "There's something else."

"Yeah?" Kenya jerked her head to the table and moved to one of the chairs. Darby followed, taking the seat across from Kenya.

"Yeah," Darby took a deep breath. "I went to my apartment on my way here. To get that article Jackson Wilcox wrote. I need to read it again, but I don't want to do it alone. Can I read it out loud, to you?"

Kenya gave her another one of those mystery looks. "Okay. . . ."

"Okay." Darby would take it. She put her purse on the table and pulled out the rumpled article. She'd crumpled it and thrown it away who knew how many times over the years. Then, retrieved it and tacked it to her wall again so she could stare at it and hate Jackson Wilcox all over again. Darby looked at Jackson Wilcox's picture now, his serious face was more stressed than critical. There was a line between his eyebrows like when he shows up at the wedding reception and faced Darby that first time. His eyes were the same though, well, except for the part where she poked them with tacks.

She wasn't proud.

Darby smoothed the paper onto the table and took a deep breath.

"I haven't read this since that first time, right before my restaurant went under. I've been hiding from something, Ken, for a long time. I think I'm ready to face it."

"Okay." Kenya nodded. "Well, then, I'm ready to face it with you." She took Darby's hand in hers and held it tightly, then moved the article so she could see it too.

"The Purple Penguin, a restaurant as unique as its name.

A food critic with a number of followers gets a lot of requests for reviews. Everything from hole in the wall taco stands to five star restaurants come through my inbox. I'll be honest, it's gotten so I yay or nay a place solely based on the name.

As you can imagine, I read this one and I was intrigued.

Adding to the mystery of the name, is the unconventional background of head chef, Darby Reynolds. Only a few years out of high school, Reynolds started this restaurant solely on grit and a passion for food. Her lack of experience shows in many administrative ways, this was definitely the most disorganized restaurant I've ever frequented, but that randomness doesn't translate to the food. Everything I tried, from Gyoza to Primavera to Pierogi was a revelation. Reynolds might be learning how to run her restaurant through the school of hard knocks, however, there is nothing wrong with her menu.

The thing that stands out most is the accommodation. If you have a large group of people with varying tastes, the Purple Penguin is your answer. There is literally something for everyone.

So, would I recommend it? Absolutely. I would also recommend Reynolds invest in some business classes to make the flow of the restaurant a little less hectic for her patrons.

Over all, four out of five stars."

Darby lifted her eyes to see Kenya's face. Kenya was still hunched over the newspaper article, studying it, rereading certain parts under her breath.

When she finally looked up, she looked terrified. "Darby?"

"Yeah?"

"This isn't a horrible review." She squeezed Darby's hand tighter, like she was afraid Darby would get up and leave like she did on the car ride home.

"I know." Darby said, pressing her lips together. "It's not."

"You know?"

Darby sighed. "Kenya, I realized something these last couple weeks while I was spending too much time in my own head."

"Yeah?"

"You were right."

"Of course I was. What are you talking about specifically?"

Darby shook her head with a smile. "I blamed the failure of my restaurant on Jackson Wilcox. On Cole. But the truth is, it was failing already. I was so excited about that review because I thought it would help me turn things around and when it didn't, it was just so much easier to blame Jackson Wilcox than to face the fact that I messed up. I had no idea what I was doing. I made so many mistakes and some of them were big enough to close my restaurant. I just rushed in. Totally impulsive. I thought I knew everything and because of that, a lot of really good people lost their jobs."

Kenya made an exaggerated frowny face. "You did your best, I know you did."

"I did the best with what I knew at the time. It just wasn't enough. I failed." Darby took a deep breath and let that word hang in the air longer than it needed to. Just to prove she wasn't afraid of it anymore. "There's something else."

"Something else I'm right about?"

Darby rolled her eyes. "Maybe."

"Well, tell me then, I love it when I'm right."

Darby laughed. "Fine, I think I'm in love with Cole."

"Of course you are."

"And I screwed up."

"Of course you did."

"And I need your help to fix it."

"Oh course you do." Kenya grinned broadly.

"I'm going to ignore you and keep talking."

"Of course you are."

"I haven't talked to Cole at all since the day of the reception. But I have missed him every single second of every single one of those days. I want him back, Ken." Darby sniffed. "Even if he is Jackson Wilcox. I don't know if I can fix this, but I'm going to keep trying until something works."

"That's my girl. I will do whatever you need me to do. What's your plan?"

# Chapter Twenty-One

*Second Chance Please (SCP)*
*Once is Just Not Enough*

Darby was swinging with new-found confidence, but she wasn't about to risk her still fragile heart in a stampede. Before she did anything, she wanted to talk to Gretta.

She knew Gretta always got to the café about an hour earlier than everyone else, so that's what Darby did the very next morning. When she knocked on the locked door to the café, Gretta jumped a mile.

"Great smokies, Darby, you scared the hair off me!"

"I'm sorry, I really didn't mean to."

"It's fine, come on in, what's going on? You're early."

"I know. I wanted to talk to you. Is that okay?"

"Now, don't you tell me you're leaving. 'Cause I won't accept your resignation. Those biscuits yesterday were the talk of the café."

"No, it's not about that. It's um, kind of personal."

Gretta's forehead wrinkled as she gestured for Darby to sit down at the nearest booth. She sat first and clasped her hands, watching Darby carefully until she was settled too.

# DARBY'S CAFE

Darby fidgeted with the napkin holder. "I wonder how much you know."

"About you and Jackson? I know everything. He tells me everything."

Darby didn't know whether to feel relieved or mortified. "So, you know he answered my personal ad?"

"Yeah, who do you think gave him that ad? I was clearing up from that young man who always comes in and saw it. It made me laugh. I thought Jackson would get a kick out of it. Life has been hard on him lately, he needed something to cheer him up. I didn't know it was you though. Not right away."

"So you know we've been talking for awhile?"

"I've never seen him so happy." Gretta smiled at the thought, then frowned. "What happened, sweetie?"

So, Darby quickly told her the story of her restaurant, her misconceptions and her horrible pride. Gretta made all the right noises at all the right places. Sympathy, understanding, empathy. If there was anyone in Hurricane who could understand where Darby was coming from, it was the lady sitting across the booth.

That gave Darby a much needed boost of courage.

"Gretta, I have to know something. Does he, um, does he still, you know, like me?"

"Well, if you count mooning around the house and checking his phone every five seconds as liking you, then I would say yes."

"Really?"

"Yes, really. I've known that boy since I diapered his bum and I'll tell you this, Ms. Darby, he seems tough, like he's got it all handled, but he ain't. Not really. He's careful, sensitive, and he don't open up easily. When he does, he goes all in. He went all in with you, and he is suffering now." Gretta reached over and took Darby's hand. "Jackson is the best kind of man there is. He has always been there for me when I needed him, even when I didn't know I needed him." Gretta stopped and swallowed. "Me and my husband, we're going through some things. Jackson left his whole life to come to Hurricane for me. He takes care of his people."

"And," Darby raised her head, "do you think I'm still one of his people?"

"I do."

Darby nodded. "Okay."

"Okay, what?"

"Okay, I'm going to talk to him. I'm going to explain and apologize. But first, can I use the kitchen? Grammie always said an apology is easier to swallow if you add some sticky buns."

"I like this Grammie of yours. I say, yes, as long as you give me some for the café, I'd call that a fair trade."

"Thank you, Gretta." Darby took a deep breath. "There's just one more thing I need your help with."

"What's that, hon?"

"I need to talk to Jackson Wilcox, I mean Cole. I mean, Jackson. I need to talk to him, face to face."

"Do you want my address? He's at home right now."

Darby shook her head. She was already scared to death that this wasn't going to work. It would be easier to talk to him in a neutral place that felt safe. Namely, the café.

"Is that okay if I meet him here?"

"Of course that's okay, if that's what you want to do."

"Could you, uh, ask him to come by in a couple hours? I'll have sticky buns ready by then."

"Sure." Gretta squeezed Darby's arm. "What do you want me to tell him?"

Tell him? Couldn't she just ask him to come by the café? That wasn't totally out of the ordinary, was it?

Gretta seemed to know exactly what Darby was thinking. "He's been staying away to make you more comfortable. If I ask him to come in without a really good reason, I don't think he'll do it. He's convinced you don't want to see him ever again."

Because that's what Darby had told him.

She sighed deeply. In that case, they would have to come up with a really good reason. "Maybe you forgot something at home that he can bring you? Or maybe you need him to run an errand?"

Gretta tapped the side of her nose. "I've got just the thing. Don't you worry about it a bit. I'll get him here."

"Thank you, Gretta, I really owe you one."

"No worries, you go make those buns." Gretta stood, her palms resting on the table. "I hope this works, Darby, for both your sakes. You deserve to be happy."

Darby looked down. "Do you think I can make your brother happy?"

The silence was overbearing enough that Darby had to look up, to check the answer on Gretta's face.

"Honey, I know you can."

\* \* \*

A little over an hour later, Darby pulled perfectly caramelized pecan sticky buns out of the oven and tried not to throw up.

Not because of the buns, those were perfect. It was more the torrential downpour of negative thoughts bombarding her for the last thirty minutes. She really wished Gretta hadn't told her what time Jackson was supposed to be there. It just made her obsessively check the clock and worry.

Kenya put a hand on Darby's arm. "Need a taste tester?"

It took a little begging to get Samson to let Kenya violate the kitchen rules. After Darby gave him her best pathetic pleading eyes, Kenya tied all her hair up, and put on a ridiculously oversized uniform, he finally relented.

The old marshmallow.

"Please, yes, please try one." Darby breathed out, holding out the tray.

Kenya reached over for some tongs and plucked a bun right out of the middle. She set it on the counter and waved a hand to dissipate the steam. Darby handed her a knife, and Kenya cut the bun into fourths.

"Something smells good." Samson said over his shoulder.

"Come try a piece."

He didn't need to be told twice.

Darby watched her friends lift the food she made to their mouths and blow, then take a bite. Her stomach churned horribly while she waited.

Kenya moaned. "Darbs, this is wrong."

"Wrong?" Darby squeaked.

Kenya laughed. "Like, sick and wrong. Seriously, so perfect. Soft and sticky, sweet but not cloying. You completely nailed this! Grammie would be so proud."

Samson didn't say a word, but reached for the other two pieces of sticky bun and took them with him to the griddle where he was frying thick slices of ham.

That was a compliment better than words.

Kenya waved a hand in front of Darby's face.

"Sorry, what?" She blinked.

"It's okay, you're nervous. Just remember to breathe, okay? It's necessary."

"Kenya, what if this doesn't work?"

"But what if it does?"

Darby grinned. "But what if it doesn't?"

"Okay, what if it doesn't?"

Then it would break her heart. Darby lifted a hand to her stomach and pressed to make the clench go away. It would hurt a million times worse than losing her restaurant.

But. . . .

She would figure it out.

Right?

She would be fine.

It was fine.

Really fine this time.

But, oh nelly, she really wanted this to work.

The bell over the door chimed so loud it was like she was standing right underneath it. Usually the bustle of the kitchen drowned it out, but today Darby was so tuned in she probably would have heard it five miles away.

"Is it him?" She whispered.

Kenya repeated the question to Samson, who peeked through his order window.

"Yep."

"What's happening? What's he doing? Does he look mad? Sad? Stressed?"

Samson gave her a look and moved away from the window, swinging his arms to invite her to come see for herself. Kenya tugged Darby by the wrist. They hunched in front of the window, then peeked over just enough to see what was going on out there.

Jackson looked good.

If there were some lines on his forehead and his eyes drooped at the corners, that did nothing to distract from how incredibly handsome he was. Darby sucked in a shuddery breath and watched as he took the seat Gretta prepared for him at the counter. He looked around before sitting and even then, he didn't relax. One leg jangled against the stool. Gretta unfolded the paper and pointed to the personal ads, then set it in front of him.

"Step one." Kenya whispered.

Jackson bent over the paper for a moment, then he looked up. He said something in a voice too low for Darby to hear. Gretta whispered back, then put her hand behind her and waved.

That was Darby's cue.

"I can't do this, Ken. I can't."

Kenya put her hands on Darby's shoulders. "Yes, you can. You can do this."

"No." She seriously felt like she was going to vomit.

"Okay." Kenya dropped her hands. "Don't do it."

Darby stumbled without Kenya's arms to support her and had to lean on the wall. "No?"

"No, don't go out there. Don't talk to him. Don't resolve this."

That was unbearable.

"No, I'm going. I'm going to do this."

Kenya grinned.

Darby lifted a finger and pointed it at Kenya's nose. "Don't even, okay. I'm totally freaking out here."

Samson appeared at her side with a plate containing one large pecan sticky bun. "Get going, little sister. It's time."

Darby took the plate with shaking hands. She was afraid she was going to drop it. She pushed her elbows into her sides to steady her hands.

Kenya kissed her forehead with a loud smack. "As Grammie used to say, you don't know anything you don't know until you try."

Hearing Grammie's words gave Darby the boost she needed to propel herself out of the kitchen. She could feel Kenya and Samson's eyes follow her out of the kitchen, and Gretta's eyes lock in on her as soon as she stepped into the café. Her own eyes were glued on Jackson as she walked towards him, trying to pretend there was no one in the world except the two of them.

He stared at the paper, even though he must have finished reading a long time ago. Whatever he was staring at held his attention so thoroughly he didn't even look up when Darby stopped in front of him.

She took a deep breath to steady herself, and set the sticky bun in front of him. "Your order, sir."

Jackson looked up, confused at first, then his eyes widened in surprise. Darby tried to get a smile to stick, but she could feel it quivering on the sides of her mouth.

"Hey, there, welcome to the Corner Café, I'm your waitress, Darby."

Jackson didn't smile.

But he didn't turn and walk away either.

So, that was something.

His deep brown eyes gazed at her steadily, like he was trying to figure her out.

Or waiting for the punchline.

Emphasis on punch.

"I see you're reading the newspaper, anything interesting in there?" She flicked her pen towards the personal ads.

Jackson looked down. "Uh, yeah, there's a personal ad that's hard to miss. Mostly because someone stuck a sticky note in here over the other ads." He smiled, but didn't look up.

Darby would take it. "That's weird. What does it say?"

"Oh, you know." Jackson traced the tape around the ad with his finger. "Someone asking for forgiveness."

"Really?" Darby said. "That's interesting. I thought people used those things to find someone to date, not to apologize. Kind of lame, actually. An apology deserves more than an ad in the newspaper. I really think that a skywriting plane would be more appropriate, don't you?"

Jackson's cheek twitched. "Probably."

"So, what does it say?"

"The sky writer?"

"The personal ad."

Jackson pressed his lips into a straight line, then said, "Idiot Seeking Forgiveness. ISF. Jackson Cole Wilcox, I was an idiot. I'm forever sorry. I miss you like crazy. I know I don't deserve it, but please forgive me."

"Wow!" Darby said in an exaggerated voice. "Someone must really care about this Jackson Cole Wilcox guy."

"You think?" Jackson stared at the paper a little longer.

Darby leaned her elbows on the counter so she wasn't looking down on him. "Jackson, I want a redo."

His eyes lifted to hers finally. "You do?"

"Do you?"

"I do." He paused. "But, I mean, do you, really? I crushed your dream, remember? I ruined your restaurant. I ruined your life. And then I lied to you."

Darby shook her head. "I read your review again. It wasn't mean. It didn't trash my restaurant. In fact, it was a really great review. All the things you pointed out that I thought were negative, were true. I rushed into that restaurant. I was so excited. I ran it haphazardly, unprofessionally. I had no idea what I was doing. My restaurant would have failed no matter what. Because of *me*."

"Darby—"

"Just . . . let me get this out, and then you can say whatever you want. Jackson, I'm sorry. I'm sorry I blamed you for my failure. I'm sorry I yelled at you and I'm sorry I didn't listen when you tried to explain what happened with Cole. Everything that went wrong was on me. Kenya and I put that ad in the personals to get the attention of this guy, Myles, who I thought I had a crush on. I couldn't ever get the guts to talk to him, and he read the ads everyday, it was a good plan."

"You thought I was someone else." He leaned back. "That makes so much sense. No wonder you were so ticked off."

"The two of you actually have a ton in common. He lives with his sister, too. He runs a franchise business and he loves food. Seriously, just about everything I talked about with Cole could have applied to Myles."

"You were disappointed it was me?"

"I was expecting Myles, but it wasn't just that. The fact that Cole was Jackson Wilcox just blew my mind in the worst possible way. I did not handle any of that well."

"That's so crazy." He ran his hands through his hair. "You know what else is crazy? I never would have answered a personal ad on my own, never in a million years. Gretta talked me into it. It probably should have been Myles that answered that ad, not me."

"No, it shouldn't have been." Darby rubbed her arms. "What happened is what should have happened. And stop being so nice. I was the biggest jerk. I was a total idiot and I'm *forever* sorry."

Jackson kept his gaze steady on Darby for a couple of breaths, long enough that she felt the connection, but not long enough to know what he was thinking. Then he looked down at the sticky bun. "Did you make this?"

"I did. Turns out, a leopard can change its spots."

Jackson looked up with the first real smile Darby had seen on his face in weeks. It broke through like the sun through gray clouds and had the same effect on Darby's heart. She was warmed from the inside out.

"Jackson, I have a question."

"What's that?" His eyes squinted when he smiled. It was so endearing, it made Darby want to run her fingers over the creases on his face.

"Is Cole busy tonight? I've been thinking about it and I'm ready to meet him. Does he . . . does he still want to meet me?"

Jackson lazily reached for Darby's hand and wound their fingers together so that when she looked down she couldn't tell which hand was hers and which was Jackson's.

"You're in luck." He said slowly. "He really does."

# About the Author

By day, Cori Cooper is the mild-mannered (sort of) Wife to her high school love, the Mother of four punny, movie-quoting, awesome-sauce kiddos who are adults and teens now, (yeah, that happened fast), and the Writer of stories that (hopefully) leave readers with a warm and slightly squishy feeling (that's not weird at all).

And by night... Cori Cooper is sleeping because that's her fifth favorite thing to do.

Writing and publishing books is a long-time dream come true. Sometimes she has to pinch herself (also not at all weird) that she's actually doing the thing she imagined when she was six years old. It's surreal, and yet, stinking amazing.

So when she's not hanging out with her fabulous family, or writing stories, Cori loves reading or listening to books that make her want to be a better person. She has a fetish for watching cheesy Hallmark movies with her girls - the cheesier the better. She's passionate about baking anything that has copious amounts of butter, and quite frequently, she can be found rearranging furniture, organizing closets, and changing the color of paint on interior walls.

You can connect with Cori on Instagram, Facebook, Bookbub, Goodreads and her website – Coristories.com.

www.ingramcontent.com/pod-product-compliance
Lightning Source LLC
LaVergne TN
LVHW041757060526
838201LV00046B/1028